MORE PRAISE FOR TIM CHAMPLIN!

WAYFARING STRANGERS
"Realistic...compelling."

—*Roundup Magazine*

"An exceptional frontier story....Purchase it, read it, and find a spot for it in your library."

—*The Tombstone Epitaph*

DEADLY SEASON
"Champlin obviously knows his area and the minutiae of his chosen period quite well....[A] good story."

—*The Tombstone Epitaph*

THE TOMBSTONE CONSPIRACY
"A nice brew of traditional western fare, that is to say, juiced up a notch or two."

RESCUE GONE WRONG

Mulroy reached for the shirt and pants, his eyes riveted on the pistol in the boy's hand. "What's this?"

"Put on these clothes."

"I could use a good bath first."

Cal said nothing, but continued aiming the gun at him. The boy had no expression on his face.

Mulroy did as he was told, glad to be rid of the filthy cavalry uniform pants he'd worn for weeks. But his mind was in a whirl. Was this some kind of joke? Why would the young guard hold a gun on him, unless he feared him as dangerous? Cal's attitude was rather nonchalant. Maybe he didn't know how to handle firearms and was inadvertently pointing it in Mulroy's general direction.

"Got any shoes or boots that'll fit me?" Mulroy asked, more to break the silent tension than anything else. He would continue to act as if everything were normal.

"You won't need any," the boy said, bringing the pistol to bear on Mulroy's chest.

Other *Leisure* books by Tim Champlin:

THE BLAZE OF NOON
TERRITORIAL ROUGH RIDER
THE LAST CAMPAIGN
A TRAIL TO WOUNDED KNEE
RAIDERS OF THE WESTERN & ATLANTIC
WAYFARING STRANGERS
DEADLY SEASON
THE TOMBSTONE CONSPIRACY
THE SURVIVOR
FLYING EAGLE
SWIFT THUNDER

Devils' Domain

Tim Champlin

LEISURE BOOKS 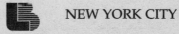 NEW YORK CITY

A LEISURE BOOK®

December 2007

Published by special arrangement with Golden West Literary Agency.

Dorchester Publishing Co., Inc.
200 Madison Avenue
New York, NY 10016

ISBN 10: 0-8439-5990-8
ISBN 13: 978-0-8439-5990-1

The name "Leisure Books" and the stylized "L" with design are trademarks of Dorchester Publishing Co., Inc.

Printed in the United States of America.

10 9 8 7 6 5 4 3 2 1

Visit us on the web at www.dorchesterpub.com.

For my granddaughter, Susanah René Champlin

Devils' Domain

CHAPTER ONE

May 20, 1864
Andersonville, Georgia

The nauseating stench struck Sergeant John Mulroy fully in the face. He stopped, and the shambling column collided with his back.

"What the hell, Sarge?" a man muttered.

Several staggered to a stop as if they'd run into an invisible wall of steaming filth. Guards in nondescript gray, thrusting long muskets with fixed bayonets, prodded the soldiers through the stockade gate.

"C'mon! Move along!" the guards yelled, trying to clear the human congestion of 100 men clumping up just inside the gate.

But John Mulroy was oblivious to everything except what lay on the long, gradual slope before him. Thousands of what he took for humans were milling—seething was a better word—on acres of open space. He tried to focus on one or two of the closest individuals, but the stink that saturated the soft May air was palpable. It had stopped him in his tracks. The pungent odor made his eyes water, and he couldn't focus. The stirrings of the human mass was like a hum in his ears. The miasma of unwashed bodies, excrement, gangrene, decay, and death combined to take his breath. He turned away, trying to draw some clean air into his lungs. As he rubbed a sleeve across his nose, he saw the yellow chevrons of a cavalry sergeant on his blue tunic and was reminded not to show an obvious aversion in front of the private and corporal with him. It wasn't as if these were new smells to him. He'd already dealt with many of the worst cruelties humans could inflict on each other during his twenty-two months of active campaigning. Disease and violent death were daily visitors in the Union ranks.

But the invisible fog he was entering was so powerful, so unexpected, he had to swallow the gorge that rose in this throat.

"In with ya, boys!" one of the youthful guards yelled, jabbing his bayonet toward Mulroy. "Get used to your new home."

In a sudden fit of pique, Mulroy slapped away the bayonet and spat in the face of the teenage guard. Then he had to jump back as the boy thrust at him, slicing the sleeve of his uniform.

"Damned Yankee scum! I'll cut your gizzard out! Git!"

The men were poised to follow his lead, but the odds were too long. Several more guards rushed in, rifles cocked. Other sentries manned roofed guard towers every twenty feet around the perimeter of the fifteen-foot-tall stockade composed of upended pine logs set in the ground.

The young guard's sallow cheeks grimaced with hate as he wiped a sleeve across his face. "I oughta shoot your ass right now. But I won't. No, I won't. . . ." The hands holding the musket shook with suppressed fury at the insult of the spittle. "I want to watch you die, inch by inch." He sneered. "I want to watch you shit your guts out, and your teeth fall out with scurvy, and your hair and beard grow until you look like a damned scarecrow. You'll wish you'd *never* spit on *me*, you blue-bellied warthog!"

"That's enough, Willie!" a grizzled guard with one milky eye admonished the thin, younger man. "Just hustle 'em on in there and get this gate shut. It's nigh onto time for the ration wagon."

The guards surrounded the cluster of new prisoners and shoved them along at gun point. Mulroy knew whatever slight chance the new prisoners might've had to rush their captors and make a break for the woods was now gone. He let himself be carried along with the rest down the sandy slope into the smothering, fetid atmosphere of the Camp Sumter, better known as Andersonville prison.

"My God, Sarge!" Corporal Zack Palmer exploded. "What a hole! And we're supposed to live in this filth?"

"Appears there're a lot of men already doing just that," Mulroy replied, looking around at the thousands of makeshift shelters and hovels squatting on the slope down to the sluggish creek and beyond. Recovering from his first shock and revulsion, Mulroy quickly assessed the situation. "Miller, you and Palmer and I'll stick together." He took in the terrain with a practiced eye. "I see a spot over on that side." He pointed. "Grab it before somebody else does." The place he'd selected was only a few feet from the stockade wall—the better to watch their backs. It was upslope from the cesspool of a stream that meandered through the compound, and possibly located where they'd catch whatever breeze there was. They could trench the slight grade for rain run-off. But there was no way to protect themselves from the sun any time of day without erecting some sort of shelter.

"Follow me." He picked his way among the narrow walkways that twisted and turned among the blanket tents and makeshift shelters that covered nearly every square yard of space.

"Fresh fish!" a man yelled as they went by.

Mulroy paid no attention.

"These boys look like they need us to show 'em a good place to light!" another man said in a strong New York accent that gave Mulroy an instinctive chill. A half dozen men blocked his way.

"Hey!"

Mulroy slapped away the hand that clutched at his arm.

"My, ain't he the feisty one!"

"He'll learn," another man said, and grinned.

"You boys got stuff to trade?"

Mulroy shoved the ragged man aside, his eyes on his spot twenty yards ahead. He didn't want to begin his time in here by getting into a fight—at least until he got the inside lay of things. But he had to assert himself quickly against any predators this prison might contain. And he didn't have to be beaten over the head to know the type of men these were.

"We'll be back tonight, Sarge!" the first man said. "Maybe you'll be in a tradin' mood once you're settled in." He waved his companions away and they descended like ragged vultures on the other newcomers who were wandering into the enclosure in small groups.

Mulroy was thankful his new, knee-high cavalry boots were muddy to the top. His captors had bypassed the footgear as not worth confiscating. In the wide tops of the boots he carried many small items such as a plug of tobacco, spare handkerchiefs, comb and razor case, a bar of soap, Case knife, matches dipped in candle wax, several sticks of beef jerky. It was his personal luggage that the Rebels had overlooked in their haste to liberate more than 100 Union captives of whatever their pockets contained—mostly script, a few greenbacks, daguerreotypes of loved ones, pocket back-up revolvers. When they were cut off from their unit and surrounded by Confederate cavalry, Mulroy had hidden several gold coins inside his thick wool socks. From the looks of this place, he was likely one of the wealthier men on the premises—for now.

He reached his chosen spot and threw down the rolled blanket he carried. "Miller, you're no longer a private. Palmer, you're no longer a corporal, and I'm no longer a sergeant." He scanned his surroundings. "In a place like this, military rank disappears. Natural leaders take over."

"This sty makes my old man's Iowa hog farm smell like a rose garden," the dark-haired Rob Miller remarked, wincing.

"You'll get used to it," a friendly voice said. "Where you boys from?" A gaunt youth crawled out of a ragged quilt shelter nearby. "I'm Luther Salsbury, Twenty-First Illinois Infantry."

They completed introductions without offering to shake hands.

"My buddies and I been here goin' on two months now. Be glad to give you a few pointers," he offered. "Easier than learnin' everything the hard way like we had to do."

"Appreciate that," Mulroy said. He instinctively trusted this man.

"I see you got two canteens," Salsbury said. "Good. Take one and split it in two at the seam. Makes a perfect tool for diggin', and a fryin' pan . . . when you got something to make a fire with."

For the first time, Mulroy noted that, except for what sticks were being used to prop up various shelters, and the planks lining the latrine trough, there was no wood anywhere. Here and there were holes in the ground that could have been anything from tiny wells to cavities left from digging up stumps.

"I share this shebang with five others. We were lucky enough to have half a tent canvas. Keeps off most of the rain, even though we have to huddle up pretty tight to fit under it." He grinned through his ragged black beard. "That the only blanket ya got? For three of ya? You'll best be usin' it over ya, like a tent, instead of puttin' it on the ground. Then you should scrape out a hollow and all pack tight in it t'stay warm. Still gets chilly at night, even in late spring."

Mulroy let the man talk. Here was a mine of valuable information.

"Directly you'll get all lousy like the rest of us. Ain't nothin' you can do about it. The ground is swarmin' with the little pests." He emphasized the point by picking a louse off his shirt and crushing it between his thumb and forefinger. "Damned gray backs are everywhere."

Mulroy tried not to show his disgust. This Salsbury and the rest of the men in the compound had not arrived in this condition in one jump. It had been a gradual thing. Men could learn to live—and die—by degrees, so, in their extremity, they could hardly remember being in any other condition.

"You bring food in with ya, by any chance?"

"Afraid not."

Salsbury looked crestfallen.

"Wait . . . I do have something here, but it's not much." In the presence of this wretched shell of a man, Mulroy felt almost guilty at being so healthy and well fed. He went to one knee and probed in his flared boot top. Pulling out a six-inch stick of beef jerky, he thrust it at the man. From the cave of bushy brows and tangled hair, Salsbury's blue eyes glinted. He reached for the dried beef hesitantly. "For me? All of it?" He obviously couldn't believe his windfall. "My messmates and I'll cook it up with some cornmeal."

"It's already smoked and ready to eat," Miller said.

"Don't matter. These teeth o' mine won't bite nothing hard. Scurvy's makin' 'em fall out as it is."

"It doesn't take much to prevent scurvy," Mulroy said. "A little sauerkraut, some apple cider vinegar . . ."

Salsbury was shaking his head. "It don't matter. They don't give us none. No salt, either I really miss the salt. Mostly cornmeal so coarse it scours out our bowels Gives us the bloody flux."

"Here, Miller," Mulroy said to the twenty-year-old, "take my knife and work this canteen apart at the center seam."

"By God, you've got a real knife!" Salsbury said. "Best hide that from the guards if you want to keep it."

Mulroy glanced at the nearest guard post on the wall a few yards away. The bored sentry was staring off toward the distant woods.

"How do you cook with no wood?" Mulroy asked.

"Swap what we can for it amongst ourselves or with the guards. Those of us still strong enough volunteer for burial detail outside the walls. The Rebs let us bring back whatever wood we can carry."

Mulroy listened with only half an ear; his mind was working on various means of escape. He would not die in here a little at a time. Being gunned down, trying to go over the stockade, would be preferable to starvation. He would compare notes with Salsbury and other older prisoners. They'd probably long since explored every feasible method of getting free.

"You got lots of stuff to trade," Salsbury was saying. "Take them brass buttons on your tunic, for instance. The Rebs is just crazy for fancy brass buttons. I think they use 'em for money. Can't imagine anyone but a woman collectin' 'em just 'cause they're pretty." He looked around to see if anyone was within earshot. "Two things I gotta warn you about right off. The first is this here deadline."

"What?"

"Behind you is the deadline," he said, pointing at an open space about fourteen feet wide to the stockade. "Don't step over that line for any reason. The guards have orders to shoot anyone who does."

"Why?"

"Captain Henri Wirz is the commandant here. He's a foreigner . . . German, Swiss, or something . . . got shot in his arm. Bone won't heal. He had to give up field service, so they put him in charge of this place. He's mean and about half crazy, and he got the idea that, if the prisoners can't get near the wall, they can't make a rush and try to climb over. So he ordered a space fifteen feet wide kept vacant all the way around the inside of the stockade. It's marked with small stakes connected with wooden sticks on top o' them."

"Uses up a lot of the available living space," Mulroy said.

"Hell, you think they care about *that?* They're crammin' more men in here every week . . . a lot more than are dyin' off."

"How many would you say are here now?"

Salsbury squinted with the effort of his calculation. "Nigh onto nineteen thousand. Maybe a tad more. It changes by a thousand or more every week."

Mulroy glanced at Zack Palmer who was reaching for one of the poles marking the deadline. In one jump Mulroy grabbed the younger man and pulled him back, just as a guard on one of the shaded towers raised his musket.

"Sarge, I need some kind of pole to prop up your blanket to make a tent," the corporal objected.

"Listen to this man," Mulroy urged. "He just warned us about touching or crossing that deadline. We'll find something for a tent pole later."

"That's for certain," Salsbury said. "It ain't called a *dead*line for nothing. I'd bet they kill two men a day for accidentally crossing that line."

"What's the other thing you want to warn us about?" Mulroy asked.

"The Raiders. Those fellas that was raggin' you when you come in the gate."

"I've heard of some of the big civilian prisons having gangs like that inside."

Salsbury nodded. "Same as in here. Bunch of New Yorkers. Mostly Irish. Camped across the crick down there. They ain't happy unless they're bashin' somebody. We figure most of them hit the recruitin' office one jump ahead o' the police." He snorted and shook his head. "Hard enough tryin' to survive, without them gangin' up on the weaker ones. They'll steal whatever they can get their hands on. And if they can't steal it, they'll use knives or clubs and take it by force."

"What do they take?"

"Money, clothes, food . . . anything they want."

"Doesn't appear there's much worth stealing in here."

"That's why they prey on 'fresh fish' . . . their name for newcomers, like you."

"I heard somebody yell that when we came in. How come nobody has fought back?"

"These are real toughs. Some of them are older members of Irish gangs who fought bloody hand-to-hand battles in New York years ago, just to dominate the street crime. I ain't got nothin' ag'in' the Irish, mind you. Even got a touch of the *auld sod* in my own bones. But these guys are different. There may be only a couple hundred of them against the nineteen thousand here, but they're organized, and they're mean."

"Too bad they didn't use some of that toughness against the Rebels to keep from being captured," Mulroy remarked. "Is there any organization here?"

"Ya might say so. We're divided into squads of one hundred for rations. A sergeant is in charge of each squad." He attempted a grin. "Trouble is we hafta stand out in the sun for hours every couple days while those stupid Rebs count us off again and again to make sure we don't draw more rations than allowed. And they ain't too good at figures."

"What?"

"New men comin' in, old ones dyin' off. They can't keep the squads at an even hundred. We slicker 'em pretty regular by overcountin' to get more food. But then that damned Wirz withholds our rations for a day every time he gets in a snit about something."

"Like what?"

"One of his spies tells him there's a big escape attempt comin', or there's a tunnel being dug under the wall to topple the logs and make an opening. Wirz punishes everybody to force the information out of us about what a few are doin'. Generally works, too," he added. "As little as we get, we can't go without food more'n a day or we'd all die."

Miller had succeeded in separating one metal canteen into halves that looked like small, circular pans. It left sharp edges for digging.

"Perfect trenching tool," Salsbury said.

Without being told, Miller set to work grooving a perimeter around their small space with the canteen half.

"Men dig tunnels twenty, thirty feet long with just that kind of tool," Salsbury said.

Mulroy was doubtful. "How can anyone tunnel in this sandy soil?"

"Oh, you dig down a couple of feet and you hit clay," Salsbury assured him. "From there it's tougher goin', but it don't cave in." He glanced away sharply toward the south. "Gotta go. The ration wagon just come in. Thanks for the jerky." Salsbury moved away to join the general migration toward an unpainted farm wagon drawn by two mules that had entered the south gate and was being driven slowly around the perimeter deadline.

Mulroy turned his mind away from reflecting on where he was and concentrated on setting up some kind of shelter. There were no rocks for a fire ring, no wood for a fire, no utensils to eat the food they didn't have. Besides the two canteens, one of which was split in two to serve multiple purposes, they had parts of three mess kits. Whatever they had would have to do.

After some discussion about which direction their shelter should face, the three men began to scoop a hollow in the sandy soil large enough for the three of them to lie down in. With only one blanket, body heat would have to suffice for chilly nights. Amenities of civilization such as toothbrushes, soap, towels, razors, scissors, underwear, socks were nonexistent in most of the shelters he saw around him. As time went on, these would become less important. Only one thing would matter—obtaining enough food to stay alive—anything edible, regardless of its nutritional value. Scurvy would show up from lack of vegetables or fruit.

Shelter was the other primary concern. Anything to keep from dying of exposure. But the lack of food and the lack of clothing and shelter would bring on debilitation that would bring on disease that would reduce them from the full vigor of health to death within a period of weeks.

One thing concerning him even more than the starvation diet was the filthy water. He had trained himself to drink very little when he was in the field to avoid the sicknesses contracted from drinking river water and polluted wells of abandoned farms. Troops on the move usually had no time to boil their water for drinking. He restricted himself to coffee in camp, except in the hottest weather when he would sip from his canteen. But, being mounted, he didn't get as thirsty as the foot soldiers.

He paused to rest and turned his gaze toward the slough that furnished water for drinking, cooking, bathing, washing, and latrine. The sluggish stream cut across the compound and had been used by a camp of Confederate soldiers just before it flowed under the log wall. It was dirty even before thousands of prisoners had a chance at it.

Mulroy silently scraped at the soil to dig their pit. If he had to live like a groundhog, he would do it. He would look upon this as a respite from such horrors as the Battle of the Wilderness in Virginia where he and others were captured on May 6th. That had been only two weeks ago, but his memory was quickly pushing the confused bloodletting into the distant past. Fighting on horseback was difficult enough in brushy terrain, but not half as bad as struggling through tangled growth, tripping over skeletons left from last year's battle at the same place. Flanking movements, troop maneuvers, shouted orders, attacks and retreats became only a jumbled mass in the two-day battle. The artillery set the woods afire, and the screams of the wounded being burned alive were ignored by those who struggled on. Darkness and fatigue finally put an end to the first day's carnage. Only the eerie, leaping fire of burning brush lighted the night sky. Above the crackling flames, exhausted infantrymen could hear muffled explosions as paper cartridges were set off by the fire consuming both Union and Confederate dead.

The next day Mulroy had been captured. The patrol he had been leading had been surprised and surrounded in a small clearing by a larger force of Confederate cavalry. His horse was shot from under him in the skirmish. Five of his men escaped, spurring through a hail of bullets into the heavy timber. He and Palmer and Miller were unhorsed and had to surrender or die.

They were taken to the rear and held for three days with 200 others from various units, then marched several miles and crammed into rickety boxcars and cattle cars, headed south. If this southern railroad was indicative of the general state of the Confederacy, the seceded states were in bad shape. Averaging about five miles per hour, the train jolted along for several days, its progress frequently interrupted by stops for repairs to locomotive and tracks.

Mulroy had gradually begun to pass the time by talking to a young soldier who had fought at the Wilderness and now served as one of his guards. His name was Curtis Packett. Through the ripped seams of his butternut shirt, he looked to be all corded muscles, without an ounce of fat.

"Where we headed?" Mulroy asked, handing Packett a dusty plug of tobacco.

The guard on the apple crate carefully shifted the musket across his knees and leaned back against the wall of the car. Taking the plug in his large, bony hand, he gnawed off a corner and worked the chew into his cheek, his eyes never leaving his captives. Before replying, he handed back the plug. "We're bound for Camp Sumter."

"In Charleston harbor?"

"Naw," he replied scornfully, as if a Yankee couldn't be expected to know anything of geography. "It's close by Andersonville, Georgia."

"That still doesn't tell me anything."

"If you really need to know, it's southwest of Atlanta and Macon." He spat a stream of tobacco juice out the car door. "It's the last stop on the way to hell." His lips split in a wolfish grin, exposing stained teeth.

"You ever been to Iowa?" Mulroy asked, thinking of the white farmhouse in the windbreak of trees where he'd lived.

"Naw. Why would I want to go to Yankeeland?"

"You a farmer?"

"Yeah. Hope I live to get back there when this is over. Raised corn and hogs."

"Then you'd appreciate the land where I come from. Dirt as black as your hat. Two to three feet deep."

"I reckon all you Yankees are liars, just like I was told."

"God's truth. Soil so rich and fertile you just throw seed corn at it and stand back to keep the stalks from jabbing you in the eye when they pop outta the ground."

"Sheeut!" Packett grinned in spite of himself.

After a ten-minute stop for water, the train jerked into motion. Mulroy covered his ears against the piercing squeal of ungreased axle ends turning in the journal boxes.

"Damn! Don't you Rebs ever grease the axles of your trains?"

Packett waited for the noise to subside as their speed increased. "We're short lots of things . . . grease being one. After three years of fighting, our government can't feed us, can't give us uniforms or boots, can't hardly keep us supplied with powder and shot." He paused with a thoughtful look, as if considering how much to tell this Yankee prisoner. "You and I was in the thick o' that fight at the Wilderness. I'd wager your quartermaster kept you fed good till you was captured. Our boys didn't have a damned thing to eat. After the first day, we was faintin' from hunger. We searched the bodies of your Yankee dead, 'cause they generally have jerky or some such eatables in their haversacks." He paused, bony hands gripping the musket. "I was so hungry I et some raw bacon, then a hunk o' hardtack . . . after I cut the bloody spots offen it."

Mulroy returned to the present and realized he had stopped scraping at the ground with the canteen half. Miller and Palmer had gone off with Salsbury to be counted and get a share of the scant rations being handed out. They took the other canteen to fill at the creek.

Mulroy rocked back on his heels and again thought of Curtis Packett. The young soldier had disappeared in the crowd when they had detrained at the Andersonville depot. Mulroy was confident Packett had told the truth about the state of things in the South. If the government was so short of food that they couldn't supply their own Army, it was no wonder they couldn't feed their prisoners. Lean times. One didn't have to be an expert in nutrition to know that dirty water and cornmeal ground up with the cob was not a diet the human body could thrive on.

"Lucky we got a few items we can use for trade," he muttered to himself. "Keep us going for a while."

He had not figured on the Raiders.

CHAPTER TWO

John Mulroy awoke from a fitful sleep when the two men beside him in the sandy hollow shifted positions. He was on one end, cupped against Palmer in the depression. The blanket had been pulled off, and he wearily reached to draw a corner of the cover back over his shoulders. Suddenly he stiffened when he sensed a close presence above him, smelled some animal odor. His eyes flew open. Part of the starry sky was blotted out.

"Hey!" He lurched up. Stars exploded in his head as something clubbed him on the temple. He fell back, losing all control of his body. Vaguely he heard yelling, and someone tripped over his legs.

A few seconds later he drifted back from his semiconscious state. Arms and legs began to work again and he struggled up onto his knees. Harsh breathing was close by.

"God-damn' Raiders!" It was Salsbury's voice. "What did they get?"

Mulroy immediately felt for his boots and tunic,

the only possessions he wasn't wearing. "The boots. The beef jerky and my razor and soap were in them."

"Too bad," Salsbury said. "I should have warned you to post a guard . . . at least for the first few nights."

"But the rest of my personal stuff was in the tunic, and it's still here."

Palmer's voice came out of the darkness. "I didn't have anything to steal."

"Where's Miller?" Mulroy asked.

"Right here, Sarge," Miller answered, breathless. "I took out after them. But they knew where they were going and I didn't. Tripped over a couple of shelters in the dark and got cussed for my trouble."

Anger burned in Mulroy. He touched the tender swelling on the side of his head. "Come morning, I'm making a search of this camp."

After several seconds of silence, Salsbury said: "We'll all keep our eyes open for anybody wearing your boots. But they're likely hid somewhere the other side o' the swamp where the Raiders got their stronghold. That good footgear will be traded to the guards for food or extra privileges right quick, I'd guess. There's lots of other stolen stuff down there. Those hoodlums got themselves pretty well set up with other people's property."

"I'll go down there and take a look, come daylight."

"Ain't tryin' to tell ya what to do, Mulroy, but that might not be the wisest move," Salsbury offered.

"Is everybody afraid to stand up to those criminals?" Mulroy asked.

"I reckon their time's coming. But not just yet.

Everybody's about got a belly full o' their antics. Just hold on for now. They'll get what's comin' to them. If you go down to their stronghold, they'll beat you or kill you. And the guards won't lift a hand to stop it. As far as the Rebs are concerned, that's just one less prisoner they have to fool with."

Mulroy took a deep breath. "Right you are. But I wish I had a gun."

"One o' those Spencer repeaters they issued us," Palmer added. "That was sure a sweet shootin' piece."

"Now and again, somebody gets inside with a pistol," Salsbury said. "But they don't have any more shots than what's in the chambers. No extra powder, balls, or caps. When a bunch of us was took at Chickamauga last September, one of my friends kept a little hide-out pistol. But the powder got wet on Belle Isle and he wound up tradin' it to a guard for some peaches. A Colt or Remington would be good enough to protect yourself, but not to break outta here. You got guards all around, day and night, and Wirz even set up artillery on the hill outside where they can rake the whole compound with grapeshot if a riot or general break out should occur."

"Good night, Salsbury." Mulroy cut off the voluble man. It was time to soothe his aching head and try to get back to sleep.

"Sweet dreams," Salsbury said, retreating into his shebang.

"Sorry I didn't get him, Sarge," Miller said as they curled up in their sandy bed once more.

"Like Salsbury says, we'll deal with it later. I should've slept with all my stuff on."

Mulroy didn't go to sleep for over an hour. A

starry blanket was spread over the thousands of men in the compound, and Mulroy lay on his back, staring up into the moonless depths of space. The night was cool and damp, but not uncomfortably chilly. He didn't huddle up next to his comrades. As a lifelong bachelor and a non-commissioned officer, he was accustomed to sleeping alone. The extra body heat was welcome, but he was self-conscious about the physical contact. Such fastidiousness would evaporate when their health began to decline and survival became the only issue.

During the jolting, noisy ride south in the drafty cattle car, he had been able to doze at intervals, although he never got a decent rest. Now, in this open prison, he was not able to sleep at all. He envisioned the lice that were probably crawling in the sand beneath him and getting into the folds of his clothing. Just the thought made him itch, and he shifted his position. Even though his head stopped aching, sleep refused to blot out the events of the day. He'd been in the field so long, he'd trained himself to remain alert at all times, even when his conscious mind told him he was safe. As a result, he slept lightly and could spring awake at any sound.

He lay, staring at the sky, its ice chip stars so crisp and clean compared to everything around him. He was hardly aware of the fetid odor as his mind replayed the days before he'd become a soldier. The war had been surging back and forth for more than a year by the time he'd turned over management of his father's western Iowa farm to a younger brother and gone to enlist. At thirty-eight, he'd been beyond the age when anyone expected him to join the fighting. War was for younger men—hotheads out to prove their manhood, to win the admiration of a lady, to save the Union, to punish the upstart slave holders, or some other such foolish notions that were endemic to youth. He had no such ideals. In fact, except for higher market prices for all the grain and animals they could produce, the war had hardly affected him at all. There'd been no reason for him to go. He'd had a reasonably comfortable existence, worked hard to support himself and his aging parents, enjoyed plenty to eat, and good health.

But he'd been bored. A bachelor schoolmaster, Raymond Streeter, who taught at a one-room country school down the road, had boarded at the Mulroy farmhouse. Streeter was seven years his junior, but the men had become good friends, fishing and hunting together in their spare time. They sat in front of the fireplace and filled many a fall and winter evening with discussions on all kinds of topics. Streeter lent Mulroy books to read—novels, biographies, a few classics, travel books, and even some works on philosophy and theology that he'd found difficult, given his lack of preparation. But gradually many of the gaps in Mulroy's spotty education had been filled in by his learned boarder.

But Streeter had fallen in love with a girl from the village, and quickly proposed. As soon as the engagement had become known, the county school board fired him for violating his contract to remain single during the period of his employment. Mulroy had been best man at the wedding, and the newlyweds moved across the state to Dubuque where Streeter had been offered a job.

Even though ruggedly handsome, Mulroy had no

steady lady friends. Streeter had accused him of being too particular, which was probably true. In addition, except for the winter months, he was busy from dawn till dusk with farm work. He attended a few parties on weekends, but was not a dancer and felt ill at ease in social settings.

So what had driven him to enlist? He stared at the starry firmament above and pondered it. In a word—boredom. His life, after Streeter's departure, grooved itself ever deeper into a rut. Yet, even given his present circumstance, he had no regrets about enlisting. A man lived only once in this world. Better to experience as much of it as he could while he was here, even if war could cut that life short.

Yet he had one inborn trait that served him well, no matter what he was doing. He could not put a name to this trait. What had Streeter called it? Stoicism. They had discussed it at length, and Mulroy had gained some insight into this ancient philosophy. Among others, even Roman Emperor Marcus Aurelius had practiced it. People called Mulroy "stand-offish" or "distant", or "unemotional". Apparently it was the way others saw his personality, and one of the reasons he had few close women friends. Nothing penetrated his inner core of calm.

Streeter had once told him: "From watching your face, I couldn't tell if you were peeking out of a storm cellar at a tornado tearing up the farm, or if you were at a Sunday picnic."

He met all situations with equanimity. No emotional highs or lows upset his balance. Triumph and disaster, pleasure and pain were treated the same. It wasn't as if he had no feelings, no emotions, he thought. It was just that he didn't let anything get to him.

Perhaps it was this coolness in the face of adversity that had gotten him promoted from private to sergeant in less than twelve months. More likely it was the mortality rate that created many openings.

He used this stable core, this stoic outlook, to assess his present situation, and reasoned that, at five feet, nine inches and a hardened one-hundred and sixty pounds, he was starting his confinement as fit as he could ever be. And his age of forty was also an advantage. Older men didn't burn up the energy that a twenty-year old did. At twice the age of his two companions, Mulroy's system had slowed down so that he could survive on less food. He would not let this prison kill him, and resolved to stay only as long as it took him to find a way out. Palmer and Miller were under his command when captured, and he felt it his responsibility to take them with him when he escaped. He had no doubt he would escape—or die in the attempt.

He had to admit that he'd joined the Union cavalry for a change of pace from a life ruled by the seasons, the weather, the crops, the weekly rides to church in town—a predictable routine. From personal observations of friends and relatives, he gathered the impression that the state of matrimony only added to one's trouble. He was well on his way to becoming a lonely old bachelor, perhaps an eccentric uncle eventually living alone on a farm he'd likely leave someone else to inherit.

So here he was. He'd gone from tilling the soil to sleeping in it. Was this the change of pace he had been looking for? He stared into the moonless sky.

The innumerable specks of light rotated imperceptibly in his vision. He squirmed into a more comfortable position on his side. His head hurt only if he rested it on the right side where he'd been struck. He rolled up his tunic for a pillow and, sometime in the early morning, dozed off.

When Mulroy woke, he was slightly disoriented. Why hadn't he heard "Reveille"? Then he remembered as the awful realization spun into focus. He had absolutely no reason to get up or do anything. But that was precisely why he had to get up and do something. Those who sat down and brooded over their misfortune soon sank down to illness and death. The mind was a powerful thing, and it would command his body to live through this. He would not begin his first morning in captivity by lying in this hole any longer.

He got up and stretched in the first rays of the morning sun. He was slightly stiff and sore, and his clothes were damp from a heavy dew. That was one reason Salsbury had advised them to use the blanket as a tent. The other reason was to ward off the southern sun that was growing stronger by the minute. It was only the 21st of May and already the southwest Georgia sun was fierce.

He still had a report notebook in the pocket of his tunic and would keep a journal of his time here, however short it might be. Keeping a record of events would give him something else to keep his mind sharp, something to occupy the endless hours, when he wasn't scrounging for food or shelter.

Rob Miller was coming toward him, carrying a full canteen by the strap. "Filled it before the crowd got down there in the crick," he said. "Want a drink?"

"No. And you better not drink much of that, either, unless we boil it and strain it, or you'll be down sick before you know it. Salsbury's mess has a little well dug over there. Maybe I can trade for some of their water."

Mulroy was conscious of something inside his wool socks. The gold coins he'd secreted there. "Where's Palmer?"

"Out exploring the camp," Miller said.

"Hope he can find his way back." Mulroy looked at the thousands of tiny shelters spread over the fifteen acres. There was no pattern to their arrangement—only tiny paths winding among them. It was like some giant, filthy maze. "Why don't you ask Salsbury if we can borrow some water for coffee."

"What coffee?" Miller asked.

"You're right. Force of habit. Just ask him for some water."

Miller went toward the next shebang where the ragged Salsbury was stooped and working on something.

While no one was observing, Mulroy sat down and pulled off his heavy wool socks and retrieved the four two-and-a-half dollar gold pieces and the three five-dollar gold pieces and shoved them into the deep side pocket of his pants. He'd find a better hiding place later. Then he folded the dirty socks and stuffed them into the pocket of his tunic. Better to start going barefoot and toughen up his feet, and save the socks for nighttime wear or to trade for some food later. He cringed at the thought of walking barefoot on the vermin-ridden ground. But the quicker he toughened himself up to this, the better. If he escaped, he'd have to run through the woods, over rocks and stickers—not a job for tender feet. He'd better be in condition, once he got his chance. He regretted losing his boots, but the tall, heavy footgear would be of little use for running.

Salsbury and Miller came over. "You're welcome to the water," Salsbury said. "There won't be but five of us using it now."

"Why's that?"

"One of the boys in my mess died last night. Neal Passerman. He'd been going downhill for a time."

"Sorry to hear that."

Salsbury shook his head. "Death used to shock me when I first came here," he said. "But no more. When a man dies of disease or starvation, or is shot by a guard, we just say he's been paroled."

"When's breakfast?" Mulroy inquired, with a grim smile to change the subject.

Salsbury peered at him through the tangle of hair. "Soon as you ring for the servant," he replied. "We generally eat once a day, along toward evening when the sun drops behind the trees and it begins to cool off some. Your man here . . . Miller . . . he got you a little cornmeal when the rations was given out last evening."

Just then Miller came up, holding half a boot by a cord. It was dripping and full of water. He set it on the ground.

"Our bucket," Salsbury said. "Let it set there a minute till that cloudy silt settles out. Don't taste worth a damn, but it's better than the water from the crick, and it's not as likely to give you the runs."

Salsbury nodded toward their shelter. "Come on and I'll show you how we dispose of the dead."

Mulroy ducked into the shelter tent to see four men in the process of stripping the clothing from an emaciated body. The shirt and pants of the deceased where swarming with lice and didn't look worth saving.

"We'll scrub 'em with sand and water," Salsbury answered when Mulroy commented about this. "We can trade 'em for some little things, or maybe use 'em to patch our tent."

One of the ragged men bending over the body straightened up with a grunt. "Should 'a' checked for any gold teeth. *Rigor mortis* got his jaw locked tight now."

"I wouldn't be for stealin' Neal's teeth, nohow," Salsbury said, taking a piece of string and tying the dead man's big toes together. The body was naked except for a pair of filthy underdrawers. They folded Passerman's arms across his chest and Salsbury took one end while one of his messmates took the shoulders to lift him.

"Need some help?" Mulroy asked.

"Naw. He don't weight nothin'. When he come in here, he was a healthy hundred and seventy. I don't reckon he goes more'n ninety pounds now."

Mulroy followed as the men carried their comrade toward the north gate in the stockade where they placed him down at the end of a double row. The ranks of the daily dead already numbered more than two dozen. As they watched, several more bodies were carried up and deposited where the wagon would come and haul them away for burial.

Mulroy was appalled. Only in battle had he seen

the grim reaper collect such a harvest. "How many die here every day?"

"Depends. Lately I'd say probably fifty to sixty. Hotter weather will fetch a lot more. Fat men die sooner. They just melt down like big candles. You'd think with all that extra stored up, they'd have enough to keep 'em goin' for a while. But they just give up, I reckon. Most of this survival business is in here." He pointed at his head. "These bodies will be collected later and hauled out to a field about a third of a mile from here and buried in trenches."

"No coffin, no prayer service, I guess," Mulroy said.

"Oh, hell no. That would be too much trouble for the Rebs. In fact, unless they have volunteers, the guards come into the stockade and recruit gravediggers at gun point."

"Good way to get outside."

"If you're thinkin' of escapin' that way, forget it. I been there. They double the guard, and won't hesitate to shoot anyone who makes a break. Besides, if you should get into the woods, where can you go on foot with no food or weapon? Men on horseback with dogs would be on your trail before you could spit."

"Cheerful prospect." He turned away. "I've got to visit the latrine."

"Git your bearin' good before you go, so you can find your way back."

"Northeast side, about halfway up the slope."

"That's it."

He thought he was getting used to the stench, but it assaulted his senses once more as he wound his way through the prisoners down to the creek. The wooden latrine consisted of long, slotted benches held together by a framework and set on the edge of the swampy downstream end of the sluggish creek.

Mulroy jumped across the water at a narrow point, then dropped his pants and sat down several feet away from the nearest customer. He tried to hold his breath against the overpowering smell, but it nearly made him sick before he was finished. The area was alive with flies. There were flies on everything in the compound, but their concentration here was much worse. He walked upstream several yards, squatted by the edge of the swamp, and washed off his bottom. Then he came back and threw his shoulder against one of the upright supports at the end of a latrine bench. The wooden two-by-four gave. He hit it again and it splintered. Twisting off a four-foot piece, he moved away, using it as a walking stick. He could make two short tent poles out of this.

While he was on this side of the creek, he meandered up through the clutter of shebangs, keeping a sharp eye out for the camp of the Raiders. Salsbury said they banded together for mutual protection. It wasn't long before Mulroy caught a whiff of frying bacon. The delicious aroma overpowered the nauseous stink. Pretending to wander with no purpose, he gradually made his way toward the smell. His empty stomach began to growl. Twenty yards away he saw several men squatting around a campfire, spooning something out of tin cups. The shegbangs nearby were made of newer, unfaded tenting, and the men themselves appeared better fleshed-out than their neighbors. He doubted these were newcomers since their clothing was only odds and ends

of uniforms. He stopped and pretended to be looking for someone, but surreptitiously studied the
men from beneath hooded eyelids. Most of them
had not shaved for some time. From their manner
and their New York accent, he felt sure he'd found
the encampment of the Raiders. There were more of
them than he expected. As he looked, a half dozen
of them walked away, two of them swinging homemade clubs.

Mulroy started to move off, then spotted a man
coming out of a shelter wearing a pair of tall cavalry
boots. Even though some of the mud had been
washed off, the boots looked very much like the new
ones stolen from him the night before. Mulroy
gripped the two-by-four, stifling an urge to use it on
the man's head. But he couldn't be sure it was the
same man or the same boots. Besides, he was out-
numbered at least 300 to one. He could wait for another time. With one last look at the shelters, a guess
at their numbers and general physical condition and
strength, he meandered away, waded the shallow
creek, and made his way back to his own camp.

The slim, blond Palmer was there, trimming Salsbury's long, greasy hair with a pair of shears.
Palmer looked up, grinning and snapping the cut-
ters. "I've gone into the barber business," he said.

"Where'd you get those?"

"Traded my half pint of cornmeal. Also gave five
dollars in greenbacks I had hid in my long johns
when we came in."

"Good idea," Mulroy said, slumping to the
ground and placing the two-by-four beside him.
"Too bad my razor was stolen, or we could do some

shaving, too. I reckon I can hone my pocket knife into a passable razor, though."

"Shaving ain't necessary in here," Salsbury said. "You might nick your skin and the cut could fester in this filth. Best to just trim your whiskers short."

"By the way, here's our tent poles. We'll saw it in half with something and prop up our blanket when you get through there." He told Salsbury about locating the camp of the Raiders, and of spotting his boots.

"You be careful o' them," he warned. "Don't be starting anything. They travel in bunches, or their friends are always close by."

"I'll wait," Mulroy said. "And keep this handy." He held up his Case knife. He looked around. "Where'd Miller get away to?"

"He volunteered to go out with the burial detail when the wagon came to load the bodies," Palmer said, raking up a lock of hair with his pocket comb and snipping it off. From behind the jungle of matted hair, a younger Salsbury was emerging.

"The Rebs snatched up Miller since he was young and strong," Salsbury said. "He said he'd try to bring us in some firewood."

"Yeah, I don't favor eating raw cornmeal mush for supper," Palmer said.

The sun climbed higher, sucking up the dew and increasing the humidity in the still air. Looking downhill over the stockade wall, Mulroy could see the compound was surrounded by several acres of stumps where the pines had stood that now formed the walls of their prison. From a distance, the thousands of stumps against the lighter soil looked like three days of whiskers on the cheek of a giant. Beyond the deunuded hillsides, the wind was waving the tops of the tall pines. Somehow, none of the breeze came into their enclosure to stir the sluggish air.

In the shade of the adjoining shebang, Salsbury's messmates were passing time with a game of cards. The worn deck didn't look as if it would last much longer.

"Salsbury, isn't anyone trying to get out of this place?" Mulroy asked. "Even the prisoners who aren't too bad off look like they're content to settle in for the duration."

Their new friend who was getting the haircut didn't reply right away. He got up, shook the trimmed hanks off his shoulders, and ran his fingers through the remaining hair that was now only four inches long. "Ah . . . much better. Since I'm plumb out of money, I'll give you my portion of cowpeas for supper," he said to Palmer. "Time for a coolin' bath in the creek." He motioned for Mulroy to join him as he walked away. When they were out of earshot of the others, he said quietly: "While you're still strong and eager to escape, I'll let you in on a secret, but you have to promise to keep this to yourself. There's a group callin' themselves the Plymouth Brigade diggin' three or four tunnels under the walls. Since the Rebels have spies in here, membership is by invitation only . . . for trusted men."

"I see."

"My diggin' days are about over. Too weak. But I'll put you in touch with some others. You can join them tonight."

Mulroy smiled. It was the most positive news he'd heard since entering this pen of starvation and pestilence. The element of surprise and the strength of numbers would force their escape.

CHAPTER THREE

Mulroy spent many hours tunneling during the next four days. He lent his toil to the secret co-operative effort of the group calling themselves the Plymouth Brigade. The tunnel he worked on was already five feet below the surface and fifteen feet toward the stockade wall. Since it extended well under the deadline, no one could poke an air hole down from the top to aid the diggers. His core of inner calm kept the claustrophobia at bay for hours at a time while he lay on his belly, arms extended in the stifling black hole. Using his half a canteen, he scraped patiently at the clay face of the passage, pulling the soil back and working it past his body to the next man who scooped it out to a third under a tent on the surface. The soil was carried off in a boot or an old shirt and spread where it would not be noticed.

One of the four tunnels finally broke surface three feet from the deadline and only ten feet from where it started. The diggers, being right-handed, had hacked more at one side than the other, lost their sense of direction and slowly curved the tunnel like a horseshoe.

By all estimates, Mulroy's tunnel was nearing the wall and would have to be angled downward to undermine the pine posts set five feet into the earth. The members held nightly discussions about whether it was better to tunnel under the wall so men could escape single file, or to undermine sections of wall so they would collapse, enabling a general rush through the gaps.

"Why should we go to all this effort so just a few men can escape?" a red-headed man from a Michigan unit argued. "Let's collapse the walls so everybody can go. We could rush the cannon and turn 'em on the camp of the reserves outside. They'll drop their guns and run. Then with several thousand armed men we could march up toward Atlanta and hook up with Sherman's Army."

"Not a good idea," a former clerk nicknamed Scrips declared. "Being underground like that, we couldn't co-ordinate it. One section would fall before another."

"Those logs could crush the diggers, too," another said. "Or smother 'em."

"The Rebs got those artillery pieces in the star forts lookin' down on us," Salsbury added. "At the first sign of a general break, they'll cut loose and rake this whole compound with grapeshot. Kill all of us, sick or healthy."

Mulroy sat listening while wiping the grime from his face with a shirt he'd soaked in well water. In spite of his resolve not to drink, his thirst had driven him to swallow several mouthfuls of water. And now he could hear his stomach grumbling at the insult.

"We've got a few days yet," Norman Blake said. A tall, black-haired former sergeant from Massachusetts, he was the acknowledged leader of the organization. He'd been a prisoner for just over three weeks, and was still healthy and vigorous. "When the tunnels reach the base of the walls, we'll meet again and decide. In the meantime, mum's the word."

But the elaborate plans and work of the Plymouth Brigade came to nothing. Either a Rebel spy had infiltrated the web, or a prisoner, trying to gain favor with his captors, gave the scheme away.

Captain Henri Wirz sent a squad of armed guards into the compound to escort Blake outside to his office.

Apprehensive muttering swept over the several hundred who were in on the plot.

"Damn!"

"I'd like to get my hands around the goozle of the man who gave us away!"

"All for nothing. . . ." Tears ran down the cheeks of a grimy, skeletal man.

Twenty minutes later, Wirz and Blake came back through the inner gate, then the commandant dispatched guards to summon the sergeants who headed the detachments of prisoners. When they'd gathered, the short, bearded Wirz stepped up onto a crate with his back to the wall to be seen and heard.

"Ve know vhat you are doing!" he shouted. "You vill not succeed."

"Too bad the little weasel didn't stay in Switzerland," Salsbury muttered to Mulroy as the prisoners migrated toward the speaker.

"Hell, they didn't want him, either," a man at Mulroy's elbow said.

"Ve vill drife heavy vagons around ze deadline and collapse your tunnels. I haf made sufficient preparations to foil your plot. I haf doubled the guard, and haf shored up the valls so dey vill not fall, efen if you undermine dem." He paused to let this sink in.

Mulroy was close enough in the crowd to get his first good look at the commandant. He was not impressed. An undersize, fidgety man, Wirz scanned the crowd with ferret-like eyes. He was dressed in gray trousers and a calico shirtwaist. A gray cap perched atop his head. Tucked under his belt was a nickel-plated English bulldog revolver secured to his left wrist by a two-foot long lanyard. A bandage on his right wrist protruded from the open cuff of his shirt—a suppurating wound that refused to heal, Salsbury explained.

"Py Got, you don't vatch dem damyankees glose enough!" he sputtered at the guards who flanked him, holding their rifles at port arms. "Dey are schlippin' rount, and beatin' you efery times." He hopped down off the crate and stepped nervously toward the gate. "Put up dat notice!" he ordered, then strode out.

Using the butt of his pistol, one of the guards tacked a sign on the log wall just inside the gate. Mulroy was carried along in the odiferous crowd as it surged close enough for him to read:

NOTICE
NOT WISHING TO SHED THE BLOOD OF HUN-
DREDS NOT CONNECTED WITH THOSE WHO CON-

COCTED A MAD PLAN TO FORCE THE STOCKADE
AND MAKE IN THIS WAY THEIR ESCAPE, I HEREBY
WARN LEADERS AND THOSE WHO FORMED THEM-
SELVES INTO A BAND TO CARRY OUT THIS, THAT I
AM IN POSSESSION OF ALL THE FACTS AND HAVE
MADE MY DISPOSITIONS ACCORDINGLY, SO AS TO
FRUSTRATE IT. NO CHOICE WOULD BE LEFT ME
BUT TO OPEN WITH GRAPE AND CANISTER ON
THE STOCKADE, AND WHAT EFFECT THIS WOULD
HAVE, IN THIS DENSELY CROWDED PLACE, NEED
NOT BE TOLD.

MAY 25, 1864   H. WIRZ

"Nice man," Mulroy said as he and Salsbury and
others of their mess worked their way back to their
shebangs.

"He's runnin' skeered, 'cause he's got way more
responsibility than he can handle. Has to act mean
to show he's in charge."

Mulroy was silently amazed that this seemingly
unlettered man had this kind of insight. But, then, in
his own experience of men he had known at home,
such was often the case.

After the big let-down of the failed escape plot, the
camp settled into a quiet, grim daily struggle for
survival.

Mulroy had not told even his closest friends about
the few gold coins in his pocket. He would part
with them only when he had nothing further to
trade.

Salsbury invited Mulroy, Miller, and Palmer to
join his mess, making a total of eight. Mulroy was
grateful to share the well water, the cooking utensils,

and all the information provided by Salsbury. The combined mess got along well, even though two of the men were so far gone with starvation and scurvy, they could hardly sit up and had to be spoon-fed. The first few evenings, the mess had no wood for cooking, so Mulroy traded brass buttons from his tunic to a guard for a thin, two-foot pine log—the "hen buttons" the guards called the shiny brass with the molded eagle insignia.

Using Mulroy's knife to slice off small shavings, the men were able to kindle tiny cooking fires for a week. Fortunately the weather was warm and they didn't need the fire for heat. Salsbury's blue eyes were startling, staring as they did from a face darkened by both the sun and the smoke of countless pine fires. With no soap for washing, Mulroy, Palmer, and Miller were gradually taking on a darker hue from the pine smoke as well. Whenever the coarse cornbread was cooked or the stew heated, Salsbury quickly held a ragged shirt or trousers over the remaining flames to singe the lice off his clothing. He had perfected the knack of doing this without burning holes in the thin cloth.

In less than a week Mulroy began experiencing gastric distress, followed by diarrhea from the coarse cornmeal and polluted water. The three newcomers in the mess were able to trade for small slices of fatback to put in the stew pot, along with a handful of cowpeas.

Then Salsbury began showing increasing signs of scurvy and dropsy—swollen ankles, pale flesh that could be dented like putty, loose teeth, aching joints. He kept up a cheerful front, but Mulroy could tell the man was in pain when he struggled to stand and could walk only a few feet before resting. Looking at Salsbury, Mulroy saw his own future and that of his two companions. At the rate they were going, it wouldn't be long in coming.

Mulroy hardly had a waking hour that he didn't think of plans to escape. But his ideas, so plentiful at first, dwindled by the day as he examined the feasibility of each. Tunneling seemed the least likely, although some men still worked at it.

During the first week of June, the weather grew hotter, and the number of bodies carried to the deadline near the gate increased. These were not always the prisoners of longest duration. Some newer prisoners shortly went mad or just gave up when they entered the compound and saw the living conditions.

Miller and Palmer made the best of a bad situation. Zack Palmer used his shears to cut prisoners' hair in exchange for whatever trifles his customers could afford to part with. The other men in the mess seemed to take heart at the optimism of Salsbury, Miller, and Palmer. One of them, Thomas Carter, even grooved a flat board with a pocket knife to fashion a crude washboard and began taking in clothing to scrub with sand and well water.

Yet, even with the hair cutting, washing, cooking, trading, killing lice, and bathing in the lukewarm, smelly creek, time hung heavily on their hands. While many men lay in the shelter of their shebangs for hours at a time to avoid the blazing Georgia sun, Mulroy forced himself to walk about the compound, if for no other reason than exercise. He noted that many who were inactive, succumbed sooner to the ravages of disease. The sights he saw in the crowded enclosure sickened him.

A man whose arm had been recently amputated above the elbow, was turned into the pen with the stump untreated. Flies quickly laid eggs in the raw flesh, and the man wandered distractedly about the compound, holding his maimed limb with his right hand and occasionally stopping to squeeze it, pressing out a stream of maggots and pus. He died within a week, apparently from blood poisoning.

Mulroy became familiar with a man known as Crazy Phil, a brown skeletal figure dressed only in ragged shorts who constantly roamed the compound, face to the sun, talking to himself, flailing his arms at imaginary foes, cursing and yelling. Everyone knew Crazy Phil and gave him snippets of food and drinks of water since the man seemed to have no place to lay his head at night, and no messmates.

One day he crossed the deadline and began railing at a guard on the wall. Three men nearby jumped up to drag him back. But they weren't fast enough. The young guard raised his musket and took aim. *Boom!* A cloud of white smoke belched from the muzzle and Crazy Phil fell back into the arms of the men, a hole through his chest. He was dead when they lowered him to the ground. Mulroy and others who saw it cursed the guard with all the epitaphs they could lay their tongues to. But the sentry ignored them as he calmly poured another powder charge and rammed a new ball home.

Later that day Mulroy related the incident to Salsbury while the men crouched around their cooking fire.

"The Rebs just changed the guards before you come," Salsbury said, stirring the stew with a stick.

"The Twenty-Sixth Alabama were sent off to fight. They were a pretty decent outfit. Been in combat. More tolerant, respectful. Knew what it was like to be shot at and to shoot an enemy. Weren't near as mean or quick on the trigger against a bunch of helpless prisoners." He paused. "Now we got the Fifty-Fifth Georgia posted around the walls. Most of them never been in a battle. Home guards mixed in. Young kids and old men. The young ones, especially, think it's some kind of game, I reckon." He squinted at the guards in their shaded towers. "Like to throw down on anybody who accidentally falls or gets shoved across the deadline. I've heard 'em laughin' about baggin' a Yank just to hear him holler."

"I saw a man commit suicide yesterday," Miller said, taking a piece of cornbread from Salsbury. "Ran right across the deadline and challenged the guard. He got shot dead."

"Yeah. Desperation," Salsbury agreed. "Happens a lot. Some use it as a quick way out of their sufferin'."

"Sad. We can't allow ourselves to come to that," Palmer said. "We got to figure a way out. I hear a lot of talk about prisoners being exchanged."

"The only thing that rumor is good for is to keep up hope for those who don't know no better," Salsbury said. "They been talkin' exchange since I come in here more'n two months ago. We got holt of a Reb newspaper a few days before you come. Can't believe much of what you read in there about who's winnin' the battles and such, but they said Grant had suspended prisoner exchanges because he didn't want the Southern prisoners of war goin' back South and fightin' against the Union."

"Well, how many in here would be capable of fighting if we got swapped?" Miller asked.

"Not many," Salsbury said. "I reckon that newspaper was right that the North don't want us back. The Rebs would be glad to get rid of us. They keep stringin' us along, promisin' a prisoner exchange. But that lie is wearin' thin. It's just to keep us from gettin' desperate and tryin' to make a mass break outta here."

The men fell silent for several seconds while they ate and Salsbury spooned some of the thin soup into the mouths of his two messmates who were propped up. Looking at the two men, Mulroy guessed they had no more than a week to live.

"Any of you three got a trade or skill?" Salsbury asked.

All three shook their heads.

"I'm a handy man," Mulroy said.

"That's a sure way outta here. The Rebs send someone in at least twice a week to recruit anyone who will go outside and work for them . . . carpenters, clerks, printers, mechanics. Any prisoner who goes out gets decent meals and a place to sleep. A lot better than this." He gestured at their surroundings.

"Are there many takers?" Mulroy asked.

"A few. But most refuse. Won't lift a finger to help the enemy. Can't say as I blame 'em. Every worker who goes outside frees up some Reb tradesman to fight our people."

"They ever try to recruit soldiers in here?"

"Yep. The only ones who go are trash like those Raiders. No loyalty to any but themselves. Bounty jumpers, mostly."

"Bounty jumpers?"

"Some of those Raiders claim New England regiments, but they're really big city fellas from New York who went over to Connecticut to join up 'cause that state offered a bounty to enlist. Then they'd desert and enlist again in another town for the bounty."

The conversation was interrupted by distant shouts of—"Raiders! Raiders!" A club-swinging fight had broken out some yards away. Then several men tore loose and ran toward the creek, dodging among the tents. There was no pursuit.

"They're gettin' bolder. Robbing in daylight," Salsbury said, spooning up the soup. "Probably left some poor fella with his head bashed in. Something's gotta be done soon."

"Maybe organize these newcomers," Mulroy said.

"Damn!" Salsbury plucked a fly out of the soup, then covered the pot with a rag. "Flies are even worse down by the swamp. I've watched millions of those white maggots crawl out of that slime and lie on the warm sand for a few minutes. Then they sprout wings and are off to bite any bare hide they can find, then they fall into the food and generally torment us."

Mulroy could have done without this graphic description just at mealtime.

Later, as the sun mercifully declined beyond the hill and the sluggish heat stifled conversation in the mess, a raucous chorus of voices rose from beyond the creek:

In Athol lived a man named Jerry Lanagan,
He battered away till he hadn't a pound.
His father he died, and he made him a man ag'in;
Left him a farm of ten acres of ground.

"They sound drunk," Mulroy said.

"Most likely," Salsbury replied. "They got plenty of stolen goods to trade with the guards for canteens of liquor made from fermented sorghum."

The Raiders' party stretched far into the night, disturbing Mulroy's attempts at sleep. The only break in the revelry came every half hour: "Eleven o'clock. Post Number One. All's well! Post Number Two. All clear! Post Number Three. . . ." With hardly a variation, except for some adolescent voices, the monotonous cry was carried from guard to guard around the entire perimeter of the stockade.

Brennan on the moor!
Brennan on the moor!
Proud and undaunted stood
John Brennan on the moor!

"These are the two favorite songs of the Raiders," Salsbury said. Verses and choruses were repeated *ad nauseum*, and Mulroy was beginning to hate the sound of them. He lay awake in the hollow under the blanket lean-to, remembering what the guard on the train had said about Andersonville—"It's the last stop on the way to hell." Maybe he was already there—the devils were manning their guard posts, while the condemned roared out drunken songs from their foul pit. In his weakened condition, the horror of the place suddenly overwhelmed him. He'd never felt so far from the eye of God.

CHAPTER FOUR

Having grown up on a productive Great Plains farm, Mulroy had never been hungry—really hungry. He'd experienced hunger pangs now and then when he occasionally missed a meal, or when he had to work long hours with the threshing crew. But then they would all troop into the farmhouse, ravenous, smelling the delicious aroma wafting from the cook stove, and sit down at the huge dining room table.

But that hunger was nothing like this. A gnawing, deep-down craving had set in, and it required strong willpower to keep from grabbing up all the food that was set out for the eight men in their mess. He was a healthy man with a hearty appetite, not a nibbler or taster. He had always cleaned his plate and usually had a second helping of whatever was being served. Now those meals of roast beef, potatoes and gravy, corn on the cob, and green beans took on mythical proportions. He found himself daydreaming for over an hour at a time about those

feasts, complete with salads of green onions, ripe
tomatoes, and vinegar. Strangely enough, he
thought little of sweet desserts, but fantasized about
heavy meat and vegetable dishes with fresh bread.

He was not alone. Palmer, Miller, even Salsbury
dreamed and tortured each other by talking about
what they would eat when they got out of here. They
conjured up all kinds of delicacies from oysters to
rhubarb pie. Comparing notes like this to stretch
their imaginations while their stomachs shrank, was
as good an entertainment as they could devise, and
it helped kill the time.

But Mulroy was careful not to let himself sink
completely into a dream world. He cinched up his
belt a notch every few days as he grew leaner, his
body burning off its excess fat. Shortly it would de-
mand more, and would begin burning muscle. He
would have to conserve his energy for survival. But
how would he balance that with his need to exercise
and stay fit for an escape attempt? He walked daily
to keep his legs in condition, threading his way in
and out among the thousands of haphazardly
placed shelters. At first, going barefoot on the filthy
ground made him cringe. But calluses were forming
on the soles of his feet, until he hardly missed the
wool socks he'd traded to one of the guards for
turnips. Picking up hookworms through the skin of
his feet was a definite possibility, but he tried not to
think about it. On his daily walks, he carried one of
his two-by-four tent poles as a protective club. He
kept an eye open for the Raiders, but ignored them
as long as they left him alone.

For several days, he'd seen a tall, white-haired

man enter the north gate and go among the men. A medical man, perhaps? But why would a doctor or a hospital steward come into the stockade when a small, rudimentary hospital was set up right outside the walls?

One stifling hot morning, he stopped near the man who was kneeling beside an emaciated prisoner, bending down to say something to him. Mulroy noticed the white-haired man wore a purple stole around his neck and carried a small book in one hand. Mulroy paused a few yards away until the tall man rose to his feet, then approached him. "You're a priest?"

"Yes. Robert Hamilton from Macon." He thrust out his hand.

"John Mulroy." Father Hamilton had a firm grip. "Why are you here?" The question was redundant— only a way to start a conversation.

The priest returned a wan smile. "Because these men need me."

"This place could use twenty like you."

"I know. I can't get to everyone."

"Father, over here. My friend is dying."

Father Hamilton went quickly to one knee by the glassy-eyed wretch on the ground, making the sign of the cross. *"In nomine Patris, et Filii, et Spiritus Sancti. Amen."* Then he began the last rites in Latin, only now and then referring to the text in the small, leather-covered manual he carried.

As this proceeded, Mulroy stood back respectfully, even though there was no such thing as privacy in this crowded pen.

By the time the priest finished, the sick man had

made his escape. Mulroy swallowed, wondering if that was the only way he himself was destined to get out of this place.

"Father, what do you hear about prisoner exchange? Is it true Lincoln and Grant have given up on prisoner exchange?"

Father Hamilton shook his head. "I really don't know."

"Some of the new prisoners say Sherman's Army is driving south from Chattanooga, and we'll be liberated if he takes Atlanta. Any truth to that?"

The priest stopped walking and looked directly at Mulroy. "John, I don't read the papers. I don't listen to rumors. Men ask me these questions every day and I tell them the same thing. I know nothing of politics or war. I purposely remain ignorant of all this, or your captors wouldn't let me in here. There are thousands who need my help. I wish I could work a miracle like multiplying loaves and fishes to feed these men, but I just stuff my pockets with a few edible things. Mostly I try to help these poor souls get ready to meet their God."

They continued walking, and the priest stopped twice more within a few rods to administer the last rites.

"I won't bother you any more, Father, since you're so busy," Mulroy said.

"No bother."

"How can you stand coming into this hole every day? Living outside, do you ever get used to this?"

"I ignore the externals, just do what I have to do, give comfort where I can. To many of these men, death is not the enemy," he said.

"They're being paroled," Mulroy muttered quietly.

"Then I leave all this misery and go home," Father Hamilton continued, "go to bed, come back in the morning and dispense the sacraments to as many as I can reach. As the mediator of Divine grace, I'm not the one who's distressed."

"Well said. If any of my messmates get to the point where they desperately need you, I'll look you up."

The priest put out his hand. "I'm here every day."

The sun suddenly went under a cloud and Mulroy glanced up. "Looks like we're about to get one of those summer thunderstorms."

"This place could use a good wash."

Thunder rumbled and the wind freshened out of the southwest, bending the tall distant pines and stirring the stinking mass of sluggish air in the stockade. Mulroy faced the breeze and drew a deep breath. Nor did he move when lighting split the black mass of clouds bearing down on them.

Thunder boomed like artillery over the Georgia hills and the cool rain slashed down, stinging and chilling his overheated skin. He took off his shirt and wrung it out, then joined a general migration hobbling toward the creek to bathe in the slightly freshened water.

The storm passed in an hour and the sun returned with a vengeance, sucking up moisture from the steaming pen. The stifling humidity drenched Mulroy in perspiration and condensation. He walked up from the creek, feeling temporarily cleansed of lice and dirt and grime. His clothes were rapidly deteriorating—frayed and worn and ripped from the hours spent digging and crawling in the tunnel. His face and hands had taken on a mahogany hue from layers of pine smoke residue that couldn't be scrubbed off except with a good soap. At least it was some protection from the sun. In a few more weeks, he'd be as dark and ragged as some of the Negroes. A few more weeks? What was he thinking? He'd probably be dead, or totally crippled by then. Even now he was beginning to show the first signs of scurvy. Salsbury, in spite of taking as good a care of himself as possible, was able to walk only with two canes, since the cords in his legs were drawing up. The man and two of his messmates were so dried out they hardly even perspired any more.

The exercise of walking, in addition to the bath in the rain and the creek had tired Mulroy. His endurance had faded considerably during his three weeks in prison. He was steadily losing weight, and he feared his sore gums and joints were early indications of scurvy. The diet of less than a pint per day of coarse cornmeal was taking its toll. A few cowpeas, and a strip of fatback now and then, when he could trade for them, were not enough for eight men to ward off disease. No—there were only seven remaining in the mess now; one had died during the night.

"Hey, mister!"

Mulroy tensed, expecting a challenge from a Raider. But the voice was too weak. It came from a man sitting under a dripping scrap of canvas.

"Yeah?"

"Do me a favor?"

"If I can."

"Cut off m'toes."

"What?" Mulroy thought he'd misunderstood.

"Take these 'ere shears and cut off m'toes. It's OK.

They're dead. Gangrene. But they bother me when I try to sleep. Rubs the nerves."

Mulroy swallowed. "I'm not a surgeon."

"Don't matter. It won't hurt." He thrust the shears out, handles first. "Go ahead. I don't have nobody to help me."

Mulroy was not usually squeamish, but he was repelled by the sight of the filthy, dead toes.

"Just snip 'em off. Won't take but a minute. I'd be obliged."

Mulroy saw his hand taking the shears and snipping off the dead flesh and bone as if the operation were being performed by someone else. Again, his inner core of calm detachment protected him from being overpowered and fleeing from this sickening spectacle.

"Thanks, mister," the man said, obviously relieved as Mulroy handed back the cutting tool. "They won't get in the way now." There was no bleeding.

Mulroy nodded and moved away without even getting the man's name. A good deed performed for a fellow human. When Mulroy looked beneath the mass of these milling thousands, he saw many individuals performing generous acts, men making gallant sacrifices for less fortunate prisoners—extra food or clothing given to the sickest, shade provided, comfort to the dying, one man aiding another to walk, or to get to the latrine, help in delousing, or washing. And those doing such things were often not much better off themselves.

As Mulroy followed the circuitous route back to his shebang, he knew that another few weeks in here might surely be the death of him. The day he'd entered this open prison, he'd resolved to escape. Yet, just like everyone else, he was slowly succumbing to the ravages of starvation and exposure.

As he lowered himself into the steamy shade of his blanket, he made up his mind that another day would not pass without some firm escape plan.

"I'm outta here in the morning," Miller interrupted his reverie.

"Sure you are," Mulroy said.

"No. I really am. A Reb came looking for people with skills. I suddenly remembered I was a baker."

"In a pig's eye you are."

"They don't know any better. I'll fake it. I've seen my mother and aunts bake all my life. I can do it," Miller said. "I'm to go out in the morning to the bake shop just outside the wall. The place turns out bread for the Reb camp and the village of Andersonville."

"Great idea," Mulroy agreed. "At least when you're outside, you can devise an escape plan."

"Yeah. I let on I was eager to get back to using my baking skills." He laughed. "How hard can it be? I'll just follow the lead of the others working there. They're bound to have recipes to follow. Once I get around all that fresh pastry and bread, I'll probably eat more than I bake."

"I'm sure they'll keep an eye on you." Mulroy's hunger had abated to only a dull longing and progressive weakness as Salsbury told him it would. But the imagined smell of fresh-baked goods stirred his gastric juices as an occasional sweet potato did.

"Once I get the lay of the place, maybe I can smuggle something in to you."

* * *

That night Miller's plan triggered a similar plot in Mulroy's mind. He confided the idea to Salsbury. Since scaling the walls or tunneling were not feasible, he decided to convince the Rebs that he should work as a hospital steward. This would take him outside the walls, and he could devise an escape from there.

None of the men in the stockade, no matter how grievously ill, wished to be carried outside to the hospital, since it was really only the last step to the cemetery. Those selected to be taken to the hospital were usually beyond human help. Thus, two more of the remaining seven in their mess begged Salsbury to let them remain inside and die with their friends.

"Act like you can hardly get around," Salsbury advised him. "If they think you're no threat to get away, they might select you."

Accordingly Mulroy tried to appear as gaunt and ragged and sick as possible when he presented himself at the gate the next morning. Even so, he was able bodied compared to the wretched applicants lying nearby.

The Confederate doctor selected him without comment, and Mulroy followed on foot under guard as the sick were lifted into a wagon and taken out the gate and around to the southeast side of the stockade to the hospital. This compound was a five-acre plot enclosed by a simple board fence. Inside were tent flies and a few shade trees. Unlike the inside of the stockade, this place was laid out in an orderly fashion with paths between the shelter tents. Board pallets were covered with straw for the patients to lie on. He was shown to an identical board bunk between two moaning patients. "This here's your spot. The doctors and other stewards will show you what to do."

Mulroy took possession by tossing down his dirty, buttonless tunic. He'd been using it for a pillow since the weather had grown far too hot to wear it.

During the rest of that day and the next, Mulroy was inaugurated into the horrors of the hospital. At least here there was shade, and something besides the ground to sleep on. In addition, drinking water was cleaner and rice was fed to the patients in place of cornbread. Pods of okra were boiled into mucilaginous soup, which was helpful in alleviating scurvy.

But these few improvements were too slight even to slow the progress of diseases of the dying thousands brought out from the stockade.

Ordinary practices of cleanliness were ignored. Men still lay in their lice-infested clothing. Their long, matted hair was not cut, their bodies not washed. Turpentine was poured on maggots.

One of the few medications given was some species of spirits made from sorghum seed. The liquid, administered by the spoonful, had a light-green tinge when cut with water. A small, undiluted taste of this convinced Mulroy that its intoxicating effects would put to shame the vilest homemade whiskey.

One day Mulroy assisted two attendants trying to arrest the sloughing gangrene by drenching the sores with a solution of blue vitriol. This produced nerve-shattering screams of pain from the agonized patients.

The surgeons resorted to wholesale amputations to check the spread of gangrene. A two-hour session of limb lopping took place each morning, resulting in a considerable pile of severed appendages. Many died shortly of shock and blood loss. If anyone actually recovered in this hospital, it was in spite of the treatment, rather than because of it.

Mulroy was a complete novice when it came to medical care. The chief surgeon, Dr. Isaiah White, and two or three others seemed, to Mulroy's inexpert eyes, to be physicians of considerable ability. But the quality fell off rapidly from there. The rest appeared to be quacks and charlatans. Daily he observed these men practicing the "healing arts" of blistering or trying to stop nosebleed by reciting a verse from the Bible. When gathering boneset—their favorite herb—three of the stewards asserted that, if they cut the stem upward, it would purge the patient, and that, if they cut downward, it would vomit them. These same "medics" held there was nothing so good for "fits" as a black cat killed in the dark of the moon, cut open, and bound while warm on the naked chest of the victim of the convulsions.

"Medicine in the Dark Ages was more advanced than what you guys are doing!" Mulroy snorted at the young man who was directing him to the next patient.

"You just shet your smart mouth and do what I tell ya!"

"Where were you raised? Can you even read and write?"

"I don't take no sass from a Yankee who's blacker than a high yaller."

Mulroy rubbed a hand over his smoke-darkened face.

"These are *your* people I'm tryin' to help," the country lad continued.

"With nurses like you, my people don't need any enemies." He threw down a towel he was carrying and walked off, shaking his head.

The next morning, Mulroy awoke early to find the man next to him dead. He quickly took the man's shoes. They were a decent fit, even though he had no socks. It was better than going barefoot. A leather coin purse in his pocket contained $7 in Confederate bills—the equivalent of one Union greenback. He traded it to one of the sentries going on duty outside for a small sack of peaches.

Carefully, quietly he ate the best food he could steal, buy, or trade for, got as much sleep as possible, and generally husbanded his strength for a week before attempting to escape.

CHAPTER FIVE

Mulroy found that the misnamed Sweetwater Creek ran through the corner of the hospital grounds. It was only three to four feet wide and a foot to eighteen inches deep in most places, but supplied their water. It came in under one wall, flowed about ten rods, and then out under the north side of the board fence.

Strolling about the grounds, Mulroy discovered that only four guards patrolled outside the vertical planks of the enclosure. Apparently the Rebels saw no need for the guard towers and earthworks that were part of the big, log stockade maybe ninety yards away.

There was room for a man to lie down in the creek and slide out under the board fence on the north end, one of the two walls of shortest length. He would have to go when the moon was down or the sky heavily overcast. There was a great risk of being seen by the sentry. Even if he got past the guard, the shallow creek flowed through an open field at least fifty yards before joining the filthy stream that exited the stockade. If he made it unseen across the open fields of stumps and into the woods, he might have a chance.

He casually studied the situation and went out into the compound at night to walk around. He listened for the sentries calling to one another, noted how the guard on the north wall tended to walk down as far as the creek, stop, take a smoke, and walk back. Mulroy wished he could see through the cracks between the ten-foot-tall boards to assess the alertness of the sentry. Guard duty was boring. He had to rely on the chance that the guard, whoever he was, had a sleepy, mind-wandering night.

Early next afternoon, an earth-rumbling, late-June thunderstorm rolled up and drenched the camp. Wind flapped the tent flies while thunder boomed.

Mulroy told the guards he was feeling sick, and went to his hard-board bunk where he slipped on his old tunic, lay down, and drifted off to sleep in the semidarkness. When he awoke, it was completely dark. A few lanterns shone here and there on posts. Now and then a hospital orderly on some errand slipped along the paths between the dripping tents.

Mulroy stepped out into the open end of the fenced acreage. The storm had passed, but the sky was heavy with clouds. Except for the partially shielded lanterns lighting the pathways between tents, the compound was in utter darkness. He made his way carefully over the grassy, muddy ground to the southeast corner of the enclosure, found Sweetwater Creek, and followed it toward the north wall. He could hear water rushing at his feet.

The creek was swollen with run-off. As he neared the fence, the moans and cries of pain-stricken and delirious men faded. With an ear close to the boards, he held his breath and listened for the sentry. But the creek was too noisy, so he walked away from it, staying close to the fence. He finally heard a light tread on the other side. The footfalls on the soggy ground grew fainter as the sentry paced along the outside, away from the stream.

Silently he hurried back to Sweetwater Creek. He was as rested and strengthened as he was ever likely to be. He regretted having to immerse himself in the cold water to slide out undetected beneath the wall, but it couldn't be helped. There was nothing worse than wearing blisters by walking in wet shoes without socks. But, if he had to make a run for it, he wouldn't have time to put them on. As a compromise, he slipped out of his tunic, rolled it up, and held it against his chest, hoping to keep at least part of his clothing dry if he floated on his back.

All at once he caught a strong whiff of pipe tobacco smoke and sensed movement on the other side of the fence. Apparently two guards were patrolling this wall. Of course! He might have guessed it. The stream was the only spot harboring the slightest possibility of escape. It only made good sense to station a guard there. But the guard stood seventeen feet up a bank from the creek and under a pine tree. Even swollen with run-off, the creek gave off a nauseating stench. Mulroy didn't blame the guard for moving away from it and lighting his pipe.

It was this or nothing. Darkness and the noise of the rushing water would have to hide him as he slipped, feet first, into the stream. The current was now two feet deep and swifter than expected. He took a deep breath and lay back. The rolled up tunic was quickly soaked as the stream took him. His shoes struck the bottom of the board fence, and he thrust himself down to pass under it. With his head under, he heard nothing for several seconds but swishing, gurgling sounds. He popped up just beyond the fence and slid along in the filthy water on his side, his face toward the guard.

Suddenly his belt snagged on a protruding root, and the current twisted him sideways, nearly blocking the flow. He struggled to free himself while the water churned over him.

The black lump of the guard's form separated itself from the trunk of the pine tree, and a straight line that was his musket separated itself from the lump.

"Who's that? Who's there?" The guard was not twenty feet away.

Mulroy's heart raced at the sound of the challenge. He threw himself down flat an instant before the musket roared, lashing out a tongue of flame. The guard had fired blindly at the noise. Mulroy wasn't hit, but he had to get away. He jerked his belt loose, ripping his pants. Clutching his tunic to his chest as padding against unseen rocks, he dove forward into the water, pushing with his feet and pulling himself along as quickly as possible.

"What's up, Bill?" a voice yelled.

"Heard sumpin' in the creek."

"Probably a muskrat."

"Don't think so. Mighty loud."

The reply was garbled. Mulroy, heart pounding, fought his instinct to jump and run. He would stay in the creek and take his chances. The water was hardly deep or wide enough to float his body. Grasping rocks and roots, he pulled himself along.

No more noise from behind him. He had reached the point where Sweetwater Creek debouched into the stream from the big stockade. The water grew even fouler, and he held his head up to avoid splashing any into his mouth.

The storm clouds blew away, and the moon came out, illuminating the field of stumps. After a half hour he cautiously peered over the bank. He was only a short distance from the hospital fence and dared not reveal himself by rising out of the creek. But it was painfully slow, dragging his body over rocks and roots that tore his clothing and skin. Briars overhung the stream and he seemed to be constantly ensnared in tangled vines.

But he persisted until he finally had to stop and rest. Another glance showed he was a quarter mile from the stockade. Ahead, the creek disappeared into a dark jungle of growth. He heard no sound of pursuit. The guard must have decided he'd fired at some nocturnal animal.

Besides being wet and smelly and tired, Mulroy was also scratched and bleeding in a dozen places where scurvy had rendered his skin thin and sensitive. If he stayed in the water, the hounds would probably not be able to pick up his scent. But there were no hounds. This creek eventually joined the Flint River, he'd been told. The distance was unknown. If he hoped to get far enough away by daylight to frustrate pursuit, he'd have to chance coming out of the water. He crawled out and lay on the bank, breathing heavily for several minutes. He was amazed at how much his reserves of energy had dwindled since he'd been a prisoner.

To have any chance at all, he'd have to get much farther away before morning roll call revealed his absence. He staggered to his feet and walked, then jogged, then walked again, following the creek through the swampy lowlands until he was approximately two miles farther. The ill-fitting wet shoes wore sore spots on his feet, but he didn't stop to examine them. And he didn't dare run barefoot in the dark for fear of risking worse injury.

A faint howl brought him to a dead stop. He cocked his head, holding his breath. The only thing he could hear was the pounding of his own heart in his ears. Then it came again, slightly louder. He knew of no wolves in this part of the country, and it definitely wasn't a dog or a coyote. A light breeze picked up the sound once more, and a prickly chill went over him. It was the distant baying of hounds, growing more distinct even as he listened. The pack would run silently until they picked up the scent, then would come on, baying in full voice. They were on his track, and he had no chance of outrunning them.

In desperation born of fear he ran for a nearby swamp where the creek slowed and spread into a broad, flooded lowland. He splashed through knee-deep water, stumbling on submerged snags and tangling willows. The baying hounds grew louder with every passing minute.

Finally he climbed up onto the knees of a giant cypress and crouched there, two feet above the water, chest heaving, exhausted, unable to go another step. The hounds came up to the edge of the water and stopped, their noses pointed in his direction while their deep-throated baying filled the moonlit night. Right behind them, a man holding a shotgun reined up his mule and dismounted.

He yelled at the dogs, quieting their mournful dirge. "OK, you son-of-a-bitch, come out of there!"

Mulroy was certain he could not be seen in the inky shadows. But this low-browed cretin was no amateur at this sort of thing, and Mulroy could only delay the inevitable. Still he kept silent and didn't move.

"Hell, I know you're in there. You can make this hard if you want to. I can send the dogs in and tear you to pieces. Or I can wait and lose a lot of sleep. Come daylight, I won't be in no mood to take you back alive."

Mulroy knew it was over. He'd live to fight another day. He climbed down and waded toward higher ground. The pack became frantic as he approached, ready to rip him apart. But their master drove them back and they obeyed his sharp commands as Mulroy stepped up the bank into the moonlight, streaming water.

"OK, get around in front of that mule and start walking."

Mulroy silently obeyed. The walk back seemed shorter, except for the pain of his blistered feet.

As the eastern sky was beginning to lighten, he was returned to the hospital compound; by full daylight, with no breakfast, he was back inside the big stockade as punishment.

"Sarge, I hate to say it, but I'm glad to see you again," Palmer greeted him as Mulroy sank down wearily at their shebang. "But you sure look whipped out."

Mulroy gave Palmer and Salsbury his story.

"Did you have to see Wirz before you come back inside?" Salsbury asked.

"One of the boys said Wirz is on sick leave," another man in the mess volunteered.

"Damned lucky for you," Salsbury said. "I've known escaped prisoners to be took to him when they was caught. Wirz acts like a wild man, they say. Rants and raves and cusses, tells them to get ready to die 'cause they'll be shot within the hour."

"Execution might be a blessing at this point," Mulroy groaned, his head lolling back on his rolled tunic.

"Been told Wirz even shot a man in his office once when the bastard was in one of his crazy rages. But I don't know for sure . . . that's just hearsay."

"How's Miller doing at the bake house?" Mulroy asked, changing the subject.

"Good. Even bribed a guard to smuggle us in a couple small loaves of real bread and a few onions. Never tasted anything so good. We didn't know you was comin' or we'd have saved some."

"No need. I won't be here long," Mulroy said.

They stared at him.

"Soon as I get my strength back, I'll try another break. There's got to be some way outta here."

"Want a trim before you eat?" Palmer held up his shears.

"Sure." Mulroy smiled. "The better I look, the better I feel."

"Rations ain't improved since you left," Salsbury said. "A few o' the fellas was able to knock down some low-flyin' swallows. With the feathers off, there warn't much meat on 'em, but that's what's in the soup pot tonight."

Mulroy took a deep breath. "Boys, I'm hungry as a wolf in winter, but I'm still not ready to munch on swallow."

"Food ain't the only worry we got," Salsbury said. "The more prisoners the Rebs cram in here, the worse the Raiders get. They're just runnin' wild now."

Mulroy didn't reply. He couldn't be taking on any more problems at the moment. After the grueling night he'd spent, he was ready for a nap.

Mulroy awoke in mid-afternoon, sweat pouring from him. He sat up and thrust his head out from under the blanket shelter. "What's all the noise up that way?"

"Rebs are enlarging this pen by a few acres," Palmer said.

Salsbury jerked his head toward the sounds. "Got niggers settin' posts in the ground to enclose a bigger rectangle at the far end. They're about done . . . made quick work of it, too. Only took a few days."

"What will they do with the original wall that's still standing?" Mulroy asked, mopping a sleeve across his sweating face.

Salsbury paused in honing a sliver of human bone into a sewing needle. "Those logs'll be scarfed up for firewood and shelters so fast, it'll make your head spin."

The next morning every last twenty-five-foot post of the original 800-foot-long stockade wall was gone.

"Amazing!" Mulroy said, gazing at the trench where the posts had stood.

"Told ya," Salsbury said. "That oughta give everybody enough wood for a while, even though the Raiders busted a few heads and got away with more than their share. But that still ain't much wood spread among almost thirty thousand, and more pourin' in all the time." He resumed scraping the bone sliver on a stone. "Now if we just had some cloth. . . ."

"What's that?" Mulroy pointed at three white cloth sacks.

"Meal bags we filched offen the ration wagon. Gotta have sumpin' to make shirts and patches with. To get thread, we unravel rags we snatch offen the bodies."

Mulroy was not that desperate—yet. Before he was reduced to it, he'd make good on his promise to escape, or die in the attempt.

Just then a tall, thin man Mulroy didn't know came up and spoke to Salsbury. "Orville died last night," he announced in a somber voice. "Fell into a well hole and busted his leg, and that finished him. He'd been moon blind for most of a week."

"Moon blind?" Mulroy interrupted.

"Yeah. Caused by sleepin' in the open with the moon shining in your face. Take care you stay under shelter these moonlit nights."

Mulroy looked at Salsbury who merely shrugged.

"I know a man can be blinded by looking at the sun, but never knew the moon would do it," Mulroy said, hoping to draw the man out about this superstition.

"Oh, yeah!" The skinny one was deadly serious.

"Well, I'm sorry about Orville," Salsbury said. "I thought for a while he had the stamina to make it."

"Just thought you should know." The lugubrious man shambled away.

"That was George Hillcox, a man from my company," Salsbury said. "When he joined up, he was six foot six and weighed close to two-eighty. We were at Belle Isle together and he held up pretty well. And even here. But this hot weather has 'fetched him', as the boys say. He's just melted. Suffers from what the doctors call *phthisis* . . . a general wasting away. Now we kid him and call him 'flagstaff', and tell him, if we put an insulator on his head, we could set him up as a telegraph pole. Or, if we braided his legs, he'd make a good whiplash. If he let his hair grow long, the Rebs could use him for a cannon swab."

Mulroy had forgotten how good a belly laugh could feel.

"Nobody could've been a better friend and nurse to Orville Jackson," Salsbury continued. "If Orville died, it wasn't from lack of care or attention. Hillcox massaged the man's legs when he got the dropsy, gave up his own rations to Orville, bought cleaner water for him . . . everything."

Mulroy felt of his soggy tunic that was spread out and drying in the sun. His unused journal notebook was still in the pocket, but was now only a pulpy mass. He'd neglected to make a single entry.

"Dry it out and we'll used the pages for toilet paper," suggested the ever-practical Salsbury.

The mid-summer weather had grown oppressively hot, and Mulroy had to relax his own resolution to drink very little water. But he and Palmer, Salsbury, and the two survivors of their mess drank only strained and boiled well water and just used the filthy creek for occasional washing.

Mulroy reluctantly parted with one of his five dollar gold pieces to buy food from one of the older guards who seemed a little more compassionate. The guard returned on his next shift and flung down from the wall a sack containing a bunch of turnip greens, a small slab of fat pork, nearly a peck of sweet potatoes, and several bunches of green onions. Then he threw down a small pine branch thick with needles. "Try makin' some pine needle tea," he said. "Helps the scurvy, I'm told."

The mess feasted for three days and traded the remaining sweet potatoes for a piece of beef that could be boiled into soup for the two messmates whose mouths were too sore to chew.

Meanwhile, the unchallenged Raiders grew bolder and more brutal each day. On the 1st of July they attacked and robbed several of the 200 new prisoners from Connecticut and upstate New York who were turned into the pen wearing newer uniforms and carrying various personal valuables. The startled newcomers fought back as best they could, but were beaten into submission, and the Raiders escaped with their loot to the sanctuary of their own fortified encampment across the swampy creek.

The new men were outraged, and their retaliatory mood began to infect others around them. Like the stirring of a placid lake as a submerged monster begins to rise from the depths, a restlessness rippled over the crowded thousands. Mulroy was reminded of the monster from *Beowulf*. But the awakening giant was not *Grendel*. "Regulators! Regulators!"—the name leaped from lip to lip as if fanned by a wind. The collective monster emerged with a low growl, then began to stretch and roar.

The roar grew from hundreds of throats as able-bodied men snatched up homemade knives and frying pans, yanked down tent poles for clubs. The vengeful monster coalesced into a mob of Regulators, and began rolling downhill, gathering strength and momentum as it went.

At the forefront was a prisoner known only as Limber Jim. A muscular giant from Chicago, he had proven to be the toughest, strongest man in the stockade. Striding at his side was a stocky New York Irishman named Michael Hoare, along with a strong Illinois sergeant named Leroy Key. They, with about three dozen of the biggest newcomers, formed the leading edge of the wave.

Mulroy, Palmer, and Salsbury stepped out where they had a good view of the Regulators who splashed across the creek and surged toward the Raiders' camp. The rest of the crippled, starving men in the stockade looked on, hunger and disease forgotten for the moment.

The Raiders were braced for the assault. From Mulroy's vantage point, the clash resembled a huge wave breaking against a rock bluff. Clubs rose and fell, smashing heads, breaking ribs and arms; knives flashed in the sun; men were trampled underfoot in the mêlée. Screams and yells, men grappling, men running.

Rebel artillerymen on the hill outside the walls scrambled to prime their field pieces, evidently fearing a mass break out.

The battle lasted only ten minutes. Weeks of pent-up frustrations burst forth as the mob maimed and killed, taking many wounded themselves. But the bloodletting and beatings didn't cease until all Raiders who could be found were captured. Several tried to sneak away, a few ran, but the righteous crowd was having none of it. They rounded up all the skulkers, including two hiding in a shebang, and pulled another out of a well. The bruised and bleeding captives were marched under tight security back across the creek and up to the north gate where Michael Hoare demanded to see Captain Henri Wirz.

Wirz came to the gate with a squad of armed guards. Mulroy couldn't hear the conference, but, after several minutes, six men were turned over to Wirz and the rest of the Raiders were penned up near the deadline.

"I don't know what's going to happen," Salsbury said. "But if I was one o' them Raiders, I'd rather be in the hands o' the Rebs than the Regulators!"

CHAPTER SIX

During the next two days a number of Raiders who'd managed to slip away into the crowd during the confusion of the battle were hunted down and arrested. Men who no longer feared the Raiders were more than willing to report their locations and turn them out of their hiding places.

The Regulators had plenty of help tearing down the Raiders' tents. Blankets, tent poles, and cooking utensils were carried off as spoils, and the ground dug up for any secreted property. The work revealed a large number of watches, chains, knives, rings, gold pens, and all kinds of loot. Led by a quartermaster, a squad of plunder-hungry Rebels even entered the compound with spades and thoroughly turned up the ground. But they were too late. All they found was one decomposing Raider body.

Captain Wirz agreed to confine, temporarily, the 125 arrested Raiders in a small stockade that formed the entranceway to the north gate while their fate was being decided.

The 4th of July came and went as preparations were made for a court-martial. Leaders of the Regulators met and organized the procedure, appointing thirteen sergeants from among the latest arrivals who were less likely to be prejudiced against the Raiders. A man named Dick McCullough of the 3rd Cavalry would preside. All the formalities of a legal court-martial were carefully observed as the trial got under way. During the several days this lasted, the accused were brought forward in small groups and witnesses called to testify against them. Dozens of victims recited a tiresome litany of beatings, slashings, robberies, and killings. There were too many eyewitnesses to corroborate the testimony for the accused to be acquitted. A Raider named Pete Bradley did his best for the defense, often directing ridicule and abuse at the witnesses, trying to discredit them.

Some men were still intimidated by the vanquished Raiders and so feared reprisals that they refused to come forward, or agreed to give testimony only at night with their faces covered.

Due to overwhelming eyewitness evidence, all the arrested Raiders were found guilty, and six of the leaders were sentenced to hang. The six were called forward, one by one. Presiding officer, Sergeant McCullough, read from a paper in front of him.

"John Sarsfield, One Hundred and Forty-Fourth New York, this court has found you guilty of the crimes of robbery and murder against your fellow prisoners, and you are hereby sentenced to be hanged by the neck until dead."

The prisoner was escorted out of the stockade under Rebel guard.

"Patrick Delaney, Company E, Eighty-Third Pennsylvania, this court has found you guilty of. . . ."

Delaney shuffled out under guard.

"Albert Muir, United States Navy, this court has found you guilty. . . ."

Sentence was pronounced and the next man stepped forward.

"William Collins, Company D, Eighty-Eighth Pennsylvania, this court. . . ."

The next man came up and Sergeant Dick McCullough's deep voice droned on over the crowd like a pronouncement of the grim reaper.

"Charles Curtis, Company A, Fifth Rhode Island Artillery, this court. . . ."

"Terrance Sullivan, Seventy-Second New York, this court has found you guilty of the crimes of robbery and murder against your fellow prisoners, and you are hereby sentenced to hang by the neck until you are dead. Dismissed."

The last of the six condemned men marched out of the compound in front of the gray-clad guards.

Although it wasn't pertinent to the charges, the improvised court discovered during testimony that two of the six condemned Raiders were born in Ireland and one was from England. All retained traces of their native accents. Since most of the Raiders were bounty-jumpers, they had probably changed their names several times. But no one knew—or cared—what their real names were.

Another two dozen prisoners were sentenced to wear a ball and chain, such as recaptured escapees were often made to do.

Punishment for the remainder came almost automatically. While the court was trying to decide something appropriate, Captain Henri Wirz sent word that he would no longer hold the arrested Raiders in confinement and was turning them back into the stockade.

When word spread that the Raiders were coming back, unpunished, thousands gathered near the gate, clubs in hand to administer their own brand of justice. The officer of the guard opened the wicket in the gate and began to force the Raiders through it, one at a time. Each was told to run for his life. Two parallel lines of prisoners formed a gauntlet and pounded the Raiders mercilessly as they ran past. Blows rained down on their arms, shoulders, heads, and backs. Three were killed before they reached the end. One burly sailor pulled a knife and slashed at his tormentors. They recoiled and he dashed away down the hill. But another prisoner thrust out a tent pole and tripped him. His pursuers pounced and clubbed him to death.

Sergeant Leroy Key, Ned Carrigan, and Dick McCullough, prominent leaders of the Regulators, requested lumber and nails to build a scaffold. The Rebels, always ready for a show, agreed.

McCullough asked several men, including Palmer and Mulroy, to act as guards while the gibbet was being constructed, both to keep the wood from being stolen for firewood and to protect the carpenters from any Raider sympathizers.

Hammers began clattering just after sunup on the morning of July 11th, while Mulroy and Palmer stood in a circle, backs to the workers, clubs looped to their wrists. The crude scaffold gradually took shape in an open area just inside the south gate where rations were usually distributed.

Raiders who had run the gauntlet and survived came to taunt them.

"You bastards will never do any hanging!"

"Come over here and I'll make you eat that hammer, Johnson! Building that thing is all a bluff!" a Raider shouted.

Johnson removed three nails from his mouth. "Wait and see," he replied.

"Chicken shits!" another Raider shouted. "You think you got us put down? Think again!"

"I've got you marked out, Palmer!" a Raider shouted, coming up close to the ring of guards. "You'll get yours later!"

"Why not right now?" Palmer asked, smacking his club in the palm of his hand.

"Later. . . ." The man backed away.

Taunts and shouts rained down on the workers, but the inmate guards stood their ground, calmly keeping the area clear around the scaffold.

By noon the job was finished and Sergeant Key sent word to the outside.

A gradual hush fell over the stockade as it became evident to everyone that the executions were actually going to take place. The July sun bore down in the windless air, wringing perspiration from the thousands of spectators.

Mulroy watched the crowd of prisoners edge forward. A human mosaic of 30,000 faces stared toward him from the packed hillside. He turned to scan the curious crowd on the sloping hill outside the wall. Through shimmering veils of heat he could make out Rebel infantry standing in the rifle pits, artillery-men grouped about their pieces, the number four man of each gun crew holding the lanyard cord ready to fire on command. A small squad of cavalry sat their horses nearby. Restless packs of hounds were held back by their masters. All the hangers-on of the Rebel camp had been drawn by the spectacle—clerks, teamsters, Negroes, hundreds of white and Negro women—in total, a crowd of about 3,000.

A few minutes after noon the south gate opened and Captain Henri Wirz rode in on his white horse, dressed in a suit of white duck.

"Death on a white horse," Palmer muttered quietly.

Behind Wirz walked Father Robert Hamilton, a purple stole around his neck and reading softly from his prayer book. The six doomed men followed, walking between double ranks of Rebel guards.

The whole party halted inside the hollow square formed by Mulroy, Palmer, and the other guards.

Wirz raised his voice above the hushed crowd. "Prizners, I return to you dese men as goot as I got dem. You haf tried dem yourselves and found dem guilty. I half notting to do wit it. Do wit dem as you please and may Gott haf mercy on dem and you. Guards, about face! Forwards, march!"

The Rebel party marched out the gate.

The six men all began talking at once, pleading for mercy. After a minute or two their voices dwindled away and they stopped, apparently realizing the futility of it.

The silence was profound. The multitude seemed

to be holding its collective breath. Thousands waited for the final act to begin.

Father Robert Hamilton stepped forward and began to speak. Mulroy was close enough to hear his plea to spare the lives of the condemned. The nearest in the crowd heard his supplication for mercy and immediately raised a shout: "No! No! Hang them!"

"Don't let them go!"

"They deserve to die!"

"Hang the rascals!"

The shouts were taken up by those farther back and spread through the entire compound until the roar of protest rolled over the log walls into the countryside beyond.

After several minutes, the tumult began to subside. Father Hamilton's plea had been thoroughly shouted down, and he stepped to one side, stone-faced and silent.

The prisoners looked stunned. Up until now, they evidently thought they would get a reprieve.

Charles Curtis yanked off his broad-brimmed hat and threw it on the ground. "By God, I won't die this way!" Holding up his arms to protect his head, he dashed through the line of guards. The nearest ones swung at him, but there were so many they broke each other's clubs and only succeeded in knocking Curtis to his knees. He staggered up and plunged into the mass.

Delaney also hurled his brawny frame toward the opening in the cordon, but Limber Jim jumped in front of him, flashing a Bowie knife. "You dare take one more step, you son-of-a-bitch, and I'll open you up from end to end!"

Delaney stopped in his tracks.

Curtis was dashing through the crowd, knocking men sideways in his downhill rush. He reached the swampy creek and plunged in, struggling through hip-deep ooze. Just as he emerged on the other side, several men caught up and clubbed him over the head.

Captain Wirz, seeing the wild rushing and shouting, ran toward his gunners yelling: "Fire! Fire!"

The outside spectators, who'd crowded in front of the cannon for a better view, screamed and trampled each other in their panic to get out of the way.

Expecting to be mowed down any second with grapeshot, the prisoners rushed every direction, many falling into wells and breaking legs.

Fortunately the Rebel officer in charge of the battery, who saw the prisoners surge *away* from the stockade gates and not *toward* them, had the good sense to hold his fire.

Within five minutes, order was restored and Sergeant Key ordered the prisoners up onto the scaffold. Curtis was returned to the cheers of the mob. He was the last to climb the stairs, still dripping filth.

Father Hamilton resumed reading the service for the condemned.

The six men asked for water, which was quickly brought. Each gulped down more than a quart.

"This hangin's thirsty work," Delaney joked, wiping his mouth with the back of his hand. Then he spotted a prominent Raider in the crowd. "Pete Donnelly!" he called. "Give Sam that gold watch o' mine. And Luke's to have the crescent ring. You and Mullins can divide up those greenbacks."

"I was not a bad man when I came in here!" Collins called out. "I just fell in with bad company."

"Oh, bad company, is it?" Delaney berated him.

"I'm a big man. And a man has to eat. I only took what I needed!" Collins shouted over the jeers of the mob.

The others began to speak, yelling out their farewells to various friends in the crowd.

Sergeant Key pulled a watch from his pocket. "Two more minutes to talk!" he called out.

"Well, good bye to all o' ye," Delaney said. "Speak up now any of ye that I've hurt and say you'll forgive me. You . . . Marion Mosley. Come forward and say you'll forgive me."

By some miracle, Mosley had barely escaped a throat-slashing three weeks earlier while Delaney was robbing him of forty dollars. Mosley was not in a forgiving mood. "Go t'hell, you murderin' Irish ape!"

"Time's up!" Sergeant Key snapped his watch closed.

One man was stationed behind each of the condemned on the scaffold, and they proceeded to tie the prisoners' hands behind them. Then a meal bag was pulled down over their heads, and lastly each man looped a noose over the head of his assigned prisoner, pulling up the slipknot.

"Father, forgive these men their sins and welcome them into Your . . . ," the priest intoned.

Sergeant Key dropped his hand as a signal and two assistants jerked out the planks that supported the prisoners. Five bodies dropped and swung in the air. The sixth, William Collins, thudded to the ground, the rope broken. Two men rushed forward, pulled off the noose and the hood.

"He's still alive."

Limber Jim came up and dashed a can of water into Collins's face. He regained consciousness and looked around. "Am I in another world?" he gasped.

"No, but you soon will be!" Limber Jim picked up the big-boned Collins as he would have hoisted a sack of cornmeal and carried him back up the scaffold.

"For God's sake, don't do it again!" Collins begged. "God has spared me once. He meant for you to have mercy on me!"

"You murdered my brother," Limber Jim said, pulling the sack over Collins's head and catching another rope someone tossed up. He pitched a coil over the crossbeam and deftly formed a hangman's noose in the loose end.

The prisoner continued to plead even as Jim jumped down and kicked the board from under him. Collins's words were choked off in midsentence as the big man jolted down to the end of the hemp and kicked twice before swaying limply back and forth.

Five minutes later, the ropes were slacked, the bodies taken down, and the hoods removed. Those of the crowd who were so inclined could file past and view the corpses. Pete Donnelly and Dick Allen knelt down to wipe the froth off Delaney's lips. "By damn, you'll rue the day you done these men to death!" Donnelly glared around at Sergeant Key and the other Regulators.

But the Raider threat was broken and everyone knew it. By request of the Regulators, the six executed criminals were buried apart from the rest of the deceased prisoners.

Life in the stockade returned to what passed for normal—blistering heat, bad water, dysentery, starvation, scurvy, dropsy, gangrene—all spiced with daily rumors of exchange.

With some additions, the stockade now contained nearly 33,000 prisoners. But, as the heat of July increased, upwards of 140 men died each day.

"Turns out the Raiders weren't the worst of our problems," Salsbury said one evening when he, Mulroy, Palmer, and the one other survivor of their mess were sipping watery soup from blackened tin cups. "The heat's beginning to take the ones I thought were the strongest."

"How are *you* feeling?" Mulroy asked.

"Holdin' my own with scurvy. Tryin' everything I can to stay healthy. But the cords in my legs are drawin' up. Have a hard time walkin', even with a crutch." He glanced at the survivor of his original mess. "Harvey's failin', though. Done everything I could for him, but he's about gone. I promised I wouldn't send him out to the hospital."

"Just as well to die here," Mulroy agreed, then proceeded to detail the miserable conditions he'd encountered at the hospital.

"We've got more trouble," Salsbury said. "No rain for two weeks. Our well's dryin' up."

"I'll go get us some from the crick," Mulroy offered. "We can boil it."

"Take the boot, and here's a little pail. That's all we got to carry it in."

Mulroy picked up the cut-off, mildewed boot they used for drawing up well water.

Mulroy would have asked Palmer to go along, but he was busy cutting a prisoner's hair.

"Be back shortly."

"We're not going anywhere," Salsbury said.

Mulroy smelled the creek before he was within forty yards of it. He paused, trying to decide where to draw the water. The lower end was the swampy "sinks" with the latrine. In the middle section, men were bathing. Drinking this water could hasten death. Dysentery itself could do it, especially in their weakened state.

He turned right and followed the sluggish watercourse upstream. He scuffed along the sandy bank, walking in the shoes he'd stolen from the corpse in the hospital. They were well worn when he took them, and had been soaked and dried out several times since. One sole was tearing loose and scooping sand at every step, but it was still better than walking barefoot on maggots and dried vomit and lice and dead flies and feces and worms.

He came to the deadline. Maybe by reaching up past the staked line, he could fill his containers with water that was at least a little fresher. He glanced around. The guard on the nearest tower was gazing off toward the long, lingering sunset. Mulroy would have to be quick and unobtrusive. He squatted by the creek with the pail and stretched under the marked deadline as far as his arm could reach, submerging the container.

His only warning was the double *click* of a musket hammer being drawn to full cock. He looked up to see a black muzzle aiming right at him. Above the breech was the face of a very young guard. Their eyes locked. The charged instant seemed frozen in time. Then the barrel swung a few inches to the right and erupted in a blast of flame and smoke.

Mulroy threw himself backward, expecting to feel a ball slam into him. Another prisoner caught him before he hit the ground, and Mulroy saw a startled, bearded face above him.

"God! You're still alive! Where you hit?"

"I . . . I'm not. He missed."

"Missed?" The man was incredulous.

They both looked up through the dissipating white smoke. The thin young guard was biting off the end of another paper pack of powder and pouring it down the barrel.

"Quick! Get outta here!" the bearded one said, giving him a shove.

Mulroy scrambled away with his empty containers. Twenty yards beyond, he paused to look back. The guard still stood in the roofed tower, looking in his direction. From this distance, Mulroy couldn't read his expression. The boy had missed him intentionally. Mulroy was sure of it. The guard had him dead in his sights, from no more than thirty feet. Yet, he'd pulled off and fired into the creek. Why? He resumed walking. It was evident the lad didn't have the stomach for murder, especially for such a minor infraction as reaching beyond the deadline. Yet more than one man was killed every day for that very thing. There was still some spark of humanity or compassion among the Rebel sentries, even though most of the younger ones had the well-deserved reputation of cold-blooded brutality against the helpless prisoners.

He reached his shebang and dropped to the ground.

"Where's the water?" Salsbury asked.

Mulroy related his story.

"Whew! You're mighty lucky to be alive."

"I'll go get some water after dark," Palmer said.

Mulroy lay there, thinking about his narrow escape. It had happened so quickly, he'd had no time to be afraid. And his stoic nature now kept any delayed nervous reaction from setting in. Instead, as dusk deepened, he began to form a plan.

"I want you to do me a favor," Mulroy finally said.

"If I can," Palmer replied.

"Take the forty dollars in gold I have and use it to buy whatever you can get in the way of fresh vegetables or meat."

"What are you going to do?"

"Before dawn I'm going to the south gate and lie down among the dead bodies. When I'm carried out on the wagon for burial with the others, I'll make a break for it."

"You'll be shot down before you get into the woods," Salsbury said. "Those burial parties are guarded."

"I've got to try while I still have the strength. If I get away, I'll figure some scheme to get you two out, and Miller, too, even though he's in the bake house."

"There must be some other way. Why don't you volunteer to go outside and work for the Rebs?" Salsbury said.

"No. I took an oath to the United States. I only went out before to give myself a better chance of escape. I can't be a turncoat by really helping them. If I'm shot trying to get away, it beats a slow death by starvation and disease. You two can use this gold to buy enough good food to see you through. I'll keep a half eagle, in case I get away and need a little money."

"They'll see right off you're not dead."

"If they do, I'll let on that I fainted, and just came to when they picked me up. I'll leave my shirt and tunic and shoes here, so it'll appear I was stripped like most of the other bodies. Just keep my pants on."

"I don't know. . . ." Salsbury was doubtful. "An awful long chance. What if there's an armed guard standing right there? You gonna let them actually bury you?"

"I understand those graves are only a couple feet deep. I'll just have to play it by ear."

"Damn!" Salsbury breathed. "You got a lot of guts."

Mulroy didn't admit that it was more desperation than courage. "Well, if I get gunned down, I'll already be right there at my grave."

CHAPTER SEVEN

Mulroy never knew how uncomfortable it was to be dead. As the sun rose over the stockade and struck him fully in the face, he realized he'd placed himself facing the wrong way when he lay down between two dead bodies shortly before dawn. He'd tied his own big toes together and lay on his back, clad only in his filthy, ragged, and torn blue cavalry pants with the yellow stripe down the legs.

His bare torso began to itch in a dozen places, and he could feel bugs crawling under him on the sandy soil. As the sun rose higher, prisoners carried more and more bodies and laid them on the ground in rows near the gate. Mulroy wondered how long he would have to endure this before the dead wagon rolled inside to collect the cadavers. The hot July sun was causing him to sweat. Dead bodies did not perspire, yet he didn't dare move to wipe it off for fear of being noticed by one of the guards on the wall.

He heard movement around him as prisoners brought more of their friends. Mulroy slitted his eyes and looked to right and left through the lashes. Men were murmuring their good byes to friends and messmates. Two men nearby were kneeling on the ground, reciting the Lord's Prayer. When Mulroy closed his eyes again, he could almost imagine himself at some civilized mortuary back home. But here there would be no washing or dressing of the bodies, no loved ones to cry, no minister or priest to conduct a burial service, no coffins. Here, death had become so commonplace as to be nearly unnoticeable. Life was cheap, and getting cheaper.

By the time the bodies stopped arriving, Mulroy estimated he was surrounded by at least 140 corpses. The fetid stench of the camp was enough; he was glad the bodies would not have to lie in the sun very long, or the odor would become overpowering. He tried to ignore the tickling perspiration and the burning sun on his face and chest while he plotted his next moves. Until he found out what was going to happen, he could not make any definite plans. If he had a small hide-out gun, he would stand a much better chance. But wishing was no good. He had to deal with what was.

To pass the time and keep his mental faculties fresh for what was coming, he retreated into his inner sanctuary of calm, and mentally escaped to another place, another time. *It was early summer in Iowa, the insects humming in the weeds along the fence rows. The leaves of corn waved in the breeze and the green stalks marched in long rows across the gently rolling terrain, marked by the black soil still visible between. He was sitting under a giant maple tree in the side yard. White, fluffy clouds dotted the azure sky. All was calm and peaceful.*

Voices and the rattling of trace chains shattered his pleasant daydream. Mulroy slitted his eyelids. Without moving his head, he could see part of a mule-drawn wagon approaching.

"Lawdy, we's got a load of 'em today. They's dyin' off like flies."

"Yeah. No sense jawin' 'bout it, though. Sooner we gets 'em loaded, the sooner we gets 'em into de shade outside."

One Negro took the feet and the other the arms and began to heave the bodies up into the back of the farm wagon.

"At least dey ain't heavy," one of them said, pausing to wipe sweat from his brow.

"Dey's jest skin and bone," the other one agreed.

Mulroy guessed he had shed at least twenty-five pounds. Even at 135, he would be heavy compared to the rest of these corpses. Lying on his back, his belly was concave. He hoped he looked properly cadaverous to fool the Negroes. He had drunk more than a quart of boiled, foul-tasting creek water before coming out here in the predawn darkness. He was definitely hungry, but it wouldn't do to attempt an escape while dehydrated.

The muscular Negroes wore leather gloves and apparently didn't notice that he was slick with sweat. Strong hands gripped his ankles and wrists and he let himself go limp and tried not break his fall as he was flung up into the wagon, landing on a pile of bodies. His flesh cringed at the feel of the cold skin, the stiff arms, legs, rib cages beneath him. Other bodies landed on him until he was nearly suffocating. He held his breath and dared not move.

A few minutes later, the wagon was piled high,

and the Negroes departed with their load. Mulroy turned his head very slightly and could see through a corpse's dangling hair two Rebel guards standing just inside, waiting to open the gate. While the wagon bumped over the uneven ground and out of the stockade, he wiggled his big toes loose from the string he'd tied them together with.

This was a job that required more than one wagon, but the Negroes would make several trips, spending most of the day picking up bodies; they were in no hurry, except to get into the shade.

The wagon stopped in the shade of a cluster of pines and oaks. He could hear shovels chunking into the earth and the grunting of the diggers as they toiled silently.

"Damn, how many more loads you got?" a voice asked.

"Maybe six or seven."

"Whew! We may have to get some relief. It's hotter'n hell," another man said.

"You gonna bring us some lunch?" one of the diggers asked.

"You ain't out here for your health, Yank," one of the guards replied. "You'll get sumpin' to eat after a bit. Just keep on diggin'."

It took all of Mulroy's willpower to keep from moving in the pile of repulsive bodies. Lice were crawling everywhere. He moved his head slightly to get fresh air, closed his eyes, and concentrated on keeping his breathing slow and shallow. Time crept by.

Finally he was dragged out and dumped on the ground. He lay on his stomach, and could see the open trench stretching away to his right. Several able-bodied prisoners toiled to extend the trench, piling the dirt to one side as they went. Behind them two other prisoners were lifting the corpses and placing them carefully in foot-deep slots, or vaults, cut in the bottom of the thigh-deep trench. Over each body, in lieu of a coffin or blanket, they placed a freshly split slab of pine. Four other prisoners were kept busy splitting thin slabs off sections of pine logs. The heavy physical toil and the heat caused the work to crawl. Mulroy lay face down in the cool grass and shade for another hour, thankful to be out of the pile of bodies, but itching fearfully from the grass and the ants against his bare chest, neck, and feet.

A prisoner carried a bucket of water and a dipper along the line of workers, letting each man drink his fill.

"All right, take a break!" one of the guards called out.

The prisoners dropped their tools and shovels, climbed out of the trench, and gathered near a shady oak. They were probably eating the usual cooked cornmeal mush and greens. The Rebel guards were in their shirtsleeves and sweating profusely in the still, humid air. They, too, joined in the food break, but ate limp bacon on corn cakes, washed down with jugs of water, or cups of hot coffee they'd brewed over a small campfire.

The men quit talking while they ate. The Negroes had driven their mules and wagon away, and it became quiet beneath the trees. In the middle distance a raucous cawing of crows ripped the midday stillness. Black vultures soared on high, silent thermals, anticipating a carnivorous feast.

The smell of cooked food caused Mulroy's stomach to give a loud growl. He cringed at the sound. The nearest guard lowered his tin coffee cup and looked curiously in his direction. Peering from under his eyelids, Mulroy recognized the pallid face of the same guard who had refrained from shooting him the evening before. For a long minute the two regarded one another, Mulroy through his eyelashes from a prone position on the grass. The guard was small and lean and didn't appear to be over fourteen years old. And he looked sick. His whiskerless cheeks had a jaundiced cast.

The guard resumed eating, but kept glancing in Mulroy's direction. Sweat trickled down his temples, but Mulroy dared not move.

At last the burial detail resumed work. Just when Mulroy began to feel safe, the thin guard sauntered in his direction, and squatted close by among the bodies. He removed his kepi and wiped the loose sleeve of his white shirt across his brow. Then he turned his head, covered his mouth with his cap, and whispered: "Keep still and I'll see that you're last in line."

Mulroy gave an involuntary start, and his eyes flew open. The boy was staring straight at him.

"Play dead and I'll get you out of here," he said. Then he stood up, replaced his cap, and stretched. Gripping his musket, he moved away and directed two of the prisoners who were splitting slabs to come and carry the bodies over to the trench and line them up. The guard pointed out which bodies he wanted moved first. The area around Mulroy began to be cleared of corpses.

Mulroy felt his heart pounding, and he was perspiring more than ever. But no one else seemed to notice.

A white headboard, crudely painted with a number, name, regiment, and company was placed on the ground at the head of each body. Two more men with wooden mauls were driving the pointed boards into the soft earth.

Two prisoners followed and scooped the loose dirt back into the trench, not bothering to tamp it down.

The work went on. The sun slid slowly down the western sky, its rays lancing between the trees to illuminate the torn, grassy meadow and the rows of white headboards.

"Come on, hurry up!" a guard yelled. "Get this batch underground before dark. You'll have just as many tomorrow."

"Aw, shit!" One of the trenchers flung down his shovel. "Get some niggers to do this pick and shovel stuff."

"You want I should turn you back into the stockade?" a guard asked.

"OK, OK." The disgusted digger picked up his spade.

The sun disappeared, but the work continued in the long summer twilight. The tired men were not talking now.

As dusk settled in, the mosquitoes came out. Mulroy gritted his teeth when the insects began to feast on his bare, sweaty back. He was nearly numb from lying for hours in one position.

Darkness softly enveloped the work party, and one of the guards lighted a pitch-pine torch.

"There's one more over there."

Mulroy closed his eyes and held his breath. He

heard footsteps thudding toward him. They turned him over. It was with relief that he felt his muscles stretching while he was being lifted and carried to the trench. With unexpected gentleness, the two prisoners lowered him onto his back, then folded his arms over his chest. Another man laid a thin pine slab over him, wedging each end into the sides of the trench.

"What's his name and unit?" he heard someone ask.

"Don't know. His friends didn't put any paper or tag on him that I could see. Just mark him as 'Unknown'."

Several seconds later, Mulroy was startled as a shovelful of dirt hit the slab. Then another. The slab was several inches above his face, allowing him a small breathing space, and he inhaled the fresh scent of pine resin. He felt a moment of panic in the blackness. Even with his arms on his chest, he wouldn't be able to dig his way out or lift the weight of the slab with two feet of dirt on top of it. The clods stopped falling.

"Gimme that shovel," he heard a muffled voice say. "Go on back. It's getting dark. I'll finish up here."

Mulroy could see cracks of light on each side of the thin slab. He lay quietly, retreating into his calm core, breathing shallowly, counting off the seconds. He stopped counting at two minutes when the air was becoming foul. Time to claw his way out of this tomb. A sudden scraping on the wood a few inches above. Seconds later someone pulled up the slab and loose dirt showered down into his eyes and mouth. He spat, then gratefully sucked in the fresh air.

"Gimme your hand," a voice said.

The guard was pulling his arm, and Mulroy struggled to climb out of the hole. It was dark above ground as well, with only a rising moon to cast a dim light.

"Thanks," he managed to gasp. He couldn't see well, but sensed the small figure in front of him was his young benefactor.

"Scrape dirt into the hole."

Mulroy, grateful to have something physical to do, grabbed the shovel and quickly scooped the end of the trench full. "Thank God I'm not underground yet," he said quietly, dropping the shovel. "And thank you for saving my life."

"This way."

The guard led him off through the pine woods at a fast pace. They trotted on some sort of footpath. Mulroy lost all sense of direction, but didn't care where he was, as long as he was being led away from the stockade. He had no idea why this young Rebel guard had taken pity on him, but was not one to look a gift horse in the mouth.

He guessed they'd gone three-quarters of a mile when they broke into a clearing and climbed over a stile into a large yard that fronted a two-story white house.

"Wait here." The guard went up onto the porch and entered the front door. Mulroy stood where he was, eyeing the frame house in the light of the rising moon, hoping no one could see him. It was not an imposing plantation house, but he could see log slave cabins out back, so the owner was a man of some means.

After several minutes, the guard hadn't reappeared, and Mulroy began to have doubts. Maybe he should retreat into the shelter of the woods. Had the boy led him into some kind of trap? But that made no sense. Yesterday the boy could have killed him for crossing the deadline, or could have exposed him today as he impersonated a dead body to get outside the walls. He remained calm and concentrated on breathing the fresh, pine-scented air—the air of freedom.

Then a light appeared behind one of the curtained windows. The front door opened and the boy came out and down the stairs.

"Come on around back."

Mulroy followed, and shortly found himself several feet underground in a root cellar. The boy lighted a small coal-oil lamp that hung on a nearby hook.

"Get outta them pants and I'll bring you some clothes. Ain't nobody home tonight. But I don't want the niggers to see ya."

"Can I have some water?" Mulroy asked, suddenly aware of a burning thirst. He'd had nothing to drink in fourteen hours and had been sweating much of that time.

The boy disappeared and returned several minutes later with a bucket of water and dipper. Shaking in his haste, Mulroy slopped water down his bare chest as he gulped dipperful after dipperful of the clean well water. He hadn't tasted anything as delightful and refreshing in weeks.

The boy stood watching him with a curious look on his face.

"Thanks." He dropped the dipper back into the bucket. "You got something I can wear? And maybe a little food?"

"Yeah." The boy seemed agitated. His face, in the yellow lantern light, looked even more jaundiced. The boy wasn't talkative, but Mulroy would find out his motives later.

It was hot and close in the dank cellar. The dirt on his bare torso was streaked with sweat and well water. He rubbed his arms and scratched several insect bites. His dirty, damp trousers still crawled with lice. Matted, filthy hair fell across his forehead.

"Name's John Mulroy. Thanks for saving my life." He didn't offer to shake hands.

"Cal Blackwood," the boy said, still looking distracted. "Wait here." He bounded up the steps and let the slanted cellar door drop behind him.

Mulroy sank down on the bottom step, feeling rather queasy and shaky. *Drank too much water, too fast,* he thought. In spite of feeling sick and weak, there was a spark of elation deep inside him. His scheme had worked! With the help of Cal Blackwood, he was free for the moment. Tomorrow he would be reported dead by his companions. With the number of men expiring each day, the lie would never be questioned. The Rebs were averse to numbers and paperwork. The only one keeping records of the dead was Dorence Atwater, a Yankee clerk who'd been recruited out of the stockade by the Rebels because of his excellent penmanship.

The cellar door opened and the boy descended, clothes draped over one arm. "Get into these," he ordered.

Mulroy reached for the clothes, then froze, his stomach contracting.

The boy had a pistol trained on him.

CHAPTER EIGHT

Without thinking, Mulroy reached for the shirt and pants, his eyes riveted on the pistol in the boy's hand. "What's this?"

"Put on these clothes."

"I could use a good bath first."

Cal said nothing, but continued aiming the gun at him. The boy had no expression on his face.

Mulroy did as he was told, glad to be rid of the filthy cavalry uniform pants he'd worn for weeks. But his mind was in a whirl. Was this some kind of joke? Why would the young guard hold a gun on him, unless he feared him as dangerous? Cal's attitude was rather nonchalant. Maybe he didn't know how to handle firearms and was inadvertently pointing it in Mulroy's general direction.

All these possibilities raced through his mind as he pulled on the cotton trousers and shirt, both of which were a fair fit, except the average-size waist was far too loose on him. Cal had anticipated this and tossed a leather belt to him.

"Got any shoes or boots that'll fit me?" Mulroy asked, more to break the silent tension than anything else. He would continue to act as if everything were normal.

"You won't need any," the boy said, bringing the pistol to bear on Mulroy's chest.

A cold chill passed over him and he braced to receive the shock. "What're you doing?" Mulroy heard his own voice as from a distance.

"I'm gettin' outta here, but you're staying."

"We'll split up, then," Mulroy said soothingly, trying to placate this obviously deranged boy.

"I'm gonna shoot you, then set this place afire. When they find your body, they'll think it's me, and won't come looking for me."

So that was it! "Good idea," Mulroy said, holding himself severely in check, "except that I'm a lot bigger than you. Who will mistake my body for yours?" His voice was calm, as if they were having a rational conversation. Mulroy had no idea what was going on here, but the longer he could keep this young boy talking, the longer he could put off the fatal shot.

"They won't know. I'll douse you with so much coal oil, you'll be a cinder." His face, in the yellow lantern light, looked waxy.

"I got an idea. Why don't we go back and dig up one of those dead prisoners who's more your size, and use him. That way, you won't be a murderer. Then we can both get away from here . . . you in one direction and me in another." Mulroy wanted to impress the idea that he had no intention of giving away this boy's whereabouts to anyone. He would play along as if he understood everything.

"No time."

Mulroy moved slightly to disguise the chill that went over him. He was still holding the belt in one hand, and thought briefly of trying to catch the boy off guard and overpower him. But the gun was too close and on full cock. Even a reflexive squeeze of the hand would send a bullet into Mulroy's chest. He would try it only as a last resort. His heart was racing. "Is someone holding you prisoner?" he asked calmly. "Maybe I can help."

"Yeah. That's why you're here." Briefly taking his eyes off Mulroy, Cal reached for a can of coal oil in the corner. "Get on upstairs. Ain't much down here that'll burn." He seemed to be talking more to himself.

Mulroy hesitated. What an ironic fate! He'd been rescued from the slow death of the stockade by this crazy guard, only to be gunned down for use as a convenient body. He started to turn toward the wooden steps, but noticed Cal's gun hand begin to waver. He looked at the boy's eyes. They were glazed. Suddenly they rolled back in his head and he collapsed. The gun struck the dirt floor and exploded, the blast deafening in the confined space.

Mulroy threw himself to one side, but there was no further threat from the boy who'd fallen unconscious in a loose heap.

"Damn!" He swallowed to lubricate his dry throat. "The kid is sicker than I am," he muttered. He took the gun and shoved it into his pants pocket, then threaded the belt and buckled it to hold up his pants before going through the guard's pockets. He removed a clasp knife, a few coins, a bandanna, and a block of matches.

Then he scooped up the limp form and staggered up the steps, bumped open the canted cellar door with his shoulder, and carried him up the back steps to the porch. He went inside the deserted house and dumped the boy onto the sofa in the living room. The lamp still burned on the marble-top table by the front window. Mulroy drew the drapes. In spite of the boy being unconscious and unarmed, Mulroy was taking no chances with someone who was determined to commit murder. He went into the dooryard and cut down the cord clothesline, using it to bind the boy's wrists to his ankles in front of him.

With the boy secured, Mulroy went out to the garden and harvested, by moonlight, two tomatoes, a cucumber, and a few onions. He didn't care whose house this was, or when they'd be home. He was now armed and had food. First things first.

The coals in the cook stove had been banked under a layer of ashes, and he thrust in a few sticks from the woodbox until he had a blaze going. A congealed pot of leftover pea soup had been set aside. He stirred some water into it, then lifted the pot onto a stove lid to heat. He cut off several slices from a smoked ham hanging in the pantry, found a plate in the cupboard, utensils in a drawer, and soon was enjoying a nourishing meal with fresh vegetables. Seated at the kitchen table, he reflected that this was the best meal he'd had in weeks, and that he'd fight to the death before he'd let anyone send him back into that prison.

While he ate, he watched his trussed-up prisoner through the doorway. Perhaps he should leave him on the sofa and take off. The owners were gone overnight, the kid had told him. Someone would be

GET
4 FREE BOOKS!

You can have the best Westerns delivered to your door for less than what you'd pay in a bookstore or online. Sign up for one of our book clubs today, and we'll send you **4 FREE* BOOKS**, worth $23.96, just for trying it out...**with no obligation to buy, ever!**

Authors include classic writers such as
LOUIS L'AMOUR, MAX BRAND, ZANE GREY
and more; PLUS new authors such as
COTTON SMITH, TIM CHAMPLIN, JOHNNY D. BOGGS
and others.

As a book club member you also receive the following special benefits:
- **30% OFF** all orders through our website & telecenter!
- **Exclusive access to** special discounts!
- **Convenient** home delivery **and 10 days to return any books you don't want to keep.**

There is no minimum number of books to buy,
and you may cancel membership at any time.
See back to sign up!

*Please include $2.00 for shipping and handling.

YES! ☐

Sign me up for the Leisure Western Book Club
and send my FOUR FREE BOOKS! If I choose to stay
in the club, I will pay only $14.00* each month,
a savings of $9.96!

NAME: _____

ADDRESS: _____

_____

TELEPHONE: _____

E-MAIL: _____

☐ I WANT TO PAY BY CREDIT CARD.

☐ VISA   ☐ MasterCard   ☐ DISCOVER

ACCOUNT #: _____

EXPIRATION DATE: _____

SIGNATURE: _____

Send this card along with $2.00 shipping & handling to:

**Leisure Western Book Club
1 Mechanic Street
Norwalk, CT 06850-3431**

Or fax (must include credit card information!) to: 610.995.9274.
You can also sign up online at www.dorchesterpub.com.

*Plus $2.00 for shipping. Offer open to residents of the U.S. and Canada only.
Canadian residents please call 1.800.481.9191 for pricing information.
If under 18, a parent or guardian must sign. Terms, prices and conditions subject to change. Subscription subject
to acceptance. Dorchester Publishing reserves the right to reject any order or cancel any subscription.

JOIN NOW!

back in the morning to set him free. But Mulroy couldn't really bring himself to leave him. What was the matter with the boy? A fever? Some kind of contagious disease?

He wiped up the last of the pea soup with a piece of cornbread and popped it into his mouth. A feast fit for a king—or at least a starving king. He let out his tightly cinched belt a notch.

A pipe from the well had been extended into the house and a pump installed by the kitchen sink. Ingenious. He filled a kettle and began heating it on the stove, while he dragged in a large washtub and two bars of homemade lye soap from the back porch. A bath was next on the agenda. He would not leave this house until he was scrubbed clean.

The boy stirred as Mulroy was pouring the third steaming kettle of water into the half-full washtub.

"What . . . happened?" The kid tugged at his ropes and nearly fell off the sofa.

"Take it easy," Mulroy said, moving toward him. "Soon as I finish my bath, I'll let you loose."

"Who are you? Why am I tied?" The boy seemed genuinely confused.

"You don't remember?"

"It's . . . kinda fuzzy."

Mulroy wondered if the boy were acting. "You said you were going to shoot me and burn the house down."

"What?"

"You mumbled something about getting away from here." Mulroy glanced at the pendulum clock on a parlor shelf. It was ten past ten. "Then you passed out about an hour ago."

"Shoot you?" Cal appeared to be shaking off the

effects of a nightmare as he struggled to fit the pieces back into place.

"With this." Mulroy pulled the pistol from his pocket.

"That belongs to Missus Anna Shackleford," Cal said.

"Who's that?"

"Wife of Lemuel Shackleford, the man who owns this place . . . and owns me. He got her that for protection when she's here alone."

"How does it work?"

"You ain't gonna shoot me with it, are ya?" the boy asked apprehensively.

"Well, you were gonna use it on me," Mulroy said. "Naw, I'm not gonna shoot you. I've just never seen a gun like this before." It was half the size and weight of the 1860 Army Colt percussion he had carried earlier.

"Press that button to the right of the hammer on the recoil shield. Yeah . . . there. That releases the cylinder and the barrel, and they tilt about a half inch to the right so you can load and unload it. That rod under the barrel punches out the empties."

"Rimfire metallic cartridges." Mulroy was fascinated. He hooked a thumbnail under one and pulled it out. "Smith and Wesson thirty-two shorts." He rotated the cylinder in its open top frame. A seven-shooter. The octagonal barrel was five inches long and scrollwork engraving decorated the nickel-plated frame. The walnut grips fit his hand perfectly. All in all, a very handy, handsome belt gun.

"Made in Brooklyn, New York, by somebody named Daniel Moore," the boy added. Obviously he fancied the weapon for himself.

"Got any more ammunition for it?"

"In the master bedroom. A drawer in the wash-stand."

Mulroy entered the bedroom just off the kitchen and retrieved two boxes of cartridges from the drawer.

"Old man Shackleford traded with one of the guards for that gun," Cal volunteered. "Took it offen a Yankee prisoner coming into the stockade. It was just the right size for me, but the old man just give me the back of his hand when I asked to buy it."

Mulroy took off his new shirt and pants and tested the temperature of the water in the elongated washtub. Then he stepped in and lowered himself carefully. *"Aahhh!"* He picked up the bar of lye soap and tried to work up a lather. For twenty minutes by the clock he luxuriated in the warm tub, soaping his hair twice and scrubbing his scalp with his finger-nails. He rinsed off and started on his chest and arms, using a stiff laundry brush. Finally satisfied, he climbed out and toweled off with a cotton dish towel hanging by the sink.

"I need some underwear and socks."

"Same bedroom. Bottom of the chest of drawers," the boy said, squirming to loosen the knots on his wrists and ankles.

Mulroy carried the lamp into the bedroom and outfitted himself with a cotton suit of clean under-wear, made for summer, cut off at the knees and el-bows. He rummaged around until he found a good pair of wool socks and then, praying they would fit, tried a pair of ankle-high shoes. They were about a size too large, but the wool socks took up the space. He even brushed his damp hair in a wall mirror.

Thanks to Palmer's shears, Mulroy's thick hair was a reasonable length. The visage staring back at him from the wavy mirror was gaunt and dark. But it would take a lot of scrubbing and soaking to remove completely the layers of pine resin smoke that coated his skin. At least it would protect his face from sunburn, since he hadn't seen a hat to borrow. Because the clean clothes Cal had earlier forced on him were now infested with lice, he rummaged around in the drawers and wardrobe until he found a clean shirt and pair of cotton pants that were a reasonable fit.

When he carried the lamp back into the parlor, he was feeling human once more, and reflected on the luxury a real bath could be. His skin tingled. For the first time in two months, he was clean, and dry, and well fed. Only a few mosquito bites still itched. He'd evicted most of his resident lice that now floated in the washtub of filthy bath water.

Now to see to the boy. He untied the clothesline cord and Cal sat up, stretching out the stiffness. From his eyes and general demeanor, Mulroy judged the young guard was not the same person who had threatened to kill him and set the house afire. Mulroy put a hand to Cal's forehead. A little too warm.

"I'm told I act kinda crazy when I have these spells o' fever now and again," the boy said, reacting to the touch.

"That's as good an excuse as any," Mulroy said coldly. "But you're sick. What else is wrong with you?"

"Hepatitis."

"Figured it was something like that," Mulroy muttered. "Now that I'm not in danger of being shot, tell me your story."

"Can I have a drink first?"

Mulroy motioned toward the pump, and the boy drew himself a large pitcher of water and gulped down half of it.

"You can eat while you talk."

"Not hungry. Hepatitis kills my appetite."

Mulroy assumed that was the reason Cal was unusually thin.

"Look, mister . . ."

"John Mulroy."

"Mister Mulroy. . . ."

"Just John will do."

"I wasn't brung up to call older folks by their first name."

"Suit yourself." The boy had had some breeding along the way.

"I ain't trying to make excuses or lie about it, but I don't rightly remember what I done today or tonight. I had the fever on me, but it's gone now. It just leaves me weak and forgetful."

Mulroy was dubious, but kept silent. He tilted his chair back against the doorjamb and watched as the boy rummaged under the sink and came up with a jug of some dark liquid. "Want some cider?"

"No."

Cal poured himself a large glass and sat down to sip it while he talked. "I guess you want me to explain," he said, his gaze dropping to the pistol thrust under Mulroy's belt.

Mulroy thought the boy looked a little more sane

and rational. His eyes didn't have that glazed, abstract look.

"Near as I can recollect, I did have some crazy plan to shoot you and burn the house and run off. But I was desperate. My folks died of the yellow jack last year. We lived on a farm thirty miles north of here. My uncle was on the place as a hired hand and he just took over after they died, without no legal will or anything. Anyway, he was lookin' to dump me and got Mister Shackleford to pay him cash money . . . just like buying a slave . . . to take me. Called me an 'indentured servant'. I was to work for Shackleford in return for room and board. He was to teach me to be a farrier. But the old man right quick forgot about all that. He works me like one of his niggers. I ain't seen a forge or nothing else inside a smithy since I been here. When this stockade was built five months ago, he seen a chance to make a little money by hiring me out as one o' the guards. Don't pay much, but he claims he needs the money to support me. I might as well be living out back in one o' them slave cabins, instead of up in the garret. When I'm seventeen, I'm free to go if I want to."

"How old are you now?"

"Fourteen."

A rather sickly fourteen, Mulroy thought, but probably accurate. He'd have no reason to lie.

"Why don't you run off?"

"I'm too weak to do a man's work. Besides, Shackleford would have the dogs track me down and bring me back. He ain't squeezed all he can outta me yet."

"But you were planning to run away tonight."

"After I threw 'em off my trail by leaving your

burned body behind as me. At least that's the story you told me. I'm fuzzy on the details." He took a long swig of the cider. "Anyways, I got me another way to throw off the dogs. I can't stand no more of this."

"Well, you better toughen up and get used to it, 'cause this is where you're staying, at least until I get clear."

"I'll kill the old man if he keeps on beatin' me." Cal sounded desperate.

"Why does he beat you?"

"He's got a hot temper, especially when he's been into the jug. He don't need a reason. If he gets mad at his wife, or somebody slickers him at cards, or he hits his finger with a hammer, he'll take it out on me."

"How old is this Lemuel Shackleford? Does he have other children?"

"No other kids. I reckon he's about fifty. Ain't sure."

"Does he treat his slaves the same way?"

"He works 'em hard, but he doesn't beat 'em. Just three on the place now . . . a man and wife about thirty, and one old man near sixty, who just takes up space and food and is stove up, so he won't bring nothing on the market."

"Where are the Shacklefords tonight?"

"Went to Americus to a wedding party. Staying overnight there."

"Why would Shackleford leave you here alone if he's afraid you'd run off?"

"I tried it before and he had a friend of his bring me back with the dogs. I got about ten miles away. Gave me good hiding, too. Said if I tried to run off again, sumpin' worse would happen."

"How'd you get hepatitis?"

"Don't know. Maybe drunk some bad water when I was on the run. When I commenced t'gettin' sick, the old man got real mad. Guess he thought he was going to lose the money he give my uncle for me.

"Good food and rest might clear it up."

"Huh! Good food? If I even had the hunger for a good meal, I wouldn't get anything but the leavin's, or what Missus Shackleford might slip me on the sly. Feeds the niggers better 'cause they do more work. He caught me sneaking truck outta the garden last week and give me a hidin'."

Mulroy wasn't sure how much of this to believe. The kid might've had a rough time of it from this surrogate parent, but it didn't make sense from a purely economic standpoint for Shackleford to mistreat the kid to the point where he couldn't work and bring in a little money. But, then, Mulroy didn't know Shackleford. Some people were just plain mean.

The clock in the parlor struck eleven. Mulroy stood up and stretched. "Whatever your reasons, I want to thank you for saving me from the stockade," he said. "I'm tired, but I have to get a move on to be as far away from here as possible before daylight."

"Take me with you!" The plea was quick and urgent.

"Can't do it. I've gotta move fast."

"They'll have the dogs on your trail before morning."

Mulroy shuddered at his previous experience with tracking hounds. "No, they won't . . . they think I'm dead."

"Not if I tell 'em different. I got those pants o' yours down in the cellar to give the dogs the scent."

"Then you'd be in trouble for helping me escape."

"I'll make up some tale about how you somehow got outside the stockade and came here after dark while I was eatin' supper, attacked me and tied me up and stole clothes and . . . well, anyway, I could make it sound good."

"I've got the gun and I could just leave you tied up again."

"I'd be free by morning, and then they'd be after you."

"I could shoot you."

"You're not a killer."

The kid had him pegged. His mind was racing. If Cal was determined to go, maybe they could travel together a few miles, then separate. It looked as if he had no choice. If Calvin Blackwood had lived just thirty miles north of here, perhaps he knew the area and terrain, and would be a great help in their getaway. But as sick and unbalanced as this boy was, Mulroy wasn't at all sure he wanted to go to sleep at night anywhere near him. Young Cal might just have one of his feverish fits and Mulroy could wake up with his throat cut or his head bashed in.

"Where did you put your musket?" Mulroy asked.

"In the other room."

"You gonna take it?"

Cal's thin face lit up in a wide grin for the first time. "I knew you'd help me."

"Not helping you as much as I'm helping myself."

"I'll go get it." He sprang from the chair and disappeared through the door.

Mulroy was uneasy about letting the boy arm himself again. But he had to trust him sometime and hope for the best. It would be good to have someone to share guard duty. And Mulroy was not about to give up the only gun.

Cal returned with the musket.

"Is it loaded?"

"Yeah, but not capped."

"Keep it that way. Take some extra powder and caps and shot."

"Got it all right here on my belt that I wear on sentry duty."

"You got any money?"

"Nope. But I know where the old man keeps a few silver dollars in a tin box under his bed."

"Unless you're against stealing, get them."

"It ain't stealin'. I'm just collectin' what I'm owed."

He came out of the bedroom rattling the tin box. Looking in the pantry, Cal found a ribbed iron hammer that was designed to break up the fibers in tough meat, and easily pounded off the flimsy lock. He divided the stack of about twenty cartwheels and put a handful into each pants pocket.

Mulroy had left all his money except a five-dollar gold piece in the stockade with his friends. And he might need that five later.

Cal looked down at the gray pants he'd been wearing while standing guard at the stockade. "I gotta change into sumpin' else. Just a minute." He disappeared up the steps. He came down a minute later, stuffing his loose, white shirt into a pair of worn cotton pants. "I'm ready."

"When are you scheduled to go back on guard duty?"

"Tomorrow morning at ten. I ain't expectin' Mister and Missus Shackleford back from Americus before that. So when they get here and I'm gone, they'll figure I'm on the stockade wall."

"Then we better make sure to leave everything as we found it," Mulroy said. "Give me a hand with this washtub and we'll dump the water out back."

With this done and the tub on the back porch, they straightened up the kitchen, put the empty tin box back under the bed, washed and put away the dishes and utensils.

"They'll figure I ate the pea soup," Cal said. "And he won't miss the clothes or the pistol or the silver dollars right away."

"Then we've got the rest of tonight and a good portion of tomorrow before anyone realizes you're gone. Won't your boss come looking for you if you don't show up for work?"

"Most o' the sentries are part o' the Fifty-Fifth Georgia. The home guards, like me, we just fill in the gaps. Captain Wirz and the officers don't bother much with us. Besides, I been off sick now and again, so they won't miss me right away."

"Do you think any of the slaves saw me tonight?"

"Don't know. I was passed out part of the time."

"Let's go."

CHAPTER NINE

John Mulroy wasn't conscious of it, but his sudden release from the grip of starvation triggered a desire to hoard. Not only did he eat his fill in the Shackleford kitchen, but he'd found an empty sugar sack and filled it with slices of smoked ham, a loaf of bakery bread, salt, six tomatoes, and as many sweet potatoes. Had he been asked his reason for doing so, he'd have said he was only making provision for the immediate future.

Calvin Blackwood poured a gallon of coal oil into a watering can that Anna Shackleford used to sprinkle her flowers.

"What's that for?" Mulroy asked as they went out the front door.

"To throw off the dogs."

They crossed the moonlit yard and climbed the stile. When they started into the open pine woods, Cal began to sprinkle coal oil in their wake. The pungent odor ruined the fresh smell of pine. With any luck, it would also ruin the scenting ability of the hounds.

"We'd best be headin' toward the village," Cal said. "The train north to Macon leaves before daylight. If we can slip aboard, we can be miles from here, come noon tomorrow."

"Not sure that's the best idea," Mulroy said. "When I escaped the first time, I made for the Flint River. It flows south to the Gulf, I'm told. A lot safer and shorter than going north, where we're bound to run into battle lines. We're liable to be taken for the enemy by some nervous picket."

"I was just tryin' to get us outta here the quickest way I know how," Cal said. "I ain't been south along the Flint River, but folks around here say it flows into a big swamp in Florida. I don't want no part o' swamps and alligators. Don't much care for snakes, neither."

"The water might throw off the dogs," Mulroy said.

"So will this," Cal said, drizzling the coal oil in their steps as they trudged through the deep shade of the woods. "When we get off a ways from the house, I'll toss the can away, and the dogs won't know which way to go."

Their footfalls were silent on the carpet of pine needles.

While they spoke in low tones, Mulroy attuned his eyes and ears to catch unusual movements or sounds.

"Hold up a minute," Mulroy said. "Let's make a plan before we go any farther." The food sack wasn't heavy, but, with every step, it seemed to be gaining weight.

Cal Blackwood paused and straightened up, the barrel of the musket slung on his back showing over his shoulder.

"Both of us are in poor condition to do much walking," Mulroy admitted. "Our best chance of escape is to hitch a ride. You're probably right that the train is the best way to do that. I have just two questions. . . ."

"What's that?"

"Is the train guarded?"

"Don't know. Sometimes they send a few men to guard the prisoners on the return trip. I ain't had to take a train nowhere since I been a sentry."

"Which way does this track run?"

"South to Albany and north to Macon. The train headin' north to Macon will likely bring back supplies and prisoners."

"That stockade won't hold any more," Mulroy said irrelevantly.

"Yes, it will," Cal answered. "It'll hold as many as they decide to put in it."

"It's got over thirty-three thousand already."

The boy appeared to shrug silently in the darkness.

Keep your mind on the business at hand! Mulroy harshly reminded himself. *Ask questions that'll get us out of here.*

"How far is Macon?"

"Sixty miles."

"Where does the train go from there?"

"Atlanta, I reckon. Not sure."

"Any east-west lines out of Macon?"

"I only been to Macon once, with my folks, when I was little. I wasn't looking for no rail connections at the time."

They were silent for a few moments.

"If we board the train near the depot in Andersonville, somebody might see us," Cal said. "To get into the village we'll have to pass close to General Winder's quarters and a few stores. And there's likely to be somebody around that depot, even this late."

"I'll leave it up to you," Mulroy said.

"That train'll roll toward us about daylight. Up yonder a bit, the road from Andersonville to Oglethorpe crosses the tracks. It's an open space with good footing along the rails. I'm thinkin' we oughta wait in the woods right by that road and hop aboard when she comes by."

"Neither one of us is in good enough shape to catch a moving train," Mulroy said. "And if we miss, we'll be ground under the wheels, or stranded here in the daylight. It's. . . ."

"Shuush!" Cal held up his hand for silence and turned his head in a listening attitude.

The faint sounds of dogs in the distance gave Mulroy a sudden chill. But they weren't baying— just some yipping and barking. The sounds were not coming closer.

"Whew! It's just the hounds over yonder in the kennel between here and the stockade," Cal said, obviously relieved. He turned back to Mulroy. "The train is pretty slow. Even at full speed. That road crossing is only seventy yards or so from the depot, so the train won't be doing over five to eight miles an hour when it gets there. We can hop one going that slow. Besides, I'm mighty near out of coal oil."

"Then lead on to the crossing. If the dogs somehow manage to track us that far, the handlers won't know if we hopped a train or got a ride in a wagon."

Cal pointed the way and they moved out toward a break in the trees that marked the road. The boy sprinkled fuel behind them. Mulroy wondered if hounds—bloodhounds in particular—could catch their scent on the air as well as on the ground when there was no wind.

They stopped in the inky shadows at the edge of the woods to survey the scene. In the moonlight, the road lay dusty and deserted. Polished rails cut parallel lines through the trees toward the village.

After a careful look around, Mulroy stepped out of the deep shadow and walked up onto the filled bank to look down the tracks where the headlamp of a locomotive burned dimly.

Moving up beside him, Cal said: "There she is."

"How do you know it'll be pulling out soon?"

"Listen close. You can hear she's got steam up. They generally leave just before daylight. Many's the mornin' that whistle's woke me up and I wished I was aboard of her, headin' away from here," Cal said. "Now that wish is comin' true."

"Hope you're right." Mulroy retreated into the shadows of the trees and set down the food sack. From it he retrieved the two boxes of cartridges and shoved them into the side pockets of his pants. He removed the small Moore revolver from his belt, so he wouldn't have to lie on it, and held it as he stretched out on a thick carpet of pine needles. He positioned himself so he could see down the tracks.

Cal set the coal oil behind a nearby pine, and lay down a few yards away, the musket still slung across his back.

Except for the chirping of crickets and a distant bullfrog's croaking, the woods were deathly still. The July night was heavy with the scent of pine, and Mulroy inhaled deeply, unable to savor enough of the fresh, untainted air. He felt as if his whole body were being cleansed—from the inside out. Mosquitoes whined in their ears, and lighted on the backs of their hands and necks, helping to keep them awake. In spite of the irritating bites, the weight of accumulated fatigue bore down on Mulroy. He lay his head on his crossed arms and closed his eyes to rest.

"Sarge! Sarge! Wake up!" A hand was shaking his shoulder.

"Huh? The Raiders coming?"

"What raiders? It's the train."

The pinewoods rotated into focus, visible now in the gray, dewy dawn. Mulroy came alert. "Why'd you call me Sarge?"

"I seen you walking around in the stockade with stripes on your jacket. You mean that wasn't your tunic?" Cal scrambled to his feet. "Never mind that. The train's coming."

Mulroy rose to his hands and knees, brushing sleep from his eyes and the twigs and pine needles from his clothes. He shoved the pistol under his belt and grabbed his food bag.

The moon shone far down the sky behind the trees as Mulroy and the boy crept out of the woods, then ran, crouching, to the railroad embankment.

Chuffing and clanking, the locomotive labored to gain momentum as it rolled out of Andersonville. The weak headlight, like a single blurry eye boring out of the trees, came closer and closer.

Mulroy squatted, testing the footing on the soft grassy bank. "We'll have to make a jump for the first car with an open side door. If they're all closed, go for a gondola or the caboose."

"There's bound to be a brakeman in the caboose."

"Doesn't matter. We have to get aboard."

The train grew louder.

"Stay still till the engine passes," Mulroy rasped in the boy's ear.

Laboring like a winded horse, the high-wheeled 4-4-0 locomotive ground past them at barely six miles an hour, billowing black smoke into the slate-colored dawn sky. The dim figures of the engineer and fireman were lit briefly by the glow of the open firebox. Then the tender full of wood slid past, followed by a closed combination baggage car. Two empty cattle cars with closed doors were next. A semidry journal box squealed past.

Mulroy saw a boxcar approaching, its side door yawning open. He sprang up and jogged alongside, hoping the boy was following his lead. He matched his speed to the slow train. The floor of the car was nearly waist high and he tossed the bag of food into the open doorway. Then he threw himself forward, sprawling his upper body into the car. He flailed with his arms to find something to grab, but felt only rough floorboards. The toes of his shoes were scraping the ground, bumping on the ends of the ties. He felt sudden panic as his body was being pulled back outside by the friction of his dragging feet. He couldn't swing his legs forward for fear of being caught under the wheels.

Finally his clawing fingers snagged a splintered hole where a floorboard was broken. Gasping, he slowly pulled himself forward. He suddenly felt someone grip his arms.

"Give him a hand, boys!"

They jerked him into the car. Fear stabbed his gut as he sat up, trying to pierce the darkness and see who his rescuers might be.

"Who air ya, mister?" came a voice.

"Who are you?" Mulroy shot back, bluffing, stalling for time as he scrambled to his feet.

"Nelson, strike a match and let's have a look at this gent."

There was some fumbling in the darkness while someone looked for a match. Mulroy had a hand on his belt pistol, but knew he was at a disadvantage, not knowing how many men were in here. He assumed they were armed. He could see the dim landscape moving past the opposite side door. He didn't dare speak for fear his Midwestern accent would betray him as a Yankee. And where was Cal? The boy must have missed the train.

A match flared, but it was held down to kindle a small pile of twigs arranged in a washtub full of dirt. Their cooking fire? The tinder caught and flared up, its flickering flame revealing four men, each armed with a musket and holstered pistol. All were dressed in Confederate gray.

Mulroy thought fast. "You boys the guards?" he asked in his best imitation of an easy drawl.

"Yeah. What's your story?" a weathered, bearded man demanded.

"Ah'm just tryin' to make a livin'," Mulroy said.

"Nothing in his sack but some ham and a few vegetables," one of the men interrupted, handing the sugar sack to the rough one who'd asked the question. He glanced inside. Mulroy was glad he'd removed the two boxes of cartridges. He still stood with his hand on the butt of the Moore belt gun. "Ah was workin' as a hired hand on a place some'ers south o' here," he said, intentionally vague. "But I was let go. Farmer gimme a little grub and ah'm workin' my way north to see if I can catch on some'ers else."

"How come you ain't in the Army?"

"You boys part o' the home guard?"

"Hell, no! We belong to the Fifty-Fifth Georgia Reserve," a third man replied, squatting on his heels by the small fire.

"I had some kinda swamp fever and dysentery," Mulroy said, "and the recruitin' sergeant wouldn't take me. But I wanted t'be in uniform, baggin' a few o' them Yankees."

"I'll just bet you would," the leathery one sneered.

"He may be tellin' the truth about being sick," the guard by the fire remarked. "He's sure skinny enough."

The first man reached out and yanked open Mulroy's shirt.

Mulroy nearly reacted by pulling the back-up pistol, but refrained when he realized the man was only looking at his bare chest. "Thought maybe you was part nigger, your face was so dark," the man said, shoving Mulroy away. "Guess I was wrong. You been out in the sun a lot. Maybe you *are* tellin' the truth about bein' a hired hand. But there's something about you that don't feel right."

"Aw, hell, Bill, let him alone. He ain't done nothin' to us," one of the others spoke up from the edge of the firelight.

Mulroy took advantage of the hesitation in the questioning to back away and slump to the floor against the wall. "You boys go right ahead and help yourselves to the grub in that sack," he said, leaning his head back, feigning weariness.

"Here, fry us up some o' those ham slices and sweet potatoes for breakfast." The sack was tossed to the man tending the fire in the washtub.

Suddenly a slim figure swung down through the open door and dropped inside. The startled guards scrambled back, clawing for their weapons.

"It's just me!"

The four froze in postures of defense.

"Cal? Calvin Blackwood?" the leathery one said, approaching cautiously, pistol in hand.

"Yep. The very one." Cal managed a sickly smile in the face of the artillery.

"Where the hell did you come from?"

"I missed my jump. Had to catch the ladder on the next car."

"I mean, what're you doin' on the train?"

"Just takin' a little ride."

"Hell you are." A guard grinned as he resumed placing ham in a small skillet he'd removed from his pack. "You're runnin' away from Shackleford, ain't you?"

"Well. . . ."

"Yeah. Figured as much. Well, kid, you'll probably make it this time. Dogs can't track you now. Unless old man Shackleford figures out you hopped this train."

Cal turned his head and seemed surprised to see Mulroy sitting where the strengthening daylight revealed his face. "This here fella helped me get away."

"So you two know each other."

"Yeah, he come to our place, lookin' for work, but the old man run him off, said he had enough help. Anyway, we got to talkin' as he was leavin' and he helped me figure out a way to get shut of that place."

"Come to think of it, this fella never did tell us his name."

"John Mulroy." He could think of no good reason to use an alias, and these men had no way of knowing he was an escaped prisoner.

"Nice to know ya."

"Long as we're cookin' your vittles, you might as well join us," one of the guards said.

The four guards seemed to loosen up, now that one of their own had vouched for Mulroy.

"Yeah," another man said. "Neither of 'em look like they've had a square meal in weeks." He pulled several tin plates from his haversack and handed them around. Minutes later, as the rising sun slanted through the open door, the six men were sitting on the floor. With their pocket knives as utensils, they feasted on fried ham and slices of sweet potato cooked in ham juice.

To Mulroy, the first hurdle was passed. If they could keep up this charade, in a few hours they would reach Macon, shake this bunch, and continue on their way. As he ate, his mind was turning toward the next step of their escape.

CHAPTER TEN

"You gonna tell old man Shackleford you seen me?" Calvin Blackwood hesitated at the open door of the boxcar.

"Naw. Go on, kid. You ain't his property, no matter what he thinks. That old bastard never done no one any favors. What d'ya think, boys?" The leathery-faced guard looked around at his three companions. "In case anybody should ask, we never saw this boy."

The others nodded their agreement.

John Mulroy knew he was getting off light. These four could have robbed him of the silver dollars and the five-dollar gold piece he carried, possibly beaten him and thrown him off the train. Two things had probably saved him. First, he'd managed to disguise his Midwestern accent. Then Cal, before coming down from his perch atop the boxcar, had evidently heard part of his story, and had the presence of mind to back it.

"You gettin' off here?"

The train slowed as it approached Macon.

"I don't want to be seen," Cal said.

Mulroy eased toward the open door and looked for an open space along the brushy right of way. They were approaching a pasture. "Better throw that musket out first," Mulroy said.

Cal unslung the weapon and pitched it into the knee-high weeds.

"I'll jump first. You follow." Mulroy gauged the speed of the train, crouched, and sprang ahead and out. He hit the sloping ground, flexed his knees, and rolled, throwing up his arms to protect his face as the thistles raked his skin and stabbed through his shirt. He slid to a stop and looked back. Cal was tumbling head over heels in the deep grass, loose arms and legs flying.

"You all right?"

Cal nodded, and they went to look for the musket. It was nowhere to be found.

"To hell with it," Mulroy said after a quarter hour of searching. "I've still got the little pistol. Let's get into those woods and out of plain sight."

"My belt busted when I landed," Cal said. "Lost all the powder, shot, and caps, too."

They tramped through the thigh-high growth, sweating in the noonday sun. Mulroy swept his gaze around, but there was no one in sight. The two men were in one of many untended fields allowed to go fallow during the war.

"Look! Here it is!" Cal shouted, reaching down to retrieve his rifled musket.

They searched for the leather ammunition pouch for a little longer, but finally gave up.

"Ain't no good without ammunition," Cal said,

slinging the weapon on his back as they plodded up over the tracks and headed for a nearby patch of pine woods.

"No matter. We can buy or steal some along the way."

They paused in the shelter of the trees, and Mulroy mopped the sweat from his face with a shirtsleeve. There was no hint of breeze on the humid air, and the July sun was ferocious. His half-length cotton underwear was damp with sweat.

Three hours earlier they'd eaten their fill, but the guards had kept the rest of the food. Mulroy was not hungry, but the back of his throat was beginning to burn with thirst. "Let's go west, circle the town, and then work our way north."

Cal nodded. "We gonna try to hook up with Yankee troops?"

"That was my plan."

"Last I heard they was still a good ways north of Atlanta."

"How far?"

The boy shrugged. "Dunno. But it's a mighty fur piece from here to be walkin'."

The hazards of overland travel were obvious to Mulroy. They were two lost souls trying to make their way cross-country without being seen or caught. "Didn't you say your folks had a farm somewhere around here?"

"Yeah. But this don't look familiar to me. I think our place was maybe fifteen miles west and south of here."

"Think you could find it?"

"We don't wanna go there," Cal said.

"Why?"

"Shackleford would figure I'd head for home. Besides, my uncle likely still has the place and he'd be only too happy t'take a finder's fee for sending me back."

Mulroy thought for a moment. "All right, then, let's head west toward the Alabama border. We'll stay out of sight as we get away from Macon. We can go a while on what we've eaten, but we'll have to find some water pretty soon."

Cal nodded, evidently willing to let an older man make the decisions. As they started off through the woods, it occurred to Mulroy that he was easily old enough to be the boy's father. He wondered what it would be like to be a parent.

Idle thoughts on a hot day. He'd better be looking to more pressing matters, such as finding clean drinking water. These lowlands should have streams aplenty, even in midsummer. Since having to use the filthy stream at Andersonville, he was even more conscious of finding good water. But if they did find water, they had nothing to carry it in. And they couldn't afford just to camp beside some stream; they had to keep moving.

After about three miles of alternating pine forest and open fields, they came to a well-trodden path and followed it. It trended west, and the woods gradually became a mix of hardwoods.

"I gotta sit down and rest a minute," Cal finally said. He was breathing heavily, sweat pouring down his face. The exertion of their fast pace had caused his face to be more flushed than jaundiced.

They moved several yards off the path and flopped down behind some thick blackberry bushes. A few shriveled berries remained, but unfortunately they were probably at least three weeks late to harvest any edible blackberries.

After a few minutes, Mulroy began to realize how weak he really was. Even though he had eaten two or three good meals in the past eighteen hours, he hadn't yet recovered from the effects of prolonged starvation. He needed at least two weeks of rest and good food, along with some daily exercise to get in condition to elude capture in this hostile part of the country. His leg muscles and endurance were not yet up to tramping cross-country, with an unknown number of miles to go before they could reach the safety of Union lines. He'd waited too long to get free. He should have escaped the first week of his internment.

And what about this boy? He was in even worse shape, his body fighting hepatitis. But at least Cal had the advantage of youth. Or was it an advantage? A growing boy needed more nourishment than just enough to subsist on. Mulroy stretched out his tired legs and lay back on the ground.

"Shhh!" Cal grabbed Mulroy as he started to speak. Something was coming down the path. A dog. The animal was some sort of short-haired mixed breed, moving as if he knew where he was going. In any case, it was obviously not tracking them. They were downwind of a slight breeze.

A Negro boy followed the dog, whistling and swinging a tin bucket along with something tied up in a white napkin. Likely somebody's lunch.

The two waited a good ten minutes after the dog and the boy were gone before they ventured out onto the trail once more. Ground cover and clumps of bushes would not have hindered them from plunging directly across country, but the creepers tripped them; they stumbled and turned their ankles on small hidden rocks and dead limbs. Besides, Cal, at least, was leery of snakes. By unspoken agreement, it was the path of least resistance for the thirsty, weary pair. They'd covered at least six miles since leaving the train.

When Mulroy could stop thinking of water long enough, he enjoyed the quiet woods, the calls of mockingbirds, cardinals, and blue jays. Nature seemed to be at peace, even if the world of man was not.

Suddenly, above the chirping and whistling of the birds, Mulroy heard the rhythmic *thunk! thunk! thunk!* of chopping somewhere ahead of them. He motioned to move forward more cautiously and presently came to the edge of an open field. A Negro man, humming to himself, was trimming some newly cut pine posts to repair a dilapidated rail fence. They watched him from cover for a few minutes. He was alone.

The two fugitives came out of the woods and approached the old black man who gave a start and silently backed away, eyes wide and axe in hand.

"What time do you have?" Mulroy inquired in an easy tone.

"Uhh . . . Ah don't have m'gold watch with me, but I reckon it's goin' on dinner time, soon's the horn blow," the man said, still cautious.

On impulse, Mulroy told the Negro, who gave his name as Sam, exactly who they were and how they happened to be here.

Sam still seemed very timid at the apparition, but

finally said: "You can have part o' my dinner when it's sent to me. Won't be long."

"We'll wait over here, out of sight in the woods."

Less than an hour later, the same boy they'd seen on the path appeared and set down a tin pail.

"You go on along home now, heah?" the old darky said, and the boy called his dog and departed.

Several minutes later, Cal and Mulroy were sharing Sam's dinner of rice, cold yams, and fried bacon. There was nearly enough to satisfy them.

Mulroy was the first Yankee Sam had ever seen and he was curious about the breed. He was full of questions as they ate, hardly removing his gaze from the former Union sergeant.

"You talks kinda funny, but you don't hardly look no different from d'other white gennemen," Sam ventured after he'd gotten over his shyness.

Mulroy attempted to convince him that Yankees were just men, and not some kind of freakish creatures.

"Da Yankee Army's comin', I heah. Dey's tearin' up Ned north of Atlanta, dey say. Dis heah war gonna break up our homes, and I won't have no place to go with my wife and chilrun," he said, worry lines creasing his brow. But then he brightened. "But we's gonna be *free!*" He sat there, chewing, and seemed to try to get his mind around this enormous fact. "Free!" he said again, nearly in a whisper. "Not beholden to no man. I can work for myself and my family. Now I belongs to Mistah Jonah Bowden. This here's his plantation."

"What's he like?" Mulroy asked.

"Oh, he be strong Sesech," Sam said. "Wish I

could help you get back to yo people, but m'master'd whip me within an inch o' my life if he caught me out here wit you."

"I'll give you a silver dollar, if you can get some food for us," Mulroy said, reaching into his pocket and producing one of the shiny cartwheels.

"I'd sho love to have that," Sam said. "But you ain't obliged t'give me nothin'. I get you some food, but you gotta stay hid till dark."

"Where's some water around here?" Cal asked.

"Dis heah's some fine land. Dey's a spring back in da woods 'bout half a mile. I'll tell you how to get dere. Mostly the critters use it, and da field hands. Mistah Bowden got him a well near the big house 'bout a mile from heah. Tonight I take you to another man I knows on the da next place, if you travelin' on west o' heah."

Cal and Mulroy thanked the man and slid off to find the spring in the woods.

Mulroy drank until he thought he'd burst. Then the pair found a well-hidden spot beneath the low-sweeping limbs of a large pine from where they could see Sam working on the fence at the edge of the field a quarter mile away.

Both Cal and Mulroy napped on the soft, aromatic bed of pine needles until the sun was well down behind the trees. As dusk settled in, they saw some dim figures approaching. It was Sam and another Negro.

"M'friend, Jacob," Sam said. "Come with us."

They walked a good two miles before Sam turned back, leaving them in Jacob's care. Before they knew it, Cal and Mulroy were in a slave cabin on the back side of the next plantation, being fed seasoned boiled turnips, cornbread, and smoked bacon, washing it down with cider. It was a meal fit for a king.

Mulroy noticed Jacob slip the bar across the inside of the plank door to secure them against any surprises. This man was younger than Sam, probably in his thirties, and lived with his wife Sadie and two children, aged about six and eight. These people were all shy at first, fearful of what might happen if they were discovered hiding a runaway boy and a Yankee. But before the hour was up and the supper finished, they were all grinning and shaking hands.

"Praise de Lord!" Jacob kept saying over and over. "Dis man's Army gonna set us free!"

"Won't be long now," Sadie added, taking their plates.

If anything, these Negroes ate better than many of the white Confederates at Andersonville, Mulroy realized. He offered them two silver dollars for their hospitality. Jacob was reluctant at first to accept such largess. "I be whipped if anybody find out I got so much money," he said, fingering the silver coins. "Dey be certain I stole it."

"Hide it," Mulroy said.

Sadie took the coins from her husband's hand and silently tucked them into a crack between the floor and the log wall.

"You know anybody who can guide us west from here?" Mulroy asked.

Jacob's mahogany face took on a conspiratorial expression in the lantern light. "I pooty sure I know da very one!"

* * *

For the next week, Mulroy and Cal were passed from slave cabin to slave cabin, hidden, fed, carried slowly westward a hundred miles across the Alabama line. Buried in a wagonload of hay, they bumped a few miles over dried clay ruts. By night, they were led afoot through fields and past homes of wealthy planters. They slept away their daylight hours in chicken coops and barns and pine thickets, and ate yams and cornbread and pilfered garden vegetables. They were given refuge by friendly slaves who vied with each other for the honor of helping the Yankee and the young white Southern boy escape as they themselves hoped shortly to escape when the invading Army reached them. To Mulroy, it seemed somehow fitting that these Negroes could operate a network that was the equivalent of the Underground Railroad in the north.

The two refugees lost all sense of time. Except for snatches of rumors they overheard from the slaves, they had no news of the war or the outside world.

Mulroy had only a vague notion of where they might find the Union forces in northern Alabama. Then they reached a point where there were no more adjoining plantations, no more friendly, helpful black folk to guide and nurture them.

That morning they awoke from sleeping in a haystack, ate the last cold, boiled yams, and wondered what to do. Beyond a rail fence to the west lay only woods and hills, with no sign of human habitation. They climbed over the low rail fence and began walking. They were often forced to change direction in a terrain broken by rocky hills and woods and small streams. Only by keeping the rising sun at their backs were they able to hold to a general westerly course. At least they had water to drink. A slave family had given them two dented Army canteens that they carried on their shoulders by twisted pieces of twine.

Since they hadn't been able to secure ammunition for the musket, Cal traded it to a huge mulatto for a twelve-mile ride in his wagon. The slave had been extremely reluctant to take a chance helping these escapees. He had been a runaway once himself and his back still bore the scars of his punishment after he was caught. Even though it left them without a hunting rifle, Cal indicated he was glad to be relieved of the heavy weapon that seemed to snag on things when they were hiding or crawling through tight places.

Although he'd come to trust the boy out of necessity, Mulroy was glad to be the only one to retain a firearm—the seven-shot .32-caliber Moore cartridge revolver.

Late that afternoon, they were forced to take shelter under an overhanging rock ledge in a deep ravine while a thunderstorm crashed across the region. In spite of their efforts to stay dry, rain blew in on them. Vivid bolts of lightning showed the run-off from the brief, but violent, storm foaming along the rocks at their feet. Afterward, they climbed out and walked as long as daylight allowed. Then, only partially dry, they lay down, supperless, under some tall pines and fell into exhausted sleep.

The day broke bright and cheerful, beads of moisture clinging to the leaves of bushes and trees.

Mulroy stretched his stiff and aching muscles. He'd grown accustomed to eating regularly and his stomach was growling. Nothing to eat for either of them except a cold yam apiece twenty-four hours earlier.

He grinned at Cal who was looking weaker and thinner than ever. "Nothing like another day of freedom!"

"Yeah." The boy nodded without enthusiasm.

"Let's be off and find some breakfast. Maybe I can get a squirrel with this." He patted the pistol under his belt.

When they began walking, Mulroy could feel his legs complaining. He was sure the boy felt the same—or worse. Mulroy had no idea what hepatitis felt like. He guessed it probably caused a listless fatigue. At least, he'd never heard Cal complain of any particular hurt. But then the boy had probably grown used to pain during his short life. Mulroy kept his eye on him for any signs of the fever's return, along with its associated madness. He wasn't completely satisfied with Cal's explanation. Perhaps he had malaria or some unknown malady that acted with the hepatitis to produce these strange fits. Mulroy was no medical expert, but he'd never heard of a fever that caused a person to go completely out of his head to the point he did things contrary to his nature, then had little recollection of them later.

They walked for several hours, and Mulroy spent about twenty minutes stalking a squirrel, finally getting off one shot at it, without success. They plodded onward, hungrier than ever.

The walking became somewhat easier as the terrain began to flatten into a wide, shallow valley. Suddenly they encountered an open field with the rotted remnants of a fence here and there around its perimeter. They halted.

"Maybe we can find a farmhouse and beg some food," Mulroy said, beginning to feel the weakness brought on by fatigue and lack of nourishment.

Cal said nothing as the older man led the way across the overgrown pasture, searching the upslope on the other side for buildings. They went over a slight rise and through the few trees, and then Mulroy spotted what he'd been looking for—a house. If it was a plantation home, it had seen better days. He paused to catch his breath and looked at it from 200 yards away. No sign of life. A shiver went over him. In spite of the bright sunshine, an air of death and abandonment hung over the big house. Four years of war had left much of this part of the country bankrupt in more than money.

He drew his pistol, took a deep breath, trying to muster up his little remaining energy. He turned to Cal. "Let's go take a look."

CHAPTER ELEVEN

As they approached, Mulroy saw the house was not as elegant as it appeared from a distance. White paint had flaked off the columns and the clapboard walls, giving the place a scabrous look. The second story verandah sagged on one end, rotten wood pulling away from the gap-toothed banister. A few scattered shakes had vacated the roof. The porch steps were missing, replaced by flat stones, evidently salvaged from a low rock wall along the driveway. All that seemed to be anchoring the house, holding it together and upright, were the massive stone chimneys on either end. Yet the windows were intact and clean, and the brass doorknob shiny from use.

Mulroy instinctively hesitated as if some melancholy force had laid a hand on him. Silent and morose, the structure bulked up, blocking the sun and exuding the miasma of a crypt. Something whispered a warning that he should bypass this ruined plantation house and go on. But he knew they couldn't. They, at least, had to search the place for some remnants of food. He was nearly faint from hunger and exhaustion and knew the sick boy probably was as well.

With a conscious effort, he stepped up onto the stone porch step. As if triggered by his footfall, the front door flew open, banging back against the wall. He flinched, his eyes locked on the rifle a woman was holding on him.

"Who are you and what do you want?" she snapped.

"I . . . uh . . . that is . . . we . . ."

"Couple o' tramps fixin' t'rob me."

"No ma'am!" Mulroy said, backing up. "We're just hungry and. . . ."

"Wish I had a ten-cent piece for every foragin' tramp and deserter who's said that! You're all the same . . . till you get a foot in the door."

Mulroy had to talk fast and be convincing. Her white knuckles gripped the Sharps at hip level. "Ma'am, I helped this boy run away from an abusive master in Georgia."

"You don't talk like you're from around here," she said. "Georgia, neither. You're a damned Yankee, that's what you are. What's worse, you're likely a deserter from your own Army."

"Ma'am, he's tellin' the truth," Cal spoke up. "If we could just get some water and a little food . . . we're tuckered out from walkin'."

"Now *you* sound like a Southerner . . . *he* doesn't."

Mulroy and Cal looked at each other, and Cal nodded his consent. They would have to take a chance on the truth and hope this young woman would not shoot him or take him prisoner. Mulroy still had the Moore .32 in his hand, but wasn't about to test his speed against this woman who held a Sharps with the hammer eared back.

She noticed his pistol at the same time that he thought about it. "You just drop that gun, then turn around and skeddadle." She snapped—"*Now!*"—when they didn't move.

The black muzzle of the .50-caliber Sharps looked as big as a cannon's mouth as Mulroy leaned forward and deposited the revolver carefully on the porch floor, just behind one of the columns.

"Yes, ma'am, I'm a Yankee. This boy helped me escape from the prison stockade at Andersonville, Georgia. Then I helped him escape from a bully of a boss. You don't look like a lady who would turn away two starving men. We have a little money and will pay for whatever food you can spare. Honest, ma'am, we haven't eaten anything since yesterday morning."

"You gonna pay with Confederate shinplasters?"

"No. Good Yankee silver."

She hesitated and seemed to waver. "Lemme see it."

Mulroy dug into his pants pocket and produced two shiny silver dollars.

Her brown-eyed gaze jumped from the coins to his face, then to Cal, standing a few feet to one side.

"We'll just eat and leave, ma'am. We won't bother nothin' . . . honest," Cal said.

"You got a funny color," the woman said. "You sick?"

"I feel fine."

"That's not what I asked. I want straight answers or you don't get a bite."

"Hepatitis, ma'am. But I'm sure it ain't catchin', or nothin'."

"In a pig's eye it ain't." She paused. "Well, never mind that. I reckon if I stay away from you, I'll be all right. Leave that shooter right on the porch, there, and come on in. Reckon if you murder me while I'm performin' my Christian duty of feedin' the hungry, the Lord'll look out for me." She stepped aside and motioned them into the house with the carbine barrel.

Mulroy caught his toe and stumbled on the porch step, he was so weak—he nearly fell on his face. He knew he couldn't go farther without nourishment and rest. Although the early symptoms of scurvy—loose teeth, sore mouth, and aching joints—had disappeared, he was still a long way from being fully recovered.

She ushered them through the entrance hall, where a straight staircase ascended to the upper floor. The house was one of very early design—two stories tall, but only one room deep. As they moved left of the hallway into what had once been a well-appointed dining room, Mulroy was surprised to notice that the inside walls were whitewashed logs.

"Hold it!"

They stopped and she walked around behind them with the Sharps. With one hand she carefully patted them down for weapons. Finally satisfied they were disarmed, she slid along the wall to the doorway. "Sit down."

They pulled out two chairs and seated themselves at the polished oval table.

"I already got a fire laid in the kitchen out back. I'll have this Sharps with me and I know how to use it. If you want to eat, just sit tight, and I'll be back in a few minutes." She backed out the door and disappeared. Then her head popped around the door frame. "Don't bother trying to steal anything. Somebody already beat you to it."

After she left, Mulroy stood up and stretched. "Beats trying to shoot a squirrel with a handgun," he said, glancing around the room. The matching table and sideboard had been dusted. A vase of wild roses formed a centerpiece on the table. The house might be falling down around her ears, but at least she was doing what she could to keep it clean and livable. He moved behind his chair and was startled by a glimpse of himself in the mirror above the sideboard. For an instant he thought a stranger had entered the room. Two weeks of dark beard surrounded his mouth and layered his lean cheeks. His smooth forehead and straight nose were darker than an Indian's. The Iowa farmer he'd been had vanished somewhere along the road of yesterday. The metamorphosis was internal as well. "Can't say as I blame her for being careful," he remarked. "Seeing the two of us coming to the door would be an unnerving sight. Especially for a woman out here alone in the woods."

The aroma of frying meat wafted through the open back door and Mulroy's stomach began to growl and rumble.

Ten minutes later, the woman, wearing an apron, returned with a platter of side meat and set it on the table. Then she brought in a bowl of hominy and a small iron pot of some kind of boiled greens. "Help yourself to plates and forks in the end door of the buffet." She left again and returned with a loaf of brown bread, already sliced.

Mulroy noted that she was careful not to put any knives on the table. He gave thanks mentally for the food as he filled his plate and fell to. He was famished.

The woman brought in a big pitcher of water and two tin cups. The cool, sweet water indicated there was probably a good well or spring nearby. She sat near the wall with the Sharps across the arms of the captain's chair and watched them.

Mulroy paid no attention to her as long as the food lasted. The loaf of whole grain bread was excellent, even without butter. It reminded him of home. About the only bread he'd eaten in the past year had been made of cornmeal. Mulroy was from a corn-growing state and wondered where all this cornmeal had come from. The quartermaster corps probably had warehouses full of dried, shelled corn. Wagonloads of it could feed horses and, ground, it provided soldiers with meal for cornbread. No yeast required. Civilians in the South probably got their corn from small, local farms. This part of the country didn't have the vast fertile prairies that made wheat a practical crop, so this bread he was eating was a real luxury.

Finally the two men were satisfied. Mulroy pushed back from the table, reached into his pocket, and laid down their last two silver dollars. The remainder he'd doled out sparingly to friendly Negroes who'd helped them along the way. Without hunger or the Sharps to distract him, he now regarded their reluctant benefactor closely for the first time.

She had risen and was leaning against the door jamb. The sleeves of her plaid cotton dress were rolled up to her elbows, and the arm that held the carbine was firm and suntanned. She was about five and a half feet tall, Mulroy gauged, lithe and graceful of movement. Voluminous black hair framed her face and brushed her shoulders. It was not held in place by combs or ribbons. Whether from excitement or fear, a touch of color highlighted her smooth cheeks, making her regular features almost beautiful. She was not a young girl. Mulroy guessed her age to be in the vicinity of thirty. Her complexion was rather dark, and he wondered if she had Indian blood or was descended from some Mediterranean race, possibly Greek. Her dialect and choice of words marked her as a woman of rural Alabama familiar with the more ragged aspects of life. He wondered what was she doing here alone. But he wouldn't push his luck by asking.

"That was delicious." He gave her his best disarming smile, hoping to show the softer side of his rough exterior. "You've literally saved the lives of two wandering strangers." He slid two silver dollars across the smooth table top.

She nodded without smiling.

"If I'm to thank you properly, ma'am, I need to know your name."

" 'Tain't necessary. Ma'am will do."

"Come on, Cal. We better go."

The pair moved past the cold stone hearth toward the door. The woman followed with her weapon. She'd fed them and accepted payment for more than the food was worth. From what she'd hinted, plus her caution, he guessed she'd been a victim of robbers—possibly foraging soldiers from either side, or brutal home guards. She was taking no chances.

Just then footsteps thudded on the porch and the front door was flung open.

She yanked up the Sharps, thumbing back the hammer, then quickly lowered it. "Damnation, Billy! Don't scare me like that."

"Just wanted to show you what I caught, Meg." A young man in his twenties stood there, holding a stringer of fish containing two bass and a good-size catfish. He looked hurt and confused by her reaction, then noticed Cal and Mulroy.

"These two were just leavin'," the woman said. "Get a bucket o' water and clean those fish out back. I'll fix 'em for supper."

"Who are they?" the young man addressed as Billy asked.

"John Mulroy and Calvin Blackwood," Mulroy said quickly before she could reply. "Just two hungry strangers your wife was kind enough to feed."

"Wife?" Billy looked confused, then laughed. "I ain't old enough for a wife. That's my sister, Meg."

The woman fidgeted, anxious for them to leave.

"Meg, many thanks for your hospitality," Mulroy said, trying to think of some reason to stall their departure. He wasn't sure why. Perhaps he'd been lacking feminine company too long—even that of an acerbic woman like this. He took two more steps and realized why he was lagging. He was absolutely bone weary. Usually after a big meal he grew sleepy, but even more so if he was already physically tired. He couldn't continue walking just now. "Meg . . . uh . . . ma'am, would you mind if we rested in your barn for a few hours? I'm dog tired."

She didn't answer immediately.

"Why can't they stay in the house, Meg?" Billy piped up cheerfully. "We got a spare bedroom upstairs."

Mulroy looked sharply at the clean-shaven young man in the ragged overalls. Something about him didn't seem quite right. He gave an impression of being totally guileless, almost immature.

"Hush, Billy! Go tend to those fish, and let me handle this." She turned back to Mulroy. "The barn is fine. I guess you saw it down the way. But I want you off the place before dark."

"Agreed." Mulroy would take what he could get.

They went out the door, Mulroy retrieving his pistol from the porch floor as they departed. Although he could feel her watching, he didn't look back.

The log barn, somewhat removed from the house, was weathered a silver gray. It was built with a wide dogtrot through the middle. It's sole occupant was a black horse that raised its head from a feed box as they entered. The muscles under its shiny coat rippled against the flies. The stall was the only one that had been cleaned and filled with fresh hay.

Standing under cover of the dogtrot was a high-wheeled buggy with front and rear leather bench seats and canvas top. It, too, was well cared for. This woman was careful and provident.

Mulroy wondered why she'd allowed them in the barn with a good horse and buggy. Not likely she was just absent-minded. Perhaps she trusted them more than she let on. They'd walked up to this house through woods and fields. Seeing the buggy suddenly made him realize there had to be a road to this place. And that road led somewhere. He'd explore the possibility for easier travel when they hiked out tonight.

"A good pile of clean hay," Cal said as he pulled off an armload from the stack to spread out for a bed. "You want I should stand first watch?"

"We'll both sleep," Mulroy said.

The boy shrugged and stretched out on the hay, far from the flies gathering near several piles of manure.

Sliding the small revolver into his side pants pocket, Mulroy lay down several feet away, near the buggy where he could see both ends of the open dogtrot. It was the last thing he knew before sleep took him.

Mulroy was just beginning to rouse up from deep slumber, helped along by biting flies in the breathless heat. He opened his eyes and sat up, perspiring, and tried to work some saliva back into his dry mouth. Dust motes drifted through the slanting rays of the late afternoon sun. He stood up and stretched, feeling more rested than he had in days. Cal was still asleep.

Suddenly the distant cry of a woman pierced the quiet. A door banged. Mulroy ran toward the open end of the dogtrot. Trees blocked his view of the house. "Cal! Get up!" Without waiting for the boy, Mulroy yanked the pistol from his pocket and ran toward the house. A saddled horse was tied to a tree near the porch. He heard a deep, male voice inside. Then a gunshot exploded and a front window disappeared in a shower of glass.

CHAPTER TWELVE

Mulroy sprang to the porch and flattened himself against the wall. He was breathing hard after his sprint, but could hear a scuffling, thumping inside. Easing one eye around the edge of the shattered window, he saw two bodies writhing on the floor, locked in silent struggle, kicking and panting. They rolled against a small table, upsetting it. A lamp crashed to the floor, splattering coal oil across the thin carpet runner.

A big, hairy man had Meg pinned down. She tried to swing the Sharps at his head, but he caught the barrel in a massive fist and wrenched it from her hands, flinging it behind him.

"Try t'shoot *me*, will ya!" he panted heavily. "I'm gonna give you sumpin' you been needin' for a long time!" The weight of his body held her down. He pinned her head with a big forearm across the throat as he fumbled with the other hand to hike up her dress. She kicked and squirmed, but couldn't get free.

Mulroy absorbed all this in seconds. He took a deep breath to steady himself, grabbed the brass knob, and yanked open the front door. He leaped inside and fired a shot at the ceiling. The explosion was deafening in the entrance hall.

The big man jerked his head around. "What the hell . . . ?"

"Get up!" Mulroy ordered, leveling the pistol at the man's head.

The big man flashed an oily grin, revealing tobacco-stained teeth through the beard. "Ah, hell, we were just havin' a little fun. Weren't we, honey?"

Meg took advantage of the distraction to rake her nails across her assailant's neck.

"*Ahh!* You bitch!" He jammed his forearm even harder under her chin.

"Get off her!" Mulroy shouted again.

With one swipe of a massive arm, he flung the woman aside and rolled to his feet with the speed and agility of a big cat. "Where the hell did you come from?" He showed no fear of the leveled gun. His hand was a sudden blur of motion across his leg and came up holding a knife from his boot top. He feinted one way, then another, wide eyes fixed on Mulroy. Weaving slowly like a cobra, he crouched and lunged.

Mulroy jerked to one side and fired. The gleaming blade ripped his shirt and grazed his ribs. The man staggered into the newel post of the stairway, the knife clattering to the floor. "You bastard!" he roared. He looked at his right hand dripping blood. "You shot me!" he said as if he couldn't believe it.

"Damn right! You're lucky it wasn't between your

eyes." Mulroy cocked the .32 revolver and warily circled the bearded man, keeping him covered. The small pistol was as easy to aim as pointing his finger, and had a very light recoil.

Meg was on her feet and had retrieved the empty Sharps. She held it by the fore end, like a club.

Out of the corner of his eye, Mulroy saw a figure descending the stairs to his right.

"Stay upstairs, Billy!" Meg warned.

The figure stopped, but Mulroy didn't take his eyes off the wounded man.

"Mister, get on your horse and get out of here before I get mad," Mulroy said.

The man moved toward the open front door, one hand gripping the other forearm, blood dripping onto the floor. It appeared the bullet had gone through his right wrist, just above the hand. His ruddy face was rapidly going pale. He looked to be in extreme pain. Clumping across the porch and down into the yard, he jerked the reins of his horse loose with his good hand.

As Mulroy, Meg, and her brother Billy watched, the man had considerable difficulty mounting his horse. He gripped the saddle horn with his left hand and tried to get his left toe into the stirrup, but the big sorrel sidled away from him, apparently sensing something wrong or smelling blood. The big man swore at the horse and finally got the animal to stand still long enough to get his foot in the stirrup and swing up into the saddle. Holding his wounded hand against his chest, and smearing his white shirt with blood, he jerked the reins savagely with his other hand.

"I'll be back. You can bet on it," he said grimly.

"There won't be enough left of you two to feed to the hogs."

"What about Billy?" Mulroy called out tauntingly. "You gonna leave him out of that hog feeding?" He was feeling light-headed and reckless.

"You forgot your hat!" Meg shouted, sailing the broad-brimmed headgear out into the dust. Catching Mulroy's reckless spirit, she turned to grin at him.

The big man growled something under his breath. He kicked the sorrel into motion and galloped down the curving driveway, leaving his hat on the ground. Dust stirred by his horse's hoofs hung in the still air behind him.

Only then did Mulroy notice Cal standing on the other side of the low, rock wall bordering the drive. The boy ambled toward them, still watching the retreating horseman.

Meg turned to Mulroy. "Thanks," she said simply.

"My pleasure."

She smiled and her face softened. "Can't say when I've enjoyed anything as much as I did that."

"You *enjoyed* that?" Mulroy thought she had an odd sense of fun.

"Only the last part."

He smiled grimly. "We might not be laughing if he comes back, or brings some of his friends."

"I don't think he has any friends."

"Even the devil has friends."

A purpling bruise was swelling on her cheek bone, and she was rubbing her throat where the big forearm had obstructed her breathing. The plaid dress and the shift under it were torn from the neck down to her waist, exposing one beautifully formed breast. He swallowed hard, his mouth dry.

She noticed his glance and, with little apparent embarrassment, pulled up the flap of material to cover herself. "Reckon I better go change," she said.

What he'd seen showed that her face and hands didn't tend toward a slightly darker complexion because of exposure to the sun; she was that same, smooth shade all over.

"Would you care for a drink?" she asked. "I'm going to have a glass of wine to steady myself. We can talk."

"Sure."

"I'll be right back." She turned toward the stairs. "Billy, show Mister . . . Mulroy, is it? Yes. Show him the whiskey jug, then get out some cups." She bounded lightly up the steps as if anticipating a picnic.

Cal came into the room and Mulroy briefed him on what had happened. The boy looked worried. "We'd best get movin', then. It'll be dark in two or three hours."

"Time enough. I don't know who that guy was, and really don't care."

"I know him," Billy said, retrieving a crock jug from under the sideboard and setting it on the dining room table. "Alford Potts. He lives over yonder, in Canfield."

"What's he doing out here?" Mulroy prompted when the young man didn't continue.

"He's been after Meg since last year when I came back from the war." His manner was bland, as if the matter held no interest for him.

"You were in the Army?" Mulroy asked before he thought.

"Yeah." He didn't elaborate.

Mulroy would get the rest of the story from the woman. Billy didn't seem quite in touch with reality. Mulroy uncorked the jug and poured a dash of the clear liquid into his tin cup. "Homemade corn squeezings?" he inquired, sniffing it.

"Yeah. Corn liquor," Billy said. "I made it. Can't afford store-bought whiskey."

"You'd better drink something else," Mulroy said to Cal. "This stuff might kill you, what with your hepatitis and all."

"Yeah. I'm thirsty," Cal replied. "Got a hankerin' for a long drink o' that good water."

Meg walked into the room barefoot and wearing a mid-calf cotton skirt and white blouse, open at the throat. She went straight to the sideboard and, opening one end door, brought out a bottle of wine and a small glass. When she turned to face him, Mulroy noticed she had brushed her hair and applied some kind of salve to the bruised cheek bone.

What kind of woman would dress this way in front of strangers, Mulroy wondered—bare feet and lower legs showing. But it *was* hot, and maybe she was in shock from her ordeal. Still, fashion dictated. . . . But it wasn't as if she were in some drawing room, receiving formal guests. She'd just escaped a beating and attempted rape. She could afford to let down a little in front of her rescuers, even though she knew them not at all.

Meg poured herself a small glass of red wine, then sent Billy to fetch a pitcher of water.

"Well, I suppose I owe you some sort of explanation," she said, setting down her glass.

"I'm curious, but you're not obliged to tell me anything," Mulroy said. "You looked like you needed some help, and I'm glad I was around to give it." He shrugged, sipping the smooth corn liquor.

"First of all," she said, "as you might've guessed, this is our old home place. Built by my grandfather. Grandparents and parents . . . all dead. And I'm trying to hang onto it . . . house, barn, and a hundred acres. The place was free and clear until my father fell into debt and had to take out a mortgage. He wasn't too good a businessman, or a farmer, and he signed an agreement whereby, if the property becomes vacant for longer than thirty days, it reverts to the man who holds the mortgage . . . even though there's only a couple thousand owing on it."

"That fella that was here, he hold the mortgage?"

"No. That's his son. The old man, Elroy Potts, is the local banker. He'd have Alford horsewhipped if he finds out what happened today."

"So the old man is a lot more upright than his boy."

"Oh, no! He just doesn't want any scandals interfering with his business deals. When the old man forecloses on this place, he wants to be sure there are no rumors his son had anything personal to do with me giving up this farm. Old man Elroy is cold-blooded and ruthless about money. His son Alford is hot and ruthless with women."

"The son might have a job explaining that bullet wound in his wrist."

Meg nodded. "And if he denies being out here, we've still got his hat and knife to say otherwise."

"How come he doesn't wear a gun, like most men?"

"He came here with something else on his mind. But I believe he generally carries a big Colt Dragoon in his saddlebags." She paused to sip her wine. "By the way," she said, brightening up, "we haven't been properly introduced. My name is Meg Sartain. And this is my younger brother Billy. His captain sent him back from the war to help me out here. Isn't that right?"

Billy nodded. "My captain said the Army wanted to thank me for doing a good job and helping out, but they didn't need me any more and I could go on home. They gave me a paper and an old horse they weren't using, and I rode back here." He advertised his good fortune with a satisfied grin around the table.

Mulroy shot a curious glance at Meg. She lowered her eyes.

This boy was definitely not normal, but he'd inquire later, if he got a chance.

"So, what's the story on this Elroy Potts?" Mulroy asked.

"When the war started, my husband Sam said he didn't want any part of it. He said he was leaving until it was over, and I could come along if I wanted. Well, we were renting a place in town and he was working as a carpenter. We were just getting by. My widowed mother was out here, and I told him there wouldn't be anybody to look after her if I left. I was torn between the two, 'cause I loved both of them. You understand?" She appealed to him with an earnest look.

He nodded.

"But it was a different kind of love," she continued. "I know the Bible says . . . 'A man shall leave his father and mother and cleave to his wife and the two shall become one flesh.' I guess the same goes for a woman. Anyway, I could just see old man Potts biding his time, waiting for my mother to die so he could get his hands on this place. Of course, I wasn't about to let that happen while I was alive. Billy and I are the only children, and he was off to war at the time, so I had to occupy the place after Mama died to keep it in the family. Guess I could have sold the place and paid off the mortgage and gone off with Sam, but there's something about a place your family has tried to build up and live on for three generations that just gets to you. Everybody belongs somewhere, and I felt attached to this farm. Wanted to keep the old home place, in case I ever have children to pass it along to. So Sam and I agreed to split the blanket for a little while. He headed West, and we arranged to meet back here after the war." She paused, looking forlorn. "Problem is, there's a lot o' West out there. . . . And this place is coming apart at the seams. Don't know how much longer Billy and I can keep it together."

"If you don't mind my asking, how do you get by?" Mulroy inquired. "You have enough money to live on?"

"We got a little, but it's running out faster than sand in an hourglass. I'm not sure we can pay this year's taxes on it and keep up the mortgage payments, too. I rent out a couple of my fields in exchange for part of the crop, but that doesn't amount to much."

"Is Sartain your married name?"

"Maiden name," she said. "When Daddy made out his will, I wasn't married and he listed me as one of the heirs under Margaret Sartain. So when I came back out here to live, I used that name. A lot simpler when dealing with the bank and such. My married name is Mortenson."

"So this Alford Potts has eyes for you," Mulroy said, thinking again of the bear-like man he'd confronted.

She nodded. "He's after whoever wears a skirt. He has a couple other women in Canfield."

"You're very attractive, but why try to rape *you* if he has other women?"

"Three reasons. First, he knows my husband is gone . . . second, his other women are whores he has to pay . . . and, third, men usually want what they can't have. Makes the prize more attractive." She laughed a bit self-consciously. "Present company excepted, of course," she added, coloring slightly. "But the big reason he thinks I'd be easy prey . . ."—she drew a deep breath and took a sip of wine—"is because of my darker complexion. A rumor's been going around Canfield for years that I'm a mulatto. If I got black blood in me, then I'm fair game for any man, according to what folks here think. A mixed-blood doesn't deserve respect. But it's a lie . . . I'm not a 'high yellah'. The Sartains are a little darker skinned than most Alabama whites 'cause my grand-pappy came from the island of Corsica. We're French from away back. My family never owned slaves."

"That explains a lot," Mulroy said.

"I'd betcha anything Alford has some kind of wager going with his drinkin' friends that he can have me, even if he has to rape me. This sort of thing would be sport for him."

"Now his pride's hurt, as well as his arm," Mulroy said. "You know him better than I do. What do you think his next move will be?"

"I don't know. He's never gotten this rough with me before. He'd been drinking before he rode out here."

"Did you try to kill him with that Sharps?"

"Yes," she said simply.

Mulroy had never met a woman so self-possessed, so confident. She was practical and did whatever had to be done to survive. Should he offer to stay and protect her if this Alford Potts should return? During his active service in the cavalry, Mulroy had seen wounds to nearly every part of the body. This wound could be very disabling. At least it would keep Potts from firing a rifle or pistol or wielding a knife with his right hand.

Mulroy knew nothing about the nearby town of Canfield or its people, other than what this woman had told him. For the moment, he'd forgotten his own past at Andersonville, his own weakness and need to escape back to Union lines. And what about Cal? He glanced over at the boy, who looked paler and sicker than ever. This boy needed a period of convalescence.

This lengthy war had cast a pall over everything and everybody. Was it the war, or chance, or Divine Providence that had put him in this position at this time? He didn't know. But no one person was isolated. People were thrown together, and interacted, for better or worse. If he and Cal had left right after the meal, instead of sleeping in the barn, they would not have been here to rescue Meg from Alford Potts. It was almost as if he had no control over his own life. "'Man proposes, God disposes,'" he muttered.

"What?"

"Nothing. Just an old proverb a schoolteacher friend of mine back home used to say."

She sniffed. "I'd best get that mess cleaned up in the hallway."

Mulroy had forgotten about the smashed coal-oil lamp from the upset table.

"I'm afraid it's soaked into the carpet runner," she added, swallowing the last of her wine and pushing back her chair.

"Why don't I drag that piece of carpet outside for now?" Mulroy suggested. "Maybe you can try to wash it later."

"Thank you. I'd appreciate that." She smiled at him.

He felt an inner glow. Probably the corn liquor. But she *was* an attractive woman. She was also married, he savagely reminded himself. He got up to join her as she picked up the bigger pieces of glass from the floor. The heavy base of the lamp was intact. She got a broom and swept up the fragments of the chimney.

Mulroy pulled the carpet strip outside and laid it across the low stone wall. When he came back in, she was swabbing the bare floor with a wet mop. "This is gonna stink for a spell," she said.

He watched her for a moment. Cal and Billy were still at the dining room table, talking about fishing. The violent events of the day hadn't distracted them.

"Billy, would you fetch me a bucket of water and a bar of soap, please?" Meg called.

"Sure." He disappeared out the back door.

Cal came into the hall. "We better go."

"How do you feel?"

"All right."

"You were sleeping pretty well, but I think you'd be better off if you could stay in one place for a time. Rest, eat right, get your strength back."

Cal took a depth breath and squared his shoulders. "We can't stop now. I can walk if we go slow. How far to your Army from here?"

"Don't know," Mulroy said, turning to the woman. "What about it, Meg? If we go straight north, how far until we reach the Union forces?"

She shrugged. "I got other troubles. I don't keep up with the war." She turned her back to swipe the mop across the floor.

Although silent, she seemed to radiate hatred of the Yankee invaders. At least that was the impression she conveyed to Mulroy.

He nodded to Cal. "Let's be on our way."

Meg followed them onto the porch.

"Cal, I left our canteen in the barn," Mulroy said. "Would you ask Billy to fill it with good water?"

The boy nodded and walked out.

"John, I can't thank you enough," Meg said. It was the first time she'd used his given name.

He waved a hand deprecatingly.

"No, I mean it," she said. "I'm sure you can tell I hate Yankees and I hate this war. You saw what it's done to Billy."

"Was he wounded?"

"Not physically." Tears welled up in her eyes, and Mulroy had to resist an urge to take her in his arms and comfort her.

"I don't know what he went through, but, ever since he found his way home, he's been like a ten or twelve-year-old boy." She wiped a tear from her cheek. "But maybe that's not bad. He's happy. He's content. He plays and fishes and helps me. He's gone back to his boyhood."

Mulroy suddenly hated the Yankees, too, and the Confederates—all armies, in fact. And prison camps. All cruel, inhumane treatment—mental, moral, and physical—was swept up together in a huge bitterness that engulfed him. This girl and her brother were only backwater casualties of the national conflict. He wanted to move farther from Andersonville, but now the idea of reaching Union lines and going back into uniform himself seemed less appealing.

He stood silently with her on the porch, gazing at the trees. Every leaf hung motionlessly in the late afternoon heat. He was already perspiring and didn't relish tramping off into the tick-infested woods. Sweat began to sting the long scratch on his left side where Potts's knife had grazed him. He went back into the house, dipped his fingers into his tin cup that still contained a little corn liquor, and rubbed it along his side.

"What're you doing?" she asked, following him back into the dining room.

"Trying to make sure this doesn't fester."

"I didn't know he cut you."

"Nothing serious. Just a scratch."

"Why don't you and Cal stay the night here?" she suggested hesitantly. "It'll be dark soon. I'll fry up those fish Billy caught and make some cornbread and slice some cucumbers and tomatoes."

"We couldn't impose on your hospitality any longer."

"You're not imposing. Didn't you just save my life? Besides, you paid me two dollars for that lunch . . . about four times what it was worth. And Cal needs some rest and good food, and he and Billy seem to be gettin' on so well, and . . . I . . . I'd sleep a lot better if I knew you were here, just in case . . . you know, if Al Potts should come back tonight." She flushed with embarrassment as she looked at him.

He noticed the bruise on her cheek bone was gradually spreading to blacken her eye. "Ma'am, that's the best offer I've had all day."

"You can sleep down here in the parlor," she said quickly, with obvious relief.

"I've got one request, though."

"What's that?"

"If we have time before supper, I'd like to take a good bath, then wash and dry these clothes."

"That can be arranged."

CHAPTER THIRTEEN

Mulroy sat on a stool in the dooryard while Meg trimmed his hair with her sewing scissors. She left it no more than two inches long anywhere on his head. When finished, she handed him a mirror.

"You missed your calling ... you should have been a barber."

"I used to cut Sam's hair," she said, obviously pleased. "When we lived in town, I even cut and styled some ladies' hair to make a little spending money."

"There is no end to your talents."

"Oh, I almost forgot." She reached into the pocket of her skirt and drew out a bottle containing a brownish-green liquid. "Here's something for you to use. Rub it into your scalp real good."

"What is it?" He drew the cork and sniffed. "Whew! That'll open the nose."

"A concoction my dad and a druggist came up with years ago. Don't know what's in it, but it's death on lice."

"Anything's worth a try, so I won't have to shave my head."

He poured a little on his scalp and began working it into his hair as he watched Cal and Billy carry a metal bathtub out to set it behind the smokehouse. Cal had a blazing pile of pine logs heating up an iron cauldron of water.

Meg disappeared into the house and returned a few minutes later with a folded shirt and canvas pants. A straight razor lay atop the stack she handed to him. "My dad's stuff. I think it'll fit you while I boil your other clothes." She pointed at the bone-handled razor. "I figure you for the clean-shaven type."

"Yeah. I don't generally wear whiskers."

"I think Billy has some outgrown clothes Cal can wear."

A half hour later, Mulroy was refreshed and feeling like a new man. He'd soaked and scrubbed with lye soap and a stiff brush, praying the homemade remedy would not cause his hair to fall out along with the lice. He'd even stropped the razor on his belt and carefully scraped the two-week's growth of black hair from his cheeks and chin.

As he toweled off, standing naked in the humid dusk behind the smokehouse, he began to sweat. Mosquitoes whined around his ears and began biting before he could pull on the borrowed clothing.

Billy and Mulroy dumped the water and refilled the tub so Cal could have a turn. Meg wrung out their boiled clothing and hung it on the line to dry.

Just after dark they all sat down to a late supper. Mulroy was as hungry as he'd been at noon and had to restrain himself from taking a second helping of fish. There was plenty of other food to eat—vegetables and bread—but he was still trying to put on flesh and was consciously fighting his natural tendency to hoard.

Meg had spread the oval dining table with a clean, white cloth and they ate from dishes with a floral pattern. Mulroy was feeling more and more like his former self before the nightmare of Andersonville. Two weeks ago, even the salt he was shaking onto his fresh tomatoes would have been an unattainable luxury. As he passed the food and filled his plate, he wondered how Salsbury, Palmer, and Miller were faring. If they didn't get relief somehow, none of them would likely live until September.

"Why you looking so glum?" Meg asked, interrupting his dark reverie.

"Oh, just thinking of my friends in that stockade," he replied. "I can only pray for them. I should be giving thanks for all this."

"That's for sure," Cal said. "Wonder what old man Shackleford is doing right about now."

"It's been long enough that he's probably stopped looking for you," Mulroy said. "From what you said, he's the type who'll take whatever he can get without putting out too much effort. Your services came cheap and easy. Now that you're beyond his reach, he's probably moved on to other things."

"Was Shackleford his boss?" Meg asked.

"Boss, taskmaster, caretaker, surrogate parent, overseer . . . all rolled into one," Mulroy said. "Too bad people can't just leave others alone. No, they have to be slave owners, greedy bankers, rapists, and everything else."

"Everybody has what somebody else wants," Meg said. "The way of the world, I guess. Just like. . . ."

"What?" Mulroy asked when she didn't finish the thought.

"Nothing."

"Go on."

"I was just gonna say it was like the Yankees invading the South 'cause they didn't like slavery, and didn't want us to break off to form another country, and wanted all the cotton we grow . . . and, who knows what other reasons."

Mulroy nodded. In the stockade he'd had plenty of time to reflect on the reasons for the war and how he'd wound up there. He'd concluded the righteous indignation of many Northern leaders was only a sham. "You're right. Relationships between individuals can be worked out a lot easier and better than relationships between groups."

Cal helped himself to a big scoop of mashed potatoes. Meg had dug them, washed, boiled, and mashed them, sliced cucumbers and tomatoes and onions in vinegar, fried the fish, and set the table with real china plates and bowls. She even provided knives and forks. No more tin cups and pans and pocket knives. They fell silent while they ate, the brass Rochester lamp above them creating an oasis of light for the four gathered around the oval table.

"I could get used to this kind of luxury," Mulroy finally said.

Meg smiled. "We're lucky. We can grow a lot of our own food. And I put up a few things for winter."

"She don't do all this fixin' every day," Billy spoke up. "Just when we have special company."

"Billy!"

"We're honored," Mulroy said. "Just like back home, except that our hostess is a beautiful young lady."

Meg put a hand to her blackened eye and bruised cheek bone, coloring slightly at the compliment.

Sam Mortenson was a fortunate man, Mulroy reflected. He wondered how the absent carpenter could have stood to leave a woman like this. The war couldn't last much longer, and he would be returning from the Western territories or from California.

"When did you last hear from your husband?" Mulroy asked.

"Eight months ago last Saturday," she answered quickly. Obviously she'd been counting the days. "Can't depend on the mail," she added.

"Where is . . . or, rather, where *was* he?"

"Wrote from Sacramento. Said he was headin' over to Carson City in Nevada where the big silver mines are." She looked rather forlorn.

"Won't be any time before he's back," Mulroy said, trying to lighten her mood. "This war will be over soon. We'll all be starting a new life."

She smiled at him, but it appeared to be a painful effort.

Two hours later Meg handed him a blanket as they prepared to retire for the night. "You want to load the Sharps and keep it down here with you?" she asked.

"No. You're more familiar with that thing than I am. You keep it by your bedside. I've got my pistol, and Cal has a stick of firewood for a club."

She took a thick candle from a drawer in the sideboard and lit it from the coal-oil lamp on the hall table. "Slide that bar across the inside of the door."

Mulroy eyed the bar. He hadn't noticed it before. "Well, if there's a mass attack, that'll hold out a few of them. But more'n likely, any visitors will come through that broken window."

She gave him an odd look. "You making fun of me?"

"Sorry. Didn't intend that at all. What I meant was, we don't know what to expect. I was just trying to figure the possibilities. Could be that Potts will sneak back here alone. He might even try to set the house afire with us inside."

She was silent as she picked up the Sharps. "Wish we had a Gatling gun or something," she said.

Mulroy laughed at the image of her cranking the rapid-fire weapon, mowing down waves of invaders. "We'll be all right. You and Billy in your two bedrooms upstairs, and me and Cal down here in the parlor. Frankly I don't think we'll see anything of Alford Potts tonight. He likely has all he can deal with, tending to that wound. But we'll be ready, just in case."

"Good night, then." She gave him a long, searching look, her dark eyes haunting in the candlelight, her black hair falling over part of her face.

"You've handled everything well so far," he assured her. "We can deal with whatever comes."

She nodded and moved away and started up the stairs, the candle flame casting wavering shadows on the log walls. She looked down once from the top of the stairs before going into her room. Billy had already retired to his room.

"Never met no woman like that," Cal observed, spreading his blanket on the rug.

"Tough as a boot, soft as a peach," was Mulroy's

assessment. "Here, you take the couch. I'll sleep in that stuffed chair over there where I can see out into the hall." He dragged the chair into position, then went out to the hall and brought the coal-oil lamp into the parlor, turning down the wick until it barely gave off any light. The damaged lamp had no chimney or shade. When they were both settled in, he blew out the flame.

The chair was comfortable enough, but Mulroy had trouble falling asleep. Even though he'd napped in the barn that afternoon, it seemed long ago. Earlier he'd slid the rod from under the barrel of his .32 Moore, then punched out the two empty shells and replaced them with fresh cartridges. It was now fully loaded. He had seven shots in the small revolver if he needed them. He tucked it under his belt near his hand, pulled the blanket over himself, and closed his eyes.

The events of the day had rolled over him like ocean waves without ruffling the inner calm that lay deep beneath the surface. Yet, part of his mind refused to allow him to relax enough to sleep. In his former days as a cavalry sergeant, he'd been able to sleep anywhere. This was probably due to two factors—exhaustion and being surrounded by armed comrades and pickets. He rarely had to remain alert and on guard. Here, he was the only adult male. And he and Meg were the only ones armed. A woman, however strong and resourceful, a former soldier, a sick boy, and a mentally deficient young man—what kind of defense could they muster, if attacked? He didn't want to imagine what might happen. He only wished he knew the situation in Canfield. Except for the violent clash today, he had no experience with the Potts family. Surely Meg and her battle-scarred brother must have *some* friends in town—somebody who would help in a crisis as he had done. He and Cal would remain for a while—at least until he felt reasonably sure the immediate danger had passed before they moved on. How long that would be was anyone's guess. He'd leave it up to Meg.

He scooted his chair closer to the parlor door. A gentle night breeze wafted the sweet scent of honeysuckle through the broken window. The rhythmic chirping of crickets, nature's sentinels, lulled him into a doze and, before he realized it, he was asleep.

Mulroy's eyes flew open and he jerked his head upright. A searing pain from cramped neck muscles seized him. The light of dawn seeped through the front windows. All was quiet. He slowly rose to his feet and stretched, thankful that the night had passed without incident. Maybe Alford Potts's threat had been only the venting of anger and frustration. More likely his revenge would be brewing down the road.

Cal was still peacefully asleep on the sofa. Mulroy moved in stocking feet into the hallway and peered out front. He slid the bar from the door and stepped onto the porch. The fresh smell of a cool, dewy summer morning greeted him. He wondered what day it was—of the week or month. He'd been surviving like an animal for so long, he'd lost all track of the civilized human calendar. He heard a *creak* behind him and whirled, yanking his pistol.

Meg was descending the stairs, Sharps in hand. "It's only me."

Mulroy let out his breath, suddenly aware of his racing heart. He'd been unconsciously wound tighter than he realized.

Meg's eye was swollen nearly shut from the bruise. "Excuse the way I look," she said, coming out the door to stand beside him.

"You look very alluring," Mulroy said, his honest first impression leaping to his lips. "Sorry. Didn't mean to say that."

She smiled. "No offense. Now, if that had come from Al Potts. . . ." She raised the Sharps like a club.

This woman struck him as much earthier than any he'd been around before. Yet, she still retained a proper decorum, even a degree of formality. Maybe it was only a forthright attitude, without a layer of artificiality.

"What's next on the schedule?" Mulroy asked.

"I gave that a good bit of thought last night," she said. "If it isn't too much to ask, would you and the boy stay for a time? I'd feel a lot easier about it. It's not so much for myself, but I'm not sure I can protect Billy."

"Yes, I think that's a good idea," he said.

"Billy's getting dressed. I'll send him out to see if he can find some eggs that aren't broke."

"You got a hen house?" Mulroy was surprised.

"No. The chickens just roost in the bushes and low trees back of the house. More wild than tame."

Mulroy and Cal remained at the Alabama farmhouse with Meg Sartain and her brother Billy for eight days.

Lacking any glass, Mulroy found several boards in the barn and nailed them over the broken window.

They fell into a routine. Meg cooked, washed, tended her garden, and took care of other chores while Mulroy used a bucksaw and a splitting axe on the wind-fallen timber in the nearby woods. He was careful never to be out of sight or sound of the house. In three days he'd managed to cut and stack more than two ricks of wood near the back door to feed the cook stove. He and Billy did some of the heavier work, such as drawing water from the well, while Cal and Billy supplied the larder with fish from the creek. Mulroy even managed to shoot a slow-moving opossum with his Moore.

"I'm not partial to greasy 'possum meat," Meg remarked as she baked it for supper one night. "But I reckon it's about as clean as any animal around, and a good deal cleaner than a hog."

"Yams, 'possum, greens, and cornbread," Mulroy said. "You're turning me into a regular Southerner."

"Good, healthy food," she said.

"Just joshing you," Mulroy said. "I'm very grateful for everything you've given us. Especially this food."

"Had to use cornmeal since we're all out of wheat flour. And this is the last of the coffee."

"How often do you go to town for supplies?"

"Whenever I can save a little money from selling produce, or a ham or some honey. I have to buy the things I can't grow or make," she said. "Sometimes I barter. Much as I'm going to dread going into town, I'll probably have to pretty soon."

As each day passed, the apprehension of Potts's return for revenge seemed to recede. Yet Mulroy was careful not to let himself be lulled into a false sense of security. Going about his tasks on the farm, he always carried his pistol in his pocket. In fact, on the second day, Meg had taken it upon herself to fashion a holster for him out of a piece of scrap leather he found in the tack room of the barn. She'd cut it out, then used a punch, and stitched it together with laces of rawhide. It fit the little revolver snugly, and she gave him an old leather belt so he could strap it on. He wore it diagonally across his chest with the holster hanging under one arm, carrying it everywhere he went. He also kept it beside him at night as he slept on a feather tick on the parlor floor.

Next day the weather was fearfully hot and close, with thunderheads building in the west. Mulroy was sitting in a rocker on the front porch, resting with a glass of cool cider when Billy and Cal came up from the creek, fishing poles in hand.

"Mister Mulroy, Cal's sick," Billy said.

"Gotta terrible pain," Cal mumbled, bent over and pressing a hand to his right side as he walked unsteadily into the house.

Mulroy followed and helped him to the couch. The boy's face was flushed and sweaty. "Probably a flare-up of that liver problem," Mulroy said, bending over him.

"Malaria, too," Cal muttered. He began to shake with chills, and Mulroy, not knowing what else to do, covered him with a blanket.

Meg came into the room, a worried Billy behind her. "What's wrong?"

"Malaria. He needs quinine."

She looked at him. "Hepatitis and malaria both. Poor kid."

Mulroy wiped the sweat from Cal's forehead. He felt helpless.

"You got a doctor in Canfield?"

She nodded. "Doc Shepherd. Amos Shepherd. I'll hitch up my buggy and we'll take him to town. Billy, can you round up Moses? He's in the pasture behind the barn."

Billy left the room.

"You think it's too dangerous to go into town?" Mulroy asked.

"Gotta go sometime," Meg answered, tight-lipped. "Running low on supplies. I'd have to make a trip in soon, anyway. Besides, I can't stand the suspense any longer. I got to see what happened to Al Potts and find out why he didn't show up here again."

"Maybe his old man, the banker, had something to do with that," Mulroy said.

"Could be, but I got to find out. I can't hide here forever." Her cheek and eye, although still slightly discolored, were healing nicely. She showed no other outward signs of the attempted rape.

"I'll go help Billy hitch up," Mulroy said.

"No. I'll do it. That horse is used to me. You stay here and cool him down with a wet rag or something." She turned to leave.

Thunder boomed in the distance. The approaching storm had turned the early afternoon into twilight.

"Be ready to go in about fifteen minutes. I'll pull up to the porch," she said as the front door shut behind her.

Mulroy looked at the boy who was hugging the blanket around him, shaking with chills in spite of the heat.

Mulroy jumped as lightning flashed. *Crack!* Thunder crashed, shaking the house. He walked to the side parlor window and looked out. The wind had picked up, blowing the curtains at the open window, drying his sweat.

What awaited them in town? Was this Doc Shepherd a good doctor, or would Cal just get sicker and die? How could they pay for the treatment? Would Meg Sartain be in danger? There were sure to be repercussions from the thwarting of the attempted rape. And here came Mulroy with her, bold as brass, an escaped Yankee prisoner who'd wounded one of their own. He adjusted the light shoulder holster. He'd better be ready to fight or run.

CHAPTER FOURTEEN

Dr. Amos Shepherd strode out of his examining room, rolling down his shirtsleeves. He was about fifty, with ginger-colored hair and side-whiskers. Focusing his blue eyes over gold-rimmed spectacles, he stared at Mulroy. "You related to this boy?"

"Just a friend."

The doctor glanced at Meg as if curious about her involvement, but withheld his question.

"He's resting right now, but he's very sick. I've given him a few grains of quinine for the fever, but there's no cure for malaria. The chills and fever will pass, but they'll recur periodically." He folded his arms and leaned against the desk. "As to the hepatitis, it's dangerous, but I don't think he has a severe case. I'm satisfied it can be cured with rest and proper food. How long has he had it?"

"I don't know. He had it three weeks ago when I met him," Mulroy said. "Can he travel?"

"Travel?" Dr. Shepherd arched his bushy eyebrows. "How? By horse?"

"Afoot. Sleeping outdoors."

"Not if you want him to get well. This boy is severely undernourished. And he's growing. His body needs rest and proper food to give him a chance to throw off this disease and let his liver heal."

"I see." Mulroy turned to Meg.

She shrugged. "He's welcome to stay at my place."

"I hate to expose you to it."

"We'd take precautions."

Mulroy turned back to Shepherd. "How long until he recovers, provided he gets good care?"

The doctor shrugged. "Hard to say. It varies from person to person."

"Weeks? Months?"

"I'd guess several weeks, at least."

"There's no medicine you can give him to help?"

"Nothing but the rest and food I've prescribed. And be sure he drinks clean water, even if you have to boil it to purify it."

Mulroy was confounded. He'd expected a better prognosis. He had to be on his way. Did he dare leave Cal? Would the boy's fever cause him to go out of his mind and harm Meg or Billy? Mulroy suspected Cal had lied about the fever causing the homicidal fit. He had never heard of such a thing.

"I'll give you some quinine to take along, and I'll write down the dosage, so when he has the next attack, it'll at least relieve his symptoms."

"Thanks, Doc," Meg said. "What do we owe you?"

"Five dollars will do it, including the quinine."

Mulroy dug out the five-dollar gold piece he'd been hoarding. "There you are."

"Ah . . . gold." The doctor grinned.

"Guess that beats produce," Meg said.

"Meg, you grow the best vegetables in the county, but a man can't spend yams and tomatoes. On the other hand"—he removed his glasses and wiped them with his handkerchief—"if you were to offer one of those mares. . . ."

"Not until I have to."

"I'd pay you in gold."

"Doc, I wish you'd quit raggin' me about that. I've managed to hide those animals from scavengers of both armies. I don't need the money just yet."

"Well, this war has scarfed up every decent bit of horseflesh in this part of the country. You've got a valuable asset in those animals."

"They're like money in the bank," she agreed.

"You'll have to buy feed for them this winter. That'll be an extra expense."

"I know. Maybe I'll sell off two or three, then."

"If you change your mind, let me know. I want to buy all five of them right now . . . for cash."

"We'll see." She was non-committal.

Doc leaned on the corner of his desk. "By the way, how's Billy?"

"About the same."

Shepherd sighed. "Wish I knew something more to do for him. He's retreated into a happier time of his life, and might stay there from now on. We just don't know much about how the mind works." He fingered the watch fob that dangled from his vest pocket. "Did you ever try to contact his commanding officer to find out what happened to him?"

"I wrote a letter, but never got a reply."

"No surprise. Troops on the move, terrible mail service. . . ."

"Actually, I'm not sure I really want to know," she said thoughtfully. "It might distress me even more."

Cal came walking unsteadily out of the examining room, looking pale and clammy.

"Feeling better?" the doctor asked, taking his arm.

"Kinda woozy. My ears are buzzing."

"That's the medicine." He put a hand to Cal's forehead. "Your temperature's come down. I'll help you out to the buggy."

The four of them went out into the darkening street, and Shepherd handed the boy up into the rear seat.

"We'll take care of him, Doc," Meg said.

The doctor turned back, averting his face from the dust-laden wind gusting up the street. Mulroy noted the storm, which had seemed imminent, was now veering off to the north and might miss them. A jagged lightning bolt stabbed through the black bank of clouds.

"Come back into the office a minute," Amos Shepherd said. "I need to talk to you two." He led them inside and thrust the door shut against the blustery wind. "You took a chance coming into town in broad daylight."

"Why?" Mulroy asked.

"Big hullabaloo about Al Potts getting shot out at your farm, Meg."

"That got around, did it?" she said.

"Bound to in a town this size. I treated the wound, but didn't say a word about it. I guess Potts was spreading the story."

"Will he heal up all right?" Meg asked.

"If it doesn't mortify, it'll heal. But he'll never have

the use of that hand again. The bullet severed the median nerve."

"I never meant for that to happen," Meg said, paling slightly and glancing at Mulroy.

"It's really none of my business," Shepherd said, "but rumors are going around about this shooting that puts all the blame on you two. Al and his father were going to get Sheriff Meigs from the county seat to arrest the both of you. But the sheriff was down with typhoid fever, and the deputy didn't want any part of serving an arrest warrant on a Yankee gunman. He's made one excuse after another for a week now."

"Yankee gunman?" Mulroy was incredulous.

"Anyway, since Al Potts couldn't get the law to go after you, he's been blowing to his friends around town that he's getting up a posse of vigilantes to go out there and clean house, as he put it."

"Does Elroy Potts, the banker, have any say about this?" Mulroy asked.

"Al's got the bit in his teeth and the old man can't rein him in," Dr. Shepherd said. "Al Potts has been wild and drunk and raving since he found out he'll be a permanent cripple. He's vowing revenge on 'the high yalla whore and her Yankee gunman,' to quote him."

"He came out there and tried to rape me!" Meg said, aghast. "This kindly stranger happened along and came to my rescue." She indicated Mulroy.

Dr. Shepherd nodded. "Figured it was something like that."

"I tried to shoot him with the Sharps, but missed," she added. "John shot him in self-defense."

"A lucky shot got his wrist when he came at me

with a knife. I could have finished him off, but I wouldn't shoot an unarmed man," Mulroy said.

"I hate to say it, but the two of you might be better off if you'd killed him. Then he wouldn't be disputing your word."

"But Billy saw it all!" Meg said, anguished.

"A sharp defense attorney would make Billy look bad on the witness stand," Shepherd said. He moved to the window and looked up and down the street.

"Cal didn't see what happened," Mulroy said. "He came up from the barn after it was over."

"All the decent people in this town know what Al Potts is like. His old man must have paid off somebody to keep him from being conscripted into the Army," Dr. Shepherd said, dropping the curtain and turning back to them. "But both of you are still in deep trouble. Meg, I've known you since you were a little girl, and I believe you. I'll help all I can. But, for now, I'd advise you to run. Get out of the county or the state. If you have any kin or friends you can go visit, leave now, or tonight as soon as it's dark."

Meg's eyes were wide in the lamplight. "I can't leave Billy."

"Take him with you."

"If we vacate the home place for thirty days, Potts can foreclose."

"Don't worry about that right now," Shepherd said. "Your life's in danger. Take your brother and run." He turned to Mulroy. "I don't know your story, or that of the sick boy outside, but you'd better decide something, fast!" Again Dr. Shepherd glanced out the window. "About an hour ago I saw Potts head for the Alhambra Saloon. He's probably not liquored up enough yet to be dangerous. Get in your buggy and go *now* . . . while you can." His expression was intense, serious. "It's only six miles to your farm. He was threatening to ride out there today, if he couldn't get the law to help him. If I see any sign that he and his friends are heading that way, I'll do what I can to stall them."

"Doc, I don't know what I'd do without you." Her eyes bright with tears, Meg kissed his cheek.

The doctor gave her a quick hug, then opened the door and peered out. "Clear. Go ahead."

"I'll drive," Meg said, untying the reins from the hitching rail and climbing into the right side of the front seat. Mulroy stepped up beside her, glancing back at Cal who lay slouched on the rear seat, eyes closed.

"Where the hell is everybody?" Mulroy asked. "The town is dead."

Two old men sat, whittling, on the porch of the general mercantile a block away.

"Most of the men gone to war," she replied. "Not more than two hundred souls here to start with. Now mostly just women and a few middle-aged shopkeepers hanging on. We've still got a blacksmith, doctor, and banker. Perkins runs the sawmill, and doubles as the preacher."

"And Alford Potts."

"Yeah. He has a couple of cronies who somehow managed to avoid the Army, too. They like to call themselves the home guard." She snorted a derisive laugh.

She urged the horse to a trot and they rolled down the nearly deserted street. At the edge of town they passed a sawmill, redolent with fresh-cut pine. Then their buggy was quickly swallowed up by heavy forest. Limbs of old growth oaks and maples arched over the roadway. The road curved downhill for a mile and the horse and buggy splashed across a shallow ford on a ledge of limestone. They began the ascent to the top of a ridge on a road that wove back and forth in long loops. Their forward motion created a slight breeze that fanned Mulroy's sweaty face. The day had grown oppressive. Thunder grumbled in the distance. The gloom of the woods and the gray sky cast a pall on the day. Without suffering any depression of mood, Mulroy mentally noted the afternoon hush—no wind, no birds or squirrels evident in the receding green depths of the forest. The only sound was the steady *clopping* of the horse's hoofs on packed earth.

Mulroy sat sideways and kept an eye on the road unwinding behind them. It was as if they were the last creatures on earth, moving through a vast forest. They wound back and forth for three miles as they ascended the ridge. When they reached the top, Meg reined up to let the horse blow and crop the sparse grass.

Cal still dozed on the leather seat as Meg and Mulroy stepped down to stretch their legs. They stood silently, side-by-side, staring out over the valley. In the distance the little town of Canfield was visible only as a gash in the solid green summer foliage.

"What are you going to do?" he asked.

She shook her head. "It's a hard choice. I hate to leave, but Doc Shepherd doesn't scare easily. If he said I was in serious danger, then I'll take him at his word."

"Anything I can do to help?"

"No." She paused. "I have an aunt in north Alabama I can go to," she said. "She'd see to us for a while. But I don't figure this problem will go away with time. And, if we're gone for more than a month, there's a good chance we'll lose the home place I've been struggling so hard to keep."

Mulroy drew a deep breath. "Why don't you move into a hotel in town?"

"Except for the county sheriff, who's sick, there's no law in Canfield," she said. Then she smiled coyly, making her look much younger. "I'd have to hire my Yankee gunman to protect me."

"Huh!" Mulroy snorted. "Ridiculous! When Potts returned to town shot up, he had to save face by spreading the story that I was some deadly pistoleer."

"Right," she said, growing serious again. "If I'm any judge, he'll have his revenge or die trying. Billy and I'll just have to pack up a few things and go."

"Why don't we lay a trap for Mister Alford Potts and company at your place? I'm sure we can figure out some way to stop him."

"He's got two or three cronies loyal to him. No telling what he's promised them to come after me. If you and I and Billy try to stand them off, they wouldn't be above gunning us down and claiming self-defense. Or they might torch the barn or lay siege to the place. Anything could happen. But don't expect any help from the law. If that deputy shows up, it'll be far too late, and he'll go along with whatever Potts says." She looked at him directly. "Billy and I are on our own. We've got to leave here, now."

"How far is your aunt from here?"

"About eighty miles."

"A far piece."

"We might make it in two days, if we don't run into trouble. The road isn't good and, with the rain, one or more bridges could be washed out. Billy's a grown man, but I can't really depend on him as one."

"I could come along and help. I'm trying to get north, anyway. I hear there are Yankee troops in north Alabama."

"What about him?" She jerked her head toward Cal. "You heard what the doctor said."

"He said Cal couldn't hike and sleep in the woods. Take him in the buggy and he'll do all right. If I had the money, I'd get him a room in town and pay the doctor to look after him until he was well enough to fend for himself."

"But he's just a kid," Meg said. "He and Billy get along great 'cause they're about the same mental age." She turned to climb back into the buggy. "Then we'll all four go. I've only known you a short time, but you've proved up. I *have* to trust you . . . there's nobody else. Hope I'm not wrong."

"I don't know what fate threw us together, but you can rely on me." He swung up into the seat. "And all that good cooking of yours has given me the strength of Samson," he said, flexing his biceps.

"All you need now is your long hair back." She smiled, slapping the reins over the horse's back.

In spite of their joking, Mulroy felt her underlying tension. He adjusted the small .32 Moore in its homemade holster under one arm. The rig was partially covered by a vest he'd thrown on before going into town.

In spite of his ingrained calm, all of Mulroy's senses became acutely alert. The condition was caused by nothing overt. On the contrary, as Meg held a loose rein on the two-mile downhill trot to the farm, the world appeared peaceful—a hot, sleepy, overcast afternoon. Yet Mulroy smelled danger, as he'd smelled it that day nearly three months ago at the Wilderness when his patrol had been ambushed out of heavy undergrowth, similar to this. He feared no attack from the woods this time. If it came at all, it would come from the road. They'd been warned, and his premonition was strong. His pores were leaking more sweat than the sultry day could account for.

But the road behind and in front of them remained deserted. Meg guided the horse through the gate and swung toward the barn. There they climbed down, and he helped her unhitch. She stored the harness in the tack room, rubbed down the horse, and turned it out to pasture. As he helped Cal toward the house, Mulroy noticed the three mares and two geldings—sleek, muscled horses—grazing near the water tank. Billy had groomed them until their glossy coats shone.

Billy greeted them, proud that he had supper almost ready, just as Meg had asked him to do before they left for town. He'd sliced ham and had a bed of coals glowing in the fireplace to bake yams.

Cal was awake, but not very alert, and he sat in the porch rocker while Meg set the table and boiled some squash.

When they sat down to eat, Mulroy selected the chair at the end of the table so he could see out the open front door. He did not remove his makeshift shoulder holster. Supper was unusually quiet. Mul-

roy was perspiring from both the weather and the
heat generated by the coals in the nearby fireplace.

By the time they'd finished, it was dark enough
that Meg lit the overhead Rochester chandelier so
she could see to clean up the dishes.

Mulroy helped Cal to his blanket on the parlor
sofa, then strolled out onto the front porch, wishing
he had a pipe of good tobacco to finish off the meal.
Better yet, he'd settle for a good, cooling breeze.
Mosquitoes hummed around his ears, and locusts
screeched in the humid dusk. Lightning flickered
through the trees, followed by a grumble of thunder. Stormy weather had threatened most of the day,
and now he'd welcome a good downpour to cool the
air, to make sleeping comfortable.

A few minutes later, Meg strolled out and stood
beside him, wiping her hands on a towel. "I guess
we'll get a good night's sleep, then start first thing in
the morning," she said.

"Yeah."

A silence heavier than the muggy air hung between them. Then Meg said: "I love this place.
Somehow it doesn't seem right that I should let that
scum run me off."

"You know, I was thinking the same thing. If
there was any justice in this county, Potts would be
the one on the defensive."

"Cal needs rest," she continued. "I'm not looking
forward to that long ride to Aunt Sarah's."

Another long silence.

Then she looked up at him and said: "I'm not
leaving."

Mulroy turned and impulsively embraced her in a

hug. It was a natural thing, triggered by sudden relief and joy, but for several seconds they clung together, knowing they were of one mind and purpose.

"It might be wise if we slept in the barn tonight," he said, stepping back. "In case anyone comes, they'll think we're gone."

"All right. But they could loot or damage the house out of spite."

"We'll be ready for them. Take your Sharps, I'll have my gun, and there's probably a pitchfork in the barn if it comes to that. We can hitch your horse to the buggy and be prepared to take off in a hurry, if we have to run."

"Good idea."

A rumble of thunder interrupted them.

"If Potts is drunk enough, maybe the weather will discourage him from riding over the ridge on a dark, slippery road."

"I'll get Cal and Billy," he said.

"I'll bring some quilts and a lamp from my bedroom."

Twenty minutes later, Billy and Cal were bedded down in the soft, sweet hay in the barn loft.

Mulroy and Meg returned to the front porch. "I'll get some candles," she said. "Easier to carry and they'll throw enough light for us to see what we're about."

Mulroy heard more rolling thunder. Yet, it wasn't exactly thunder. He paused on the dark porch and took her arm as she started inside. "Listen!"

The rumble gradually grew louder, and his stomach knotted. It was the approaching drumming of hoof beats.

A long, wavering flicker of lightning lit up the yard for several seconds, and Meg gasped. There, hardly forty yards away, sat four hooded riders, as grimly spectral as the Four Horsemen of the Apocalypse.

CHAPTER FIFTEEN

Mulroy's stomach contracted as if struck by lightning. He recoiled, numbed by a burst of thunder that rattled the windows. The brilliant lightning blinked out, leaving shiny silhouettes of hooded horseman burned into his vision. Hallucination? The painful grip of Meg's fingers on his arm assured him the sight was real. Expecting the devil and seeing him appear were two entirely different things. The reality of their worst fears stood before them, engulfed in velvety darkness.

"Quick. Inside," he whispered.

They ducked into the front hall and quietly shut the door. Mulroy was suddenly glad he'd boarded up the broken front window. He edged up to the other and peeked out.

"Did they see us?" Meg whispered, sliding the bar across the door.

"I'm sure they did."

He silently cursed their luck. In a few more minutes they'd have been safely ensconced in the barn with Cal and Billy. But, then, they probably wouldn't have seen or heard the horsemen approach, and a lighted candle could have given them away. Now they would *have* to fight—Meg with her Sharps and he with his revolver.

He stared hard through the wavy glass, but the lightning failed to co-operate and give him a second look. A long minute passed before the next flash came, showing—nothing. The horsemen had vanished.

Would they make a frontal assault? Not likely, if they knew they might be greeted with leaden hail. And wearing white hoods over their heads, they probably wouldn't come knocking at the door.

What, then? Mulroy tried to put himself in their place. If they were bent on revenge, they might just torch the house and barn. But that wouldn't be the smartest move if the elder Potts planned to foreclose. He suspected the banker had no control of these night riders. He tried to recreate the image of the horsemen. Did one of them have a bandaged hand, or carry his arm in a sling? The sight had been so quick and startling, he couldn't recall.

With the sound of rushing wind, the rain roared in. Having threatened for several hours, the storm finally unleashed its fury over the isolated farmstead. In the glare of lightning, every detail of the front lane, the rock wall, and the barn were revealed. Trees tossed their limbs wildly, leaves flying through the air. Then the light winked out in utter blackness, and every sound was drowned in booming cannonades of thunder.

"Get those candles," Mulroy said.

Meg went to the sideboard and retrieved them, intermittent flashes from outside the only illumination. He didn't have a plan for their use, but wanted them handy, just in case.

"Shall we slip out the back way?" she asked, returning to his side, gripping the carbine.

"They're not out front now," Mulroy said. "They've either taken shelter in the barn, or they've gone around back. I think our best chance is to go upstairs and watch from the windows."

They felt their way up the steps, clinging to the banister, watching, and listening, but the storm was blotting out all other sounds.

"My room has the best view out back," she said.

They hurried to the window and crouched to one side as she swung the two framed panes inward on their hinges. Unlatching the wooden shutters, she pushed them open. In spite of driving sheets of rain, a torch flickered below. Probably rags saturated with coal oil and dipped in tar, Mulroy thought. If they'd brought torches to see their way, they were of little use now. More likely, they were intended to set some buildings afire. The driving rain had literally dampened that possibility, unless they hurled one of the firebrands through a window or onto the porch.

Mulroy drew the .32 Moore, cocked it, and rested his forearm on the windowsill, sighting on the blaze. The next flare of lightning showed the mounted man holding the torch to one side. Mulroy quickly adjusted his aim and fired. The torch waved wildly and dropped to the ground, still flickering, as the darkness returned. Mulroy ducked back, hearing a shout below.

"The Sharps," Mulroy whispered. He would have

exposed himself to take the shot, but knew Meg was probably better than he with the weapon.

She slid the barrel over the sill and sighted into the darkness below. At the first hint of lightning, she fired. The .50-caliber carbine bucked with the blast, jetting flame. If the horsemen had any doubts about where the first shot had come from, there was no doubt now. Two seconds later, the shutter exploded into splinters as several bullets tore through the window opening.

"Into Billy's room!" she cried, scuttling toward the door.

The next bedroom also had one window that overlooked the dooryard and one on the end of the house next to the chimney.

They saw nothing from either window. The men below had taken shelter or ridden back around front.

"I think I wounded one. Did you get anybody?" he asked.

"Don't know. Had one in my sights for half a second. But it went dark again just as I pulled the trigger." She was breathless with exertion and excitement, and her hands shook as she reloaded.

"They'll bust in downstairs," he said, guessing.

"Unless they want to smoke us out. But the outside of this place'll be too wet to burn."

Mulroy strove to think quickly, yet calmly. He had to devise the best strategy. "Well, they won't be sittin' their horses, carrying lighted torches in their hands," he said with grim satisfaction. "You probably know them. What's likely to be their next move?"

She took a deep, audible breath. "Maybe break in and loot the place . . . and try to gun us down," she said.

"All this because I shot Potts in the hand and ran him off!"

"He lost face," she shrugged, hunkering by the window. "Nobody in sight. They're either up close to the house or headed for the barn."

"Let's hope not," Mulroy said, thinking of Cal and Billy; neither was in a position to protect himself. They would have heard the shots, and were probably wondering what'd happened. Cal, sick as he was, would at least know enough to stay under cover and not show a light. Possibly the two of them had gone outside to hide in the woods where they would never be found on a night such as this.

"Come on." He guided her from the bedroom and they crouched behind the railing overlooking the front hall. "I'm guessing they'll either toss a torch inside or they'll come through that front window. If I were in their place, I'd have a man stationed out back in case we ran."

"We're not going to run?"

"Whatever works best. They know we're in here on the defensive. I'm for giving them a dose of their own medicine."

"You at least wounded the man with the torch," she said.

"And you might have gotten another one. But we'll have to be ready just in case all four of them are still in fighting shape," he said in a hoarse whisper.

Crashing glass interrupted him. Splintered wood and shards of glass showered the floor below.

A flicker of lightning showed a bulky figure by

the window, and Mulroy fired three quick shots. The figure disappeared and everything was silent for the space of a minute. Mulroy pulled the rod from under the barrel and punched out the three empties, his eyes hardly leaving the shattered window that showed only as a faintly lighter square in the front wall.

Meg's reloaded Sharps rested on the railing. A man swung a pair of saddlebags at the remaining glass in the window. Remnants tinkled down as jagged pieces were cleared from the frame. The Sharps exploded with a deafening roar and the saddlebags were knocked back outside. She jerked down on the lever to open the breech. A strong smell of spent gunpowder seared Mulroy's nostrils.

His heart was pounding, this time from anger, not fear. He would give as good as he got. Without waiting for Meg, he sprang to the stairs and descended nearly to the bottom where he could have a level shot at the window.

"John, get back! They can see you there!" she cried, moving toward him.

The front door thudded as someone jerked the latch, but the bar held. Mulroy's ears were ringing from gunfire in the confined space, and he couldn't hear movements outside.

Just then, in a flicker of lightning, he caught a slight movement out of the corner of his eye. He swung and fired in the direction of the dark figure moving through the dining room from the back of the house. Then the Sharps exploded behind and above him, and Mulroy sensed the dark figure scrambling toward the back door.

How long could they hope to hold off this assault? He fired two more shots at the faint window opening, to cover his retreat back up the steps. Three or four answering shots slammed into the wall and splintered the banister a few feet below. He emptied his revolver at the flashes from the front porch, probably to no effect.

Trying to work some saliva into his dry mouth, he crouched again at Meg's side in the upper hallway, fumbling to reload his seven-shot Moore.

"God, John, what can we do? They've got us trapped!" she gasped.

"At least they're not trying to burn us out," he replied as he completed his loading and locked the tilted barrel and cylinder into position.

Another fusillade of shots from the front came so quickly they sounded like one long roar. Muzzle flashes reflected inside the front hall. Glass shattered as flower vases and framed pictures disintegrated. Mulroy returned fire with little hope of hitting anything, unless one of his bullets ricocheted. If they were to die here, he wanted to go down fighting.

Suddenly the firing ceased and the house became still except for the rain that sluiced down outside, splattering off the roof onto the hard-packed ground. Mulroy thought he could even hear water splashing into the rain barrel at the back corner of the house.

The silence was eerie and nerve-wracking. What were they up to now? The silence stretched out, and he shifted his position to ease the strain on his cramped legs.

"Take a look out the back window," he said.

She crept into the bedroom. A few seconds later

she returned. "Nothing. The lightning gave me a view, but nobody's out there that I can see. Think we should try to get outside and make a run for it?"

"No. I'm sure they have the front and back covered. They'd gun us down. As long as we stay holed up here, they can't get at us without exposing themselves." He wiped a sleeve across his sweating face. The storm had cooled the overheated air, but the atmosphere inside the house was still close and muggy. "They may decide to give it up as a bad job," he added hopefully, while the silence continued.

"I haven't heard their horses," she said.

"You probably wouldn't, in these conditions. We barely heard them ride up before the storm started." Mulroy realized he was trying to convince himself, as well as her.

The cease fire continued interminably. He wished he had a watch. It probably seemed much longer than it was. From his former battle experience he knew that five or ten minutes could seem like an hour.

"Yo! You in the house!"

Mulroy started at the sudden shout. He and Meg turned toward each other in the darkness, but didn't speak.

"Hello, in there!" The shout came from the front porch near the broken window.

"Yeah!" Mulroy yelled back.

"You can't come out and we can't come in!" the man shouted.

Mulroy said nothing.

"Gotta proposition for you!"

Mulroy waited.

"We won't hurt these two . . . Cal and Billy . . . if you throw down your guns and come out."

"Oh, no!" Meg cried softly.

"They may be bluffing."

"No. They might know Billy's name, but they wouldn't know Cal's unless they'd captured him," she said.

"You're right. They must have searched the barn." He raised his voice. "How do we know you've got them?" he yelled.

There was a pause. Then Billy's voice answered. "Help, Meg! They said they're gonna shoot us!"

Mulroy took a deep breath. "Would these men actually hurt those two if we don't give up?" he asked under his breath.

"I'm not sure who they are, even though that voice sounded familiar. But the way they came in here, shooting, I'd guess they'd do 'most anything."

"Reckon we don't have a choice, then. We'll have to surrender and take our chances."

"Yes. I won't do anything to put Billy in danger."

"What's your answer?" the shouted voice came again. "We ain't gonna stand out here in the rain all night!"

"All right, we're coming down!" Mulroy yelled, standing up. "We'll leave our guns at the top of the stairs." He shoved his Moore back into the shoulder holster, slid out of the belt, and put it on the floor with Meg's Sharps. He kept the remaining cartridges in his pocket.

He took Meg's hand and they slowly descended the stairway. "Don't shoot, we're coming out!"

Meg slid back the bar from the door and swung it inward. A man, armed with a long-barreled Army Colt and carrying a torch, shoved Cal and Billy ahead of him as he entered the house. Two other hooded men followed, one holding a Spencer carbine and the other a nickel-plated Smith & Wesson.

"Douse that torch," said the second man in as he found a lamp and prepared to light it. The wick came alive with a soft yellow glow, illuminating the entrance hall and glittering off the broken glass on the floor. Rivulets of water ran off the shiny slickers as the man with the smoky torch retreated outside.

"Let's all go into the parlor and make ourselves at home," the man with the lamp said, gesturing with the Smith & Wesson.

Cal and Billy sat on the horsehair sofa. Billy appeared wide-eyed with fear while Cal looked pale, but alert. Mulroy and Meg sat on two upholstered chairs.

The man returned without the torch, closed the front door, and joined them in the parlor. All three men removed their hats, but retained the hoods.

Mulroy wondered if the fourth man was taking care of the horses, but said nothing. From here on, it was their game to call. He and Meg had done their best, but fate had put them into the hands of these raiders.

"Meg, you should have sold those horses when you had a good offer for them," the man with the nickeled pistol said.

She glowered at him, as if trying to place the voice, but didn't reply.

"Now, since you put us to all this trouble, we'll have to take them with no compensation."

Mulroy gave her a questioning look. Was this raid not about revenge, then? Had he been duped into fighting for something besides her honor and her life?

"Lock these two young men in the smokehouse," the raider continued. "Leave them a lamp, some matches and food and water."

This man was clearly the leader, Mulroy realized as one of the other two gestured with the Spencer for Cal and Billy to get up and go ahead of him.

When they'd left the room, the man with the Smith & Wesson continued. "One of you shot Al Potts. Probably won't live through the night. He's unconscious on the front porch with a couple of saddle blankets over him." The voice was cold, clinical. "He'd probably want it this way if he had a choice. Don't think he could have lived the rest of his life as a cripple." The man paused, and paced to the darkened side window and back, his boots leaving muddy tracks on the thin carpet.

The other raider stood silently, holding the Colt and watching them through the two eyeholes cut into the white sugar sack.

"Actually, Al Potts was undisciplined. He wasn't worth a damn for this sort of thing. Not dependable, so we're probably better off without him."

Mulroy and Meg exchanged a questioning glance.

"Too bad he has to die like this, though. I abhor violent death. As a man of peace, I want this war to end while thousands of lives can still be saved."

"What're you talking about?" Mulroy asked, confused. "You didn't come out here to help Potts take his revenge?"

"Of course not. Potts was here, to be sure, but under my strict orders. Now it doesn't matter, since one or both of you shot him."

"You just came to steal my horses, then?" Meg asked.

"That's right. We came hooded, in case you were still here. Thought we could snatch them and go. But the storm interfered, then you decided to put up a fight. . . ."

"I know that voice!" Meg interrupted, her face paling.

"Of course you do." He reached up, grabbed the sugar sack by the top and pulled the homemade hood off his head to reveal the bushy auburn hair of Dr. Amos Shepherd.

CHAPTER SIXTEEN

Mulroy was stunned. He never dreamed this kind, caring physician would be the leader of a band of raiders.

"I was hoping I was wrong," Meg said, apparently not as taken aback. She seemed disappointed, more than surprised.

"Ah, Meg," Shepherd said with a tone of regret, "I warned you to leave right away. If you'd followed my advice, you wouldn't have been here and none of this would've happened. We would've just taken your horses and disappeared." He raked a hand through his tousled hair and turned to the other man. "Take off your hood, Charlie."

"Charlie Bowen!" Meg said. "I wouldn't have thought you'd be mixed up in something like this."

"Had to. My contacts were needed."

"Who's minding the mercantile?"

"My wife. She has a better business head."

The third hooded man reëntered the room. He looked around, then pulled off his own hood, revealing lanky blond hair. "Whew! This thing's hot, but it keeps the mosquitoes off."

"Willis Aston, editor of the *Canfield Clarion*." Meg shook her head.

"You the Yankee gunman I been hearing about?" Aston asked.

Mulroy laughed harshly without answering.

"Get the rope off my saddle and tie this one up," Shepherd said.

"Doc, what's this about taking my horses?" Meg said.

"Well, rather than someone else stealing them, we'll put them to good use for the Confederacy."

A few minutes later they had Mulroy bound, hand and foot, to a captain's chair.

"These ropes are cutting off my blood circulation."

"Yours is temporary . . . Potts's isn't."

"What the hell you up to?" Mulroy demanded. "Even horse thieves don't go to this much trouble."

The heavy set, balding Charlie Bowen back-handed Mulroy across the mouth, snapping his head sideways. "Don't be callin' me no horse thief."

Mulroy tasted blood in his mouth. "I don't know you, or this other guy, but I never thought Shepherd would stoop to stealing horses from a defenseless woman. Where I come from, that's like stealing chickens or taking money from the church poor box." He spat blood and saliva. "Shepherd, I guess you're on the same level with that whiskey-soused, hog-fat rapist, Al Potts. You're a real Southern gentleman, you are! Yes, sir, a professional healer, a pillar of the community!"

"Shut up!" Shepherd snapped, his face reddening.

"You don't know a damned thing about what's going on. This is bigger than all of us."

"The 'butcher, the baker, and the candlestick maker' all out for a night's adventure and some gun play to enrich their dull lives with some expensive horseflesh," Mulroy continued, taunting. "You fellas going to sell them to the highest bidder? The war must have made business mighty slow if you're stooping to this to put gold into your pockets."

"Shut your mouth or I'll gag you!" Shepherd almost shouted. "You're ignorant, like most Yankees I've met."

"Then enlighten me."

Meg stood to one side, wide eyes looking from one to the other.

"Maybe it's pride, but I don't want even a Yankee thinking I'm a horse thief," Shepherd said. "This raid has nothing to do with revenge, or stealing horses for personal profit. We've been commissioned by Jefferson Davis himself to. . . ."

"Don't tell him anything, Doc," the newspaper editor warned.

"Will, I think since we've lost the services of Potts, we should take these two along with us. They'd make perfect hostages in case anything goes wrong. Besides, a mission like ours would look much less suspicious if a woman is present. But, I'll leave it up to both of you." He looked from Charlie Bowen to Willis Aston.

Finally the pair nodded their silent agreement.

Shepherd turned to Meg and Mulroy. "You may not know this, but, in June, the Republicans nominated Abraham Lincoln for a second term. He's

been calling for more volunteers and more con-
scripts to replace the thousands of troops that the
incompetent Grant and the bloodthirsty Sherman
are getting slaughtered. Lincoln and Grant and
Sherman are trying to outlast our boys and win the
war by attrition. People of the North are heartily
sick of this war. To put it in a nutshell, if we kidnap
Lincoln while our General Lee is winning major en-
gagements, the Confederate government can bar-
gain Lincoln's life for a quick end to this brutality on
terms favorable to the South. That's our mission."

"Are you mad?" Mulroy was incredulous.

"No. As I said, I'm a man of peace who wants this
war to cease while thousands of lives can still be
saved."

"How do you plan to get Lincoln?"

"Normally that would be the difficult part. However, fate is playing into our hands. Since the nomi-
nation in June, many Republicans have tried to
convince Lincoln not to run. He's refused. So a
splinter group of the Republican party is meeting
now with plans to nominate former General John C.
Frémont to oppose him as an Independent. This will
effectively split the Republican vote, allowing the
Democratic candidate, General George McClellan,
to win the election." Shepherd paused, as if to organize his thoughts.

"So Lincoln has decided he must actively campaign. He must appear among the people, acting
like a strong, capable leader. He'll travel by train to
Chicago, Springfield, and Saint Louis to make campaign speeches. He'll then go south to Nashville
where he'll confer with the generals of his occupy-

ing forces, and travel to Chattanooga so he can be reported meeting with his recently victorious generals in the field before returning to Washington.

"There are many loyal Unionists in Tennessee who would vote for Lincoln, if there was a mechanism for casting ballots. But it's irrelevant, anyway, since Congress won't accept electoral votes from states they consider in rebellion. But there's a move to furlough as many Yankee soldiers as possible just before the election so he can get their votes." Shepherd seemed charged with energy as he spoke, pacing back and forth in the parlor, raking a hand through his auburn hair. "That's the background as to why Lincoln will be traveling to Nashville, where he'll be within our reach."

Mulroy thought he'd better humor this madman. "How do we fit into your scheme?"

"You'll be our shield . . . our hostages . . . in the event of trouble. You'll obey me without question, or I'll leave your dead bodies behind on our trail."

"I'm sorry I asked," Mulroy said.

"If you give us any trouble while we travel North to carry out our plans, I'll be forced to sacrifice your lives. It would be regretful, since I'm not only a man of peace, but I'm dedicated to saving life, not taking it."

"I can see you're a caring soul."

"Sometimes the few must be lost to save the many."

Mulroy thought it wiser not to reply.

Shepherd turned away. "Charlie, you and Will go check on Potts," he ordered. "If he's still breathing, carry him into the front hall. Sweep up that glass and pull the drape over the window opening. Meantime, since Meg was in no hurry to leave, she can fix us something to eat."

The two men obeyed without comment. At Amos Shepherd's direction, Meg went to light the chandelier in the dining room and lay out cold ham, biscuits, and sweet potatoes.

Shepherd, heedless of the July heat, thrust several sticks of wood into the coals in the fireplace left from Billy's cooking fire. The small sticks flared up. "We'll dry our boots and clothes overnight," he said. "Can't afford to ride in wet things. Besides being damned uncomfortable, it could lead to lumbago."

Meg threw two handfuls of ground coffee into a pot of water and hung it on a swinging hook over the fire.

Mulroy squirmed in his chair, flexing his legs and arms under the ropes in an attempt to restore some of the circulation. He listened to the storm fading into the distance. Rain was dripping from the eaves, and the low grumble of thunder had all but ceased. Now that the strain and uncertainty had passed for the moment, he felt very tired. In spite of the danger, he could hardly keep his eyes open. He remembered leaving their guns at the top of the stairs. No one had retrieved them.

The two raiders came back into the room. "Potts is still alive . . . barely." The balding Charlie Bowen threw a hard look at Mulroy. The three raiders sat down and ate heartily as if they were invited dinner guests.

When they'd eaten their fill, Shepherd got up and gestured at Mulroy. "Untie him." Aston pried the knots loose and shook off the coils.

"Come with me. I want you to see your handiwork." Shepherd carried a lighted lamp into the hallway. Mulroy followed. The doctor held the lamp down close to the blanket-covered patient. The big man's hair was plastered down by the rain, and what showed of his face above the beard had an odd color to it. But what struck Mulroy was the ragged, labored breathing. He'd heard that sound before. The doctor crouched and set the lamp on the floor, then pulled back the blanket and blood-soaked jacket and shirt. Mulroy didn't even need to see the massive chest wound to know that Potts wouldn't see another sunrise. If Mulroy's bullet had done that much damage, it must have hit a major artery. More likely, Potts had gotten in the way of a big lead slug from the Sharps.

Poetic justice. But Meg needn't know that hers was the shot that finished her attacker. Maybe he'd tell her later after the danger had passed. But when would that be? One or both of them might be on the other side of the great chasm by then.

"He's gone," Shepherd said, rising to his feet.

Only then did Mulroy realize the stentorian breathing had ceased. The broad chest was no longer heaving up and down. He was surprised he felt nothing but curiosity—no remorse, no relief— simply curiosity at what the man's soul must be experiencing wherever it was at this moment. Mulroy's only contact with Potts had been an unpleasant one. And he'd seen too many strangers die of wounds in the past two years to have any feeling about this one. He'd trained himself always to turn toward the living, to look to the immediate future and the welfare of those in his charge.

Dr. Shepherd pulled the damp blanket over the dead man's face. "We'll bury him in the morning. He won't be missed right away. When we return in triumph, the folks in Canfield will be told he died a hero in the Confederate cause."

Mulroy again wondered at the mentality of such men. He followed Shepherd back into the dining room.

"Doc, why don't you take the big room at the head of the stairs?" Willis Aston suggested. "Charlie and I will split the watch until dawn, and guard these two in the parlor."

"You trying to pamper an old man?" Shepherd said, arching his eyebrows.

"You're the leader . . . you need your rest," Aston replied. "Not playing favorites. Just good sense. Besides"—he grinned—"you got a good ten years on me."

"All right," Shepherd said, ignoring the levity. He pulled the watch from his vest pocket. "Time to get some sleep. We have a long day tomorrow."

"Are you going to leave those boys locked in the smokehouse?" Meg asked.

"No. They will have to come with us. I can't afford to leave anyone behind who could tell what happened here. If they go blabbing to town about a gun battle, the sheriff might come to investigate. If he happened to find a fresh grave, Billy and Cal could be arrested on suspicion of murder. Potts's death and the stolen horses would get the small minds of the local constabulary in an uproar. In their bumbling way, they might interfere with our clandestine operation. That's why we're taking you all with us. Besides, you're smart, and I can use you. Your Yankee friend might come in handy as well."

"Why don't you just leave us alone, take the horses, and go away?" Meg pleaded, her voice trembling.

"I've just told you why."

"God, I can't believe this is happening," Meg said, blinking away tears.

Mulroy put a reassuring arm around her. "We'll get through it." Then to Shepherd: "Where do we sleep?"

"In the parlor on the floor. Your hands will be tied to one side of the base of that upright piano and Meg's hands to the other. Al Potts will be sleeping much sounder than either of you, but you'll manage. And, as a precaution, should you somehow figure a way to get loose, Will or Charlie will be on guard with orders to shoot."

Mulroy had many questions, but they could wait. He and Meg and the two young men were in the custody of these raiders. Mulroy had learned not to antagonize people he suspected of being fanatics, especially those who tended toward violence. Their actions could never be anticipated. And, in spite of what the doctor had claimed about being a man of peace, anyone who would seriously entertain a plan of kidnapping the President of the United States might be mentally unbalanced and couldn't be trusted to have normal reactions.

If he and Meg were left alone, he'd suggest they play along and humor these men, as if their mission were the most logical thing in the world. Sometime in the next few days, the two of them could figure out a plan of escape.

An hour later they were lying on the worn rug, arms stretched out and tied to each end of the heavy piano. Meg had fallen into exhausted sleep. Within a couple of minutes, Mulroy heard her regular breathing. But he could not relax enough to sleep. Images of the gun battle and other events of the day paraded through his mind. Could he have done anything differently to avoid this? Yes. He and Meg could have taken Billy and Cal and fled in her buggy. But she—and he—had decided to stay and fight. They'd gambled and lost. But this was only one hand. The game wasn't over yet. He'd always been able to adjust quickly to any situation.

Their captors were fanatics. Apparently these three leading citizens of Canfield were desperate enough to attempt this seemingly impossible task. The doctor, the mercantile owner, and the newspaper editor—three unlikely prospects for political kidnappers. Where had Alford Potts fit in? Perhaps that reckless bully was to take care of any necessary violence.

Mulroy pulled himself closer to the piano to ease the uncomfortable position of his arms. He and Meg were now unwilling members of this group. Shepherd had said they would be hostages, if needed. Not a pleasant prospect.

From where he lay on his stomach he could see the reflection of the lamp burning on the front hall table. Charlie Bowen paced from room to room, the floorboards creaking under his heavy tread.

The storm had moved away to the east. Meg slept soundly a few feet away. She was a sensible, capable woman, and quite desirable. He sighed and laid his cheek on one outstretched arm. What a situation! If he could fall asleep, perhaps he'd awake to find that this whole thing was only a complicated nightmare.

Dr. Shepherd and the editor had retired upstairs to the two bedrooms. They would have seen and confiscated the Sharps and his pistol at the top of the stairs. He was glad they'd forgotten to search him since he still had the two boxes of cartridges in his pocket. These men were not trained lawmen or soldiers; they were only political patriots. Yet, why were they chosen as agents of the Confederate government for such a dangerous, critical mission? Surely others in the Confederate secret service or the signal corps were more capable of such an assignment. These men were just civilians. It made more sense—if such a plot were afoot—to abduct Lincoln near Washington and spirit him away to the capital at Richmond, or some other protected place in the South. Then it suddenly occurred to him that these three were probably not agents of the Confederate government at all—they were only eager patriots of Secession who'd hatched this scheme on their own, and had no official connection with the Confederate high command.

He grew weary of speculating. He had no choice but to be patient and let it unfold. His thoughts jumped to his farm in Iowa. The corn would be high now, the hogs fat. Had it rained enough this summer? What about the snow melt from last winter? It'd been so long since he was home. Once, those scenes had bored him. Now, they seemed like some unattainable heaven in his imagination.

* * *

Just before sunup, Shepherd untied Meg and Mulroy and, at gun point, ordered them to accompany him to the smokehouse, while Aston and Bowen buried Potts.

Shepherd administered the quinine to Cal, then put the remainder of the drug into his own pocket. "Billy, Al Potts was shot and killed here last night," the doctor said, speaking slowly. "You understand?"

"He won't be bothering my sister any more," Billy said with no emotion.

"That's true. He's being buried out by the rock wall along the driveway. You and Cal are coming with us and we're all taking a ride up north to Tennessee."

"What for?" Billy asked, distrust in his voice.

Cal cast an apprehensive glance at Mulroy.

"My friends and I have some business to take care of there. We'll all be back in a few days. Wouldn't you like to make a little trip away from the farm? See the sights?"

"Are Meg and Mister Mulroy coming, too?"

"Yes. The four of you can ride in your buggy. It'll be fun. My friends and I will go on horseback."

"I don't know. What do you think, Cal? I don't want to leave. I have to take care of the horses."

"Oh, we're taking the horses with us," Shepherd said. "Meg wants to sell them, and I know a man, on the way, who will pay three thousand dollars for those horses. What do you think of that?"

"That's a lot of money, but I want to talk to Meg. She always lets me take care of them."

"Well, here she is," Shepherd said, stepping out of the way. "Ask her yourself."

"Are you really going to sell them, Meg?" Billy asked.

"We have to. They're worth lots of money, and we need money to pay our bills and pay for our farm so we can always stay here."

"Can't we keep them for just a little longer?" he asked.

Meg shook her head. "One or two of them might get sick and die, then what would we do? We can't take a chance. We have to sell them now while they're strong and healthy."

Billy looked crestfallen.

"We'll still have the buggy mare," Meg said. "Lady will need you to groom her and take care of her. She's a beautiful Morgan."

"Oh, that's good." Billy grinned and thrust his hands into his overall pockets. "What do you think, Cal?"

"I think we better do what the doctor says," Cal replied, sidling away and eyeing Shepherd as if he were a coiled rattler.

"Tell you what, Billy," Shepherd said, "you go get cleaned up and shave and put on some clean clothes while we hitch up the buggy." The doctor stood aside and held the smokehouse door open for the two young men to leave.

The early sun was lancing obliquely through the wet foliage as the entourage left the Sartain farm. Shepherd and Aston rode ahead, followed by the black buggy with Mulroy driving and Meg beside him. Cal and Billy rode in the back seat. Two of the sleek horses and Al Potts's unsaddled mount were tied to the back of the buggy, and the remaining three were trailed by Charlie Bowen who brought up the rear of the caravan.

The four captives had been allowed to stuff one change of clothing into a grip. Meg had changed into a divided skirt, in case she might have to ride astride.

"Where's the old cavalry horse Billy rode home from the war?" Mulroy asked, hoping to distract Meg from her brown study.

"Sold him last year while he was still worth a little cash," she replied, giving him a wan smile.

"Don't let them get you down," Mulroy added under his breath. "Ignore them. Just think of this as a picnic with only the four of us."

"I'll try. Oh, my arms are so stiff and sore from being tied up all night!"

The road was still muddy from the overnight rain. Shepherd kept a steady pace, pausing several minutes every hour to rest the horses and allow them to drink from small streams or puddles, and to rip off mouthfuls of the lush grass that grew everywhere in the open. Members of the group got a chance to stretch their legs during these hourly stops.

Shepherd avoided the main roads. He seemed to know exactly where he was going. Part of the time they followed a single track through heavy timber, fording shaded streams in rocky bottoms. Nothing was mentioned about a midday meal. Each of them had filled a canteen before leaving the farm. In late afternoon Shepherd turned off onto a little-used side road, and the pace slowed. Knee-high weeds grew rank between puddled ruts. The route twisted and turned through hilly country on good roads and bad. They seldom saw other riders or wagons. Occasionally they passed an isolated farmhouse in a cleared field; mostly the country appeared wild and deserted. Mulroy could tell by the sun that they were riding north by west.

The sun dropped behind the trees and dusk crept over the land. Finally it grew too dark to see. Mulroy figured it had to be at least eight-thirty. Shepherd called a halt at the edge of an overgrown meadow. Lightning bugs were winking on and off, flying silently around them in the dark. They reminded Mulroy of long summer evenings in his childhood, and he felt a sudden pang of nostalgia for those past days.

"Meg, help me collect some firewood," Mulroy said as the others were unsaddling and unhitching. Billy busied himself rubbing down the sweaty coats of the led horses with handfuls of grass.

Aston pulled the Spencer carbine from its scabbard and tossed it into the crook of his arm. "Don't wander off," he warned.

When the two were twenty yards away, picking up pieces of dead limbs at the edge of the woods, Mulroy lowered his voice. Without looking up, he asked: "How much did Shepherd offer for your horses?"

"Five hundred."

"Figures. You heard him say he had a buyer who'd give him three thousand."

"I know. The war has caused a severe shortage of good horses. It's a seller's market, but Doc has the contacts to get the best price. That kind of money would keep me going for a long time."

Mulroy glanced back at Aston who was still holding the Spencer and staring in their direction. "I think I know why Shepherd was so desperate to grab your horses when you refused to sell."

"Why?"

"Shepherd is paying for this entire operation himself. The Confederate government is probably not even aware of what these three are doing."

She shrugged. "Doc can likely afford it."

"I don't think so, since he's been bartering his services for produce and such. I'll wager he's into Elroy Potts at the bank for a loan. And that's why son, Al Potts, was let in on this scheme. If there's no reimbursement coming from Richmond, Shepherd is looking to pay himself back for all the gold he'll have to lay out for livery, food, and lodging bills, not to mention some sizeable bribes along the way. And I'll bet Shepherd aims to make a decent profit for the risks he's taking, too. That's why your horses were a quick and convenient means of cash."

"All right, you two, that's enough wood," Aston interrupted, wading through the tall weeds. "Get back up there and start the fire."

The men soon had a fire going, and they sat on blankets, eating ham and corn muffins from their saddlebags that Meg had packed that morning.

As they ate their cold supper, Shepherd said: "We'll stop tomorrow night at a hotel and get a proper meal and sleep."

"What town?" Mulroy asked, trying to pry out as much information as he could.

"We should make Winchester."

"And what about the Union soldiers?"

Shepherd didn't answer at first, then said: "I guess it's all right to tell you now. As far as any inquisitive Yankees are concerned, I'm a physician with Union sympathies called by Nashville's commanding general to deal with an outbreak of vene-real disease among the troops. And I have the forged papers to prove it."

This scheme had taken some advance planning.

"How far is Nashville?" Meg asked.

"Two more days of hard riding, honey. You're lucky that soft little butt isn't in a saddle," Bowen leered.

Meg cringed at the storekeeper's remark.

"Keep your mind on business, Charlie," the doctor snapped.

Billy nudged Cal. "Hand me a drink from that canteen, will you?" He seemed oblivious to the conversation around him, concentrating on his food as if he were at a picnic.

"I haven't seen a newspaper in weeks," Mulroy said. "Last I heard, Sherman was marching toward Atlanta."

Willis Aston removed a slim cigar from his mouth, the blond stubble on his chin glinting in the firelight. "Yeah, but our boys are makin' him pay something fierce. Lincoln's trying to conscript more and more soldiers to throw into the grinder. If Sherman takes Atlanta, he'll be victorious on a mountain of dead bluebellies."

"I'm curious about one thing," Mulroy said.

"What's that?"

"If Lincoln is so hated by his own party that they're about to nominate somebody else, what good will it do to kidnap him? They'll just say good riddance. You'll be doing them a favor by taking Lincoln out of the picture."

"Lincoln is still their President, and he's still supported by many of the common people. His kidnapping will disrupt the North. It will cause chaos and fear when they realize the South is still capable of grabbing their leader, their commander in chief, by the throat, and snatching him out of their midst. He's playing right into our hands because Allan Pinkerton and a couple of his men can't protect him as well when he's traveling."

"There's an alternate plan to abduct Lincoln from Washington," Bowen spoke up. "Special agents are arranging to lay mines in the rivers to discourage pursuit when they bring Lincoln south to Richmond. And our troops will protect against pursuit by rail."

"In case your plan fails?" Mulroy said. "Nashville is a long way from Richmond."

"What makes you think we're taking him to Richmond?" Shepherd asked. "We don't need troops or mines as a rear guard."

"No?"

"That's the beauty of this plan. Lincoln won't be taken out of Nashville. We've arranged to hide him in the city until it's safe to smuggle him south."

"Jefferson Davis doesn't have high-placed, experienced agents around him who could accomplish this?" Mulroy asked, trying not to sound sarcastic.

"The high, the mighty, the experienced, the famous are not necessarily the best men to accomplish a clandestine task," the doctor said. "Skill, nerve, and daring can do wonders. Lincoln, the great bloodthirsty ape, will be taken for ransom. We'll save thousands of human lives by forcing the North to capitulate and end this war!" The leaping firelight lit up the wide, blue eyes of the fanatical patriot. Shepherd's ruddy face glistened with sweat. "Whatever you may think, you're in this with us, and you'll carry out your orders or die!"

CHAPTER SEVENTEEN

Mulroy slept like a dead man. He awoke, stiff and sore, in the dew-drenched dawn. If he took solace in anything, it was the fact that he felt this way from his rough treatment and sleeping on the ground, rather than from the effects of scurvy and starvation in the Andersonville prison camp. He had so much on his mind of late that he seldom thought of that experience, except in disordered dreams. Andersonville already seemed years in the past.

Meg's eyes were puffy and her movements a little rusty, so he surmised she was as sore as he was. He gave her a reassuring hug, which drew the comment from big, balding Charlie Bowen: "Mighty friendly for a married woman." He gave a harsh laugh. "Huggin' on a Yankee before breakfast. Gawd! Like chewin' on a green persimmon."

"How would you know?" Meg snapped.

"Shut up and get saddled," Shepherd ordered. "This girl didn't come along for your amusement."

Bowen's face clouded. "Yeah? Then just why *did* she come along?"

"Would you rather have left her to spread the word about our mission? Possibly get us captured or killed? You have contacts in the secret service in Richmond and Washington, so you ought to know that absolute secrecy is essential to our success."

Bowen grumbled something under his breath as he shook out his blanket and began to roll it up. "We don't get nothin' to eat this morning?"

"Whatever's left in your saddlebags," Shepherd said, scraping dirt over the still smoking coals of the fire with the edge of his boot.

No symptoms of Cal's malaria and liver problem were bothering him this morning, and the fourteen-year-old had taken Billy under his wing, helping him hitch the mare to their buggy.

Mulroy took a good drink from his canteen and handed it to Meg.

In less than a quarter hour, the horses were moving out at a walk in the fresh dawn. The sun was poking its head through the trees, and Mulroy could feel the heat of the day already stoking up. He wondered what the date was. After some calculations, he guessed it was probably late July.

The noon sun was boring down when the party paused near the Tennessee River to rest, eat the last ham scraps and crumbs of cornbread, and reconnoiter their way across. The wide, green river slid along in front of them as deep and broad as the Ohio. Definitely not fordable.

Shepherd removed his hat and, wiping a sleeve across his sweating brow, squinted downstream.

"Wish I had a pair of field glasses," he muttered, replacing his hat.

A mile away, a wooden bridge on solid stone supports spanned the stream. Teams and wagons were crossing it, and small figures could be seen at either end.

"Blue coats swarming all over that thing," Shepherd muttered, rubbing his unshaven chin.

"Your fake correspondence from the Yankee brass should be enough to bluff us across that bridge," Willis Aston said. "If those forged documents work here, they'll work anywhere."

Shepherd was silent for a few moments. Finally he said: "No, not until I have to. Some really astute officer might question why a Union commander would be asking for an Alabama doctor's help."

"Simple. In a war, the number of casualties demands that you get medical help from anybody willing and able to offer it," Aston said. "I've run articles in the *Clarion* about Southern surgeons working on the wounded of both sides. It's a common practice. The medical profession is almost neutral in this war."

Bowen grinned. "Besides, they probably really do need you in Nashville, Doc. The bluebellies in town aren't fightin' or marchin'. They got lots of time on their hands to get in trouble. We oughta hand out medals to those Tennessee whores for laying the Yankees low . . . in a manner o' speaking." He gave a harsh laugh, glancing at Meg. "Yes, sir, venereal disease was so rampant a few months ago, the commanding general rounded up all the prostitutes he could find and shipped 'em north by riverboat to

Louisville and Cincinnati. Then those cities shipped 'em right back."

Willis Aston grinned. "There's more than one way to fight a war."

Shepherd didn't appear to be listening. He continued his original thought. "If the Yankees control that bridge and are restricting travel, the locals probably have a ferry around here somewhere."

"Want me to take a look?" Mulroy taunted.

"Not likely. Will, ride on down the hill and see if this road goes to the river. Scout around for a ferry."

The four captives were resting in the shade provided by the canvas buggy top when Aston rode back into view. "Like you figured, Doc. There's a ferry landing right at the end of this road, about a half mile from here. Steam ferry is coming back across right now."

"Let's go."

They tightened their horses' girths and mounted up.

When the flat, barge-like ferry nosed into the bank, the party was waiting. After an old couple in a buckboard drove off, Mulroy got down and led the mare and the buggy aboard. The others followed, crowding their mounts and the led horses around it. Shepherd paid the operator, a grizzled river man. Ten minutes later the boat angled upstream, bucking the current as the small, rear paddle wheel churned the dark water to white foam. Mulroy leaned on the railing, breathing the fresh, cooler air. Breeze blowing over rivers always carried a peculiar, although not unpleasant, odor. Crossing the river was a pleasant break after the heat and humidity of their morning ride.

The afternoon was stifling hot, but, an hour later, Shepherd led them off the road and up a long, curving drive to a plantation house surrounded by cleared fields.

"Don't say a word," he warned, dismounting.

Someone had seen them coming, and a man in loose shirtsleeves and whipcord breeches came out the front door. He was a big man with wavy, graying hair and a florid complexion. He and Shepherd went around to inspect the sleek led horses that stood, hipshot, tails swishing at the biting flies. There was a muttered conversation Mulroy couldn't pick up. As the two men came around the buggy, Shepherd could be heard saying: "I'll even throw in that extra horse and saddle for sixty more."

"Done!" The big man gripped Shepherd's hand. "Come on into the parlor."

Fifteen minutes later Shepherd emerged, adjusting his shirt and vest over a bulging money belt.

Two Negro grooms appeared from the stable, untied, and led away Meg's prize animals and Potts's horse.

Shepherd heaved himself into the saddle, impeded by the weight of gold coin he carried in the money belt. He kneed his horse close to the buggy. "We're rid of all those extra horses, so we can make better time."

Mulroy could smell whiskey on Shepherd's breath.

"I think the mare has a bruised foot or picked up a stone," Mulroy said.

"That Morgan is fine . . . I've been watching her," Shepherd replied, reining away.

Mulroy had never been a convincing liar.

They reached Winchester, Tennessee that evening without encountering any Yankee patrols along the way. Shepherd didn't have to show his altered credentials at the hotel. The desk clerk barely glanced at their names in the register. He was more interested in the color of their money as the doctor paid for three rooms with gold coin, rather than Confederate paper.

Mulroy saw a few Union enlisted men on the street, but had no chance to get their attention. Any escape would have to include Meg and the two young men, or their lives would be forfeit. Shepherd impressed him as a man of his word, and he'd declared he'd put a bullet in any or all of them if they tried to get away. And Shepherd's nickled, Model Number Two, Army Smith & Wesson was never far from his hand. In spite of his Hippocratic oath, he wasn't above sacrificing one or two to save the many. To his way of thinking, it was like amputating a gangrenous limb to save the life of the patient.

Before going to dinner, Aston and Bowen boarded their four horses at the livery a few doors away. Here again, gold bought the best service and grain.

For the moment, Mulroy banished any thoughts of escape. Shepherd was buying, so, in the hotel dining room, Mulroy treated himself to steak and potatoes and boiled okra. He finished off with apple pie and coffee. Cal and Billy also ate well, but in silence.

Shepherd handed out slim cigars. Bowen and Aston accepted, but Mulroy shook his head. "No, thanks, Doc. I'm trying to get myself back into condition after that six weeks' of room and board your government gave me at Andersonville."

"From all appearances, you've about done it." Shepherd gave him a critical look. "You could still use a little more meat on your bones."

"I'm trying." Mulroy patted his stomach. It would be easy to like Shepherd—if it weren't for the physician's dark purpose.

"You really ought to throw in with us," Shepherd said. "It's hell holes like Andersonville we're trying to get rid of . . . and all similar prisons, North and South."

Mulroy was beginning to understand Shepherd's single-minded effort to end the bloody conflict, even though he didn't agree with his method of doing so.

Shortly after supper, they retired to their rooms. Shepherd was careful that none of the prisoners came within speaking distance to anyone they passed in the hotel. The banner headline of a newspaper on the registration desk caught Mulroy's eye.

ATLANTA FALLS!
SHERMAN'S ARMY LOOTS, BURNS CITY

He could read no more, for Shepherd hustled them toward the stairway to their rooms.

The captives were separated, Mulroy to a room with Bowen, while Shepherd and Meg, posing as man and wife, took the adjacent room. Aston was in charge of Cal and Billy in a third room. There would be no plotting or planning between Mulroy and Meg this night. But after two days of hard travel, followed by the heavy meal, Mulroy was so tired, he had nothing but sleep on his mind.

"I sleep light," Bowen said, patting the big Army Colt he slid under his pillow.

"Don't blow your ear off," Mulroy said, dropping his clothes on a chair and slipping between the clean sheets of the narrow single bed. He was glad to see the hotel windows were shuttered to let in the cool night air while frustrating some of the larger insects.

In the morning, fortified with a hotel breakfast, they hitched up, collected their horses, and started the last leg of the journey to Nashville.

Hours later, they trotted up the Nashville Pike, passing mule-drawn wagons driven by Negroes—wagons evidently headed to market, loaded with unshucked corn, melons, and baskets of fresh tomatoes and squash. Civilian buggies and military wagons rolled along the pike bordered by low, mortarless, vine-covered stone walls. Mounted Union soldiers patrolled in both directions. The porticos of white-columned mansions peeked through the greenery of oaks and magnolias. Mockingbirds, blue jays, and cardinals flashed their colors in the foliage.

The conspirators and their four captives blended into the flow of traffic on the packed-dirt road. No one bothered them. Mulroy sensed no urgency in the movements of the Union soldiers. This was part of the occupation force. The closest active war was miles away in Georgia where General Sherman's Army was driving beyond Atlanta.

At sunset, the lights of Tennessee's capital city came into view on the hills ahead. Shepherd apparently knew his way, for he rode straight in with no hesitation. As they entered the city, stores and wooden buildings began to crop up along the rutted road. They rode slowly downtown, past elegant townhouses with deserted, forlorn aspects, their owners likely fled or gone to fight. Gradually four-story, commercial, brick buildings and warehouses with heavy cornices rose up on either side of the street. Blue-clad Union troops were everywhere. Surely, Mulroy thought, among so many of his own, some opportunity for escape would present itself. He noticed Billy had not spoken since they entered the city. The lean young man was gazing, wide-eyed, at the Union soldiers. Mulroy wondered what memories were being stirred in the ex-soldier by the sight of the enemy.

Shepherd stopped in front of a three-story brick building on Summer Street next to St. Mary's Catholic Church. "This used to be the Planters' Hotel," he said, eyeing a sign attached to a wooden balcony that read:

U.S. SANITARY COMMISSION
SOLDIERS HOME

"Stay here." Shepherd dismounted and went inside. Several minutes later he returned and swung into the saddle. "This place is now a hospital for officers," he said. "Most of the larger buildings around here have been converted for use by wounded or diseased soldiers. The Watson House on Market Street and the Jones Hotel on the square are both convalescent hospitals."

He led them two blocks down a gradual hill to the public square where the City Hotel still functioned as a hostelry. The building was typical of other hotels—three-story brick with a front wooden verandah on each story running the full width of the building. Besides the hotel and a U.S. sutler's store, a few other buildings faced away from the Cumberland River, forming one side of the public square.

"I think I can squeeze you and your party in on the top floor," the proprietor said after examining Shepherd's forged letter from the U.S. Army Medical Corps and endorsed by General Thomas.

"Where can we stable our horses?"

"There's a livery about two blocks from here, but it might be full."

"Full?"

"Yeah. Two years ago, seventy thousand Yankee troops descended on us like a plague of locusts. Most of 'em are still here. They took over nearly everything. Put a helluva strain on those of us still in business. The Union Army even uses the Southern Methodist Publishing House next door to print their damned forms and report blanks." He turned to pluck their room key from one of the pigeonholes behind the desk. "And with President Lincoln in town on a visit, it's even worse. Town's bustin' at the seams with people."

The man brightened up enough to smile when Shepherd paid in advance with gold for the single available room. "Gonna be a mite crowded for seven of you, but it beats sleeping in the park."

Aston stayed outside with the horses and buggy while Shepherd, Mulroy, Meg, and Bowen lugged their saddlebags upstairs. The room, under the sloping roof at the back of the building, reeked of stale cigar smoke, even after they threw open the window overlooking the river bluff.

"Go help Aston stable those horses," Shepherd ordered Bowen.

A half hour later the two men returned.

"Couldn't afford to live in this town very long," Aston remarked, handing Shepherd his change. "Cost extra to wash the mud off the animals' legs and flanks, and to give 'em some grain. Even at that, they're out in an open corral. All the stalls are full. Parked the rig there, too."

"Wish my mercantile was located here," Bowen said. "I'd be a wealthy man in no time."

"If you could stand to trade with Yankee scum," Shepherd said.

"Yankee dollars don't have no politics," Bowen said.

"Spoken like a true businessman," Aston said, grinning.

Bowen looked disgustedly at the room. "One bed, and it's sagging like it'd break your back."

"We'll round up some pads or pallets and sleep on the floor," Shepherd said. "At least it's better than camping out, and we're close to our objective." He moved the pitcher and bowl to make room for a seat atop the wash stand. "Here's the plan."

Aston and Bowen sat on the bed while Mulroy was glad to stand after twelve hours on the buggy seat.

"What are we doing here?" Billy asked.

"*Sshh!* You'll find out," Cal replied, keeping him out of the way against the wall.

Mulroy squeezed Meg's hand when she came close to him, standing near the open window. He glanced out at the darkening scene. Too bad it was a three-story drop, straight down. From a ground floor window, he and the others might be able to escape. And they could easily lose themselves in the dark, labyrinthine byways of the crowded city.

"Lincoln is scheduled to tour a couple of the hospitals with his generals," Shepherd said. "After that is a reception for him with various dignitaries and military brass. Then there will be a grand supper. . . ."

"Where?" Aston interrupted.

"Not sure. But it doesn't matter. Our business won't start until he returns to his private train car near the depot, five blocks southeast of the capitol building. By then it'll be dark, so we'll create a diversion and snatch Lincoln from his private car. We'll spend tomorrow setting it up." He paused, looking at Meg. "Since you declined to sell your horses, I had to confiscate them. Just consider it your contribution to stopping the war." He gave her a tight smile. "Now, here's what we'll do. Start with this sutler's store on the square, then check second-hand clothing shops to buy remnants of Confederate gray uniforms or hats, enough to outfit three men. Then we round up that many derelicts on the streets or saloons, each of whom can ride and wants to earn a ten-dollar gold piece and a free horse. Each of these bums will wear parts of a uniform . . . enough to pass for a Confederate raider in the dark. Bowen, Aston, you'll supply each of these derelicts with one of our saddled horses and, after dark, scatter them among the cars in the freight yard within a hundred yards or so of Lincoln's train.

"Aston, when I scouted Nashville weeks ago, my railroad contact pointed out a tool shack in the freight yard where the construction crews store their kegs of black powder. You'll bust the lock and lay a fuse to this powder, a fuse long enough for you to get safely away before it blows. The signal to light it will be when you see me start to enter Lincoln's private car at the end of the train."

"How you going to manage to get in there?" Bowen asked.

"Leave that to me," Shepherd said. "But we must all look clean, well dressed, and presentable. Not like we just came off a week on the trail. So, first thing in the morning, we'll visit a bathhouse and buy some new clothes. I'll get a doctor's bag to go with my credentials, then present myself as a physician called to attend one of Lincoln's aides who's ailing. Meg, posing as my nurse, you're to use your good looks to distract the guards. Once inside, I'll lock the door, pull the gun from my bag, and capture everyone in the car." He looked directly at Mulroy and Meg. "You two understand any resistance will get you killed," he said. "And Billy and Cal, too," he added.

"The sound of gunshots will attract attention," Mulroy pointed out.

Shepherd pulled back his vest to reveal a large sheath knife at his belt. A hush fell on the group. Mulroy had no reason to doubt that Shepherd was deadly serious. He now understood the role Alford Potts would have played in this drama.

"I'll chloroform Lincoln and the others," Shepherd continued. "While this is going on, Aston will set off the explosion, the bums will gallop off in all directions, whooping and hollering like Confederate raiders who've just blown up something. Aston, you are to fire a few shots as if you're trying to keep them from escaping, then fade away into the dark. All this will draw the attention of any Pinkertons or bystanders outside the train long enough for us to hustle Lincoln off between the cars on the dark side away from the depot."

"Sneaking him away's going to be the most dangerous part," Aston said.

"As I said before, heroes come from lowly places. Tomorrow I'll contact the man I was put in touch with three months ago when I was here. He's a rail yard switchman who'll be waiting with a handcar behind some parked freights nearby. We'll take Lincoln and pump the handcar three miles up the tracks, away from town. The switchman lives near the tracks, so we'll hide Lincoln in the cellar of this man's house. In a few days, after the first excitement's over, we'll arrange to smuggle that warmongering President South." He looked at the other two raiders. "Aston, you and Bowen will disappear during all the uproar and meet me later as we arranged."

"What happens to the four of us after all this is accomplished?" Mulroy asked.

"If you give us no trouble before Lincoln is safely out of Tennessee, you'll go free. Then it won't matter what you do or who you tell."

"You can't fit that many of us on a handcar," Mulroy said.

"These two will be left behind," Shepherd said, indicating Cal and Billy.

"To tell the police and the soldiers where you went?" Aston said.

"I'll take care of them . . . never you mind."

"What do you mean by that?" Meg demanded.

"That's no concern of yours. They'll be dealt with."

Shepherd was wound tighter than ever, so Mulroy said nothing, although he had a sinking sensation in the pit of his stomach. He glanced at the grip of his own .32-caliber Moore revolver protruding above the doctor's money belt. So near and yet so far. If only he could do something to divert the course of events, without endangering Meg, her brother, or Cal. Shepherd had been wise to bring them along as insurance. In spite of his lingering weakness, Mulroy knew, if he were the only captive, he would have jumped at his first reckless chance to get away, or to thwart this scheme. The next twenty-four hours would be the longest of his life.

CHAPTER EIGHTEEN

Mulroy slept soundly for five hours. Early the next morning he awoke on his floor pallet, thinking immediately of how he might escape with the other three. But, as time for the kidnapping grew short, Shepherd anticipated his desperation and was careful not to let Mulroy stray more than a dozen feet from him.

They ate flapjacks and coffee in the hotel dining room, then went to shop for the cast-off remnants of Confederate uniforms and bought three tunics, missing buttons and insignias, two pairs of pants with yellow cavalry stripes, and one kepi. These they hauled back to their room in a canvas bag. Since they would need the room for a staging area during the day, Shepherd paid for another night's lodging.

The next order of business was a bathhouse. Aston had been given charge of Meg and stood by alertly while she splashed in a wooden tub just behind a portable screen.

Mulroy noted how white and thin Cal looked without his clothes. But the boy didn't act as if he felt weak or was in any distress. He was still growing. With enough good food, he'd recover from his mild case of hepatitis, Shepherd had predicted. As long as a supply of quinine was available, his malaria could be kept in check. In time, Cal would likely make a full recovery. But did any of them have that much time left?

After they'd all bathed, it was a barbershop for the men—haircuts and shaves, beards and side whiskers trimmed. The Gay Paree ladies' salon on Summer Street performed magic on Meg's dark, thick hair, sweeping it back into a voluminous French twist.

"I feel silly," she confided to Mulroy, as they stepped out onto the sidewalk. He was distracted from their hostage status for a long moment as he stared at her. Dark skin and eyes combined with the new hairstyle to transform her into a striking woman.

"If you can't distract the guards at Lincoln's car, nobody can," he remarked under his breath.

They worked their way through the crowds on the sidewalk, toward a men's emporium a block away. As they were being herded along the street by the three conspirators, Mulroy edged up beside Cal. "How're you holding up?" he asked in a low tone.

"I've been a sight better. Is Shepherd gonna kill us . . . ya know, what he said about dealing with us?"

"Naw. Shepherd just wouldn't admit he didn't have all the details of his plan worked out." Mulroy glanced back to make sure he was several steps ahead of the others and out of earshot. "Shepherd's crazy, but he just wants Lincoln. He's mostly bluff when it comes to killing."

"Sarge, I got a gut feeling he's gonna put that chloroform on me and Billy like we was two stray cats."

"Even if he does, it'll only put you to sleep for a short time." Mulroy tried to make light of it; he had no idea what was in Shepherd's deranged mind.

"If you get a little too much of that stuff, it'll kill you," Cal said. "I seen it happen in the Andersonville hospital."

"Once all this starts, Shepherd won't have time to fool with you and Billy," Mulroy said, trying to sound confident. "Besides, he wouldn't be dosing you with that quinine for malaria if he meant to kill you."

"He can't leave us alive," Cal insisted with a desperate, pleading look. Mulroy couldn't tell if the boy's pale face was a result of his sickness or his fear. For a fourteen-year-old, he'd certainly shown his mettle so far. Although he hadn't fully recovered his own strength, Mulroy had no chronic disease, and silently vowed somehow to save this boy and the President, no matter the cost to himself.

"What the hell you two whispering and plotting up there?" Charlie Bowen asked, striding forward to catch up.

"Nothing," Mulroy answered quickly. "I was just telling him to quit eyeballing these good-looking women on the street. They're all too old for him. Besides, a lot of them in this part of town are probably prostitutes." He chuckled. "Don't want my young friend, here, to come down with some social disease."

Bowen guffawed. "Yeah. Sick as he is, catchin' sumpin' else would likely do him in. But whatta way to go, huh, boy?" He laughed again. "I've never been to Nashville," Bowen said as they turned a corner and the turret-like tower of a massive stone building came into view on a hill. "But I know I've seen a likeness of that capitol somewhere recently."

"There's a picture of it on the February issue of the Confederate twenty-dollar bill," Shepherd informed him.

"Ah, that's it. Somebody spent one of those in my store a couple weeks ago," Bowen recalled.

They gazed briefly at the square structure on the bluff above them. Overlooking a bend of the Cumberland River and visible for several miles in any direction, it dominated the city.

They reached the store and the men outfitted themselves with new clothing, from the skin out. Surreptitiously the three raiders took turns watching the prisoners. Shepherd was careful to create an appearance that was tasteful, but not ostentatious— white shirts and cravats, broadcloth suits of gray and black, new shoes or short boots as each man preferred. He even bought them each a new hat. "Businesslike and presentable," he said, "but nothing that will draw attention to ourselves." Shepherd carried their old clothes in a sack to be disposed of later. While all this was going on, he kept Cal and Billy under close scrutiny.

"Don't we get to buy new clothes?" Billy asked as they left the store.

"Never mind," Cal said, distracting him away from confronting Shepherd. "Our old clothes are plenty good enough."

"I guess you're right," Billy said with a grin. "Can't go hunting or fishing in those fancy outfits. They'd get all torn or muddy." He looked at Cal. "Ask them when we're going home."

Mulroy again noted the young man's cultured speech, unlike what he'd come to expect from a backwoods Alabama lad. Billy and Meg had apparently been well schooled by educated parents. What a catastrophe that his mind had been damaged, maybe for life.

"Last but not least," Shepherd announced as the men ushered Meg into a ladies' boutique that advertised the latest fashions.

In spite of being a prisoner, she obviously enjoyed the unaccustomed shopping. Shepherd paid for it all without flinching, yet Mulroy knew the value of Meg's five top-grade saddle horses would more than cover the cost of the entire trip.

"This is really nice," Meg murmured to Mulroy as they emerged from the dress shop. She smoothed the material of the long, pleated dress over her hips. "I could close my eyes and almost forget where we really are."

"You'd look even more stunning if you had your Sharps," Mulroy whispered back.

By the time they'd been bathed, shaved, coifed, and clothed, it was mid-afternoon, and they gathered in a Market Street restaurant a few blocks from their hotel on the square to have a meal before beginning the deadly serious business of the evening.

Mulroy was surprised he was hungry, but noticed Meg eating lightly. Shepherd forbade any alcohol, even beer.

Back on the sidewalk, Shepherd handed their bag of old clothing to Bowen. "Throw these in the first trash barrel you see, then get those odds and ends of uniforms from our room. Round up three derelicts, if you can find that many who aren't too drunk to sit a horse. Keep Cal and Billy with you. We'll meet you at the Silver Dollar Saloon at eight and take it from there. I have one more stop to make with these two." He jerked a thumb at Meg and Mulroy.

"Meg Sartain, John Mulroy, this is Howard Kenny," Shepherd said, making quick work of the introductions.

"Howdy."

Mulroy stared into the switchman's intelligent eyes. In his overalls, cap, brogans, and thick, graying mustache, Kenny looked every inch the railroad switchman. Broad shoulders and thick chest added to the impressive look of this short man.

"Want all of you to know each other, 'cause we'll be working the handles of the car tonight," Shepherd explained.

The four of them stood in the shadows of a smokegrimed brick house a stone's throw from the freight yards. Tumble-down piles of bricks and stark chimneys advertised where other houses had stood nearby. Swallows fluttered and darted in the twilight. There were no neighbors close by. The odor of boiled cabbage emanated from the open door behind Kenny. He reached to pull it shut on the voices of his children inside.

"She gonna be in that outfit?" Kenny asked, nodding at Meg and her long dress.

"Yes. But don't worry about her. She's got the stamina for it. And, at that point we won't be worried about her dress. It's not tight, so she can run."

"All right. I'm going on duty at eight, just before dark. I'll arrange to be down below the depot before ten. That'll clear me of the blast, then, quick-like, I'll work my way up opposite Lincoln's car. As soon's you're aboard, we'll slip in behind two long parked freights and pump like hell for this place. Shouldn't take us more'n fifteen minutes to get here. Then it's inside and down cellar. I got a place all set up with food and water. The missus is in on it, but the kids are too small to know. They'll be sound asleep, anyhow."

"As soon as the blast goes off and all hell breaks loose, watch for us. We'll be hoofin' it," Shepherd said. "If anything should go wrong, you wait only five minutes. If you don't see us, then go. Understood?"

"Yeah," said Kenny. He pulled a silver watch from his overall pocket and he and Shepherd coordinated their timepieces.

An hour later the seven of them sat in the Silver Dollar Saloon. If Meg hadn't slipped in, unnoticed, among them and behind a throng of boisterous soldiers, she would probably have been refused admission to this rough waterfront saloon. But once they crowded their way into a corner where their conversation was drowned by a piano, she could be mistaken for a working prostitute.

"Can you trust this Kenny?" Aston inquired. "He's crucial to our plans."

"Yes. Not only has he suffered the indignities heaped on him for two years by these Yankee invaders, but he and his family are in need," Shepherd said.

"He won't be in need after you pay him a thousand in gold," Bowen said. "Patriotism has a steep price."

"Since he has a chance to take revenge on the Northern aggressors and make money at the same time, why not?" Shepherd snapped. "The point is this man is reliable." He glanced out the window at the deepening dusk. "Bowen and Aston, take our saddlebags from the room and leave them at the livery for us to pick up later. Bring along our three saddle horses. You didn't have any trouble rounding up enough volunteers, I take it?"

"Hell, no. We had our pick. Got three I think will do fine. Not too far gone, and they're ex-cavalry who can ride, drunk or sober. They're waiting in an empty shed a half block from here. Had to give 'em a bottle to share to make sure they'd stay put. The promise of a ten-dollar gold piece and a free horse each should keep 'em in one place for at least a half hour." Aston grinned. "Besides, I jammed the door of the shed. They'd have to bust out."

"It's almost dark," Shepherd instructed. "Bowen, have 'em put on those pieces of uniform, then meander down to the rail yards. Split up and go slow so you won't draw any attention." He consulted his watch. "Aston, I'll be waiting on the uphill side of the passenger depot. If anything goes wrong, signal me by coming into the waiting room and taking off your hat. If I don't see you by nine-thirty, I'll proceed with my act. That'll give you time to bust the lock off the black powder shed, and set the fuse.

When you see us start to enter the car, light the fuse. Bowen, make sure those bums take off, whooping and hollering at the sound of the explosion." He looked at each of the two men. "Everything clear?"

They nodded in unison.

"Let's get at it," Shepherd announced as he picked up the small black bag and motioned for the four hostages to go ahead.

As they started for the door, Mulroy noted that his own .32 Moore was tucked handily into the doctor's waistband, beneath the money belt and partially covered by the new vest. Shepherd's own nickel-plated Smith & Wesson was hidden in the bag, along with the chloroform and the tightly rolled blanket they planned on using to conceal Lincoln's unconscious body.

The key grated in the lock and Cal's heart sank as the hollow thumping of feet receded down the stairway. He twisted his head to one side. A lingering twilight cast just enough light through the open window of their hotel room for him to see Billy, hogtied and gagged three feet away.

Bowen had done a very thorough job. Each of them had been placed on the floor, belly down, and held at gun point by Aston while Bowen worked the knots. Cal had been tied first, wrists behind the back. Then his knees had been bent and the ankles tied together with the rope extended from the ankles to form a noose around the neck. Thus, if they struggled to get free, they would only succeed in pulling the slipknot and choking themselves—a cruel, but effective deterrent. Gags made from the torn sheet cut off any chance of yelling for help.

Would anyone come back for them? Cal knew a moment of panic when he thought of lying there for hours, or maybe far into the next day until the hotel maid or the desk clerk found them. By then they might be dead, or their blood flow restricted for so long that their limbs would have to be amputated. His heart began to pound with fear, causing him to pant. Suddenly he realized he could actually breathe through his mouth around the gag. While Bowen was gagging them, he'd been in a hurry. Cal had had the presence of mind to thrust out his narrow jaw and press his tongue forward in his mouth, so that when Bowen was finished, Cal could relax and find he had a little slack. It was similar to a trick he'd seen horses do when being saddled. By expanding the rib cage while the cinch was being tightened, the animal could relax afterward and have a little slack.

For fifteen minutes he worked his jaw and his tongue, trying to enlarge the tiny space in his mouth. Sweat stung his eyes, and he paused to rest and breathe. Finally he got just the amount of slack he needed. Worming his way across the floor to the bedstead, he managed to hook the gag on the corner of the wooden bed frame. A sense of desperation ate at him as he worked. Again and again his head slipped off the edge of the wood, pulling the rope tighter around his windpipe. Finally, with one hard yank, he ripped the gag loose, cutting his lip and bruising his cheek. He lay for a minute, gratefully sucking in the fresh air.

"Billy," he croaked. "I got my gag out. I'm coming over to see if I can use my teeth on the knots tying your hands."

It was nearly completely dark as he wiggled his

way to Billy, who turned away, presenting his tied hands to the probing teeth. Ten more agonizing minutes and Billy's hands were free.

Meg and Mulroy stood with Shepherd in the dim light emanating from the doorway of the depot. Every few minutes Shepherd glanced into the waiting room. He consulted his watch. 9:30 came, and crept past. No Aston. Everything was on schedule.

At 9:45, Shepherd snapped his watch closed. "As soon as Lincoln arrives, we'll go into action. Let me do the talking. Remember, you're my assistants, so act like it. If either of you try to tip off a guard or do anything to stop this, remember, Billy and Cal won't live to see the morning." He pulled a pair of gold-rimmed spectacles from a breast pocket and put them on, immediately assuming a more studious, professional aspect.

At that moment, a team of spirited blacks, pulling an open carriage, swung in a half circle and the driver reined them up. The President's party had arrived. A company of two dozen uniformed cavalry followed as an escort to Lincoln's carriage, their shod hoofs clumping a hollow tattoo on the cobblestones.

"Company, diiiss-MOUNT!" The troopers dismounted as one, then secured their horses to a long hitching rail. They fell into an honor guard stretching from the carriage to the depot door, twelve men on each side.

"Pree-sent . . . ARMS!" came the sharp command from the captain. With a sibilant shriek, twenty-four shiny steel sabers slithered out of their scabbards in unison to be held vertically in front of each man.

The driver opened the carriage door and a corpulent general stepped down, followed by the tall, gangly figure of the President, dressed in black. He was followed by two men in civilian suits.

"Probably two of Pinkerton's men," Shepherd said under his breath.

The four men passed between the rows of the honor guard, and Mulroy got a good look at the hatless Lincoln who stood at least a head taller than his companions. His coarse black hair and chin whiskers were shot through with gray. Three years of war had worn deep furrows into his angular face. So this was the man they were to kidnap, the man who was to be held hostage by the South to force an end to the war.

"Order . . . ARMS!"

Sshhuunk! With the sound of a dropping guillotine blade, twenty-four sabers were sheathed.

Mulroy swallowed, trying to work some saliva into his dry mouth. He took a deep breath to calm his racing heart, and wiped his sweaty palms on his pants. He thought it incredible that everything seemed so calm. Events were going on as if the world had no idea what was about to take place. Bugs *buzzed* around the coal-oil chandelier in the waiting room. A half dozen men were scattered on benches throughout the big room. Two were reading newspapers, one dozing, one was having his boots blacked by a young boy. The station agent was stamping a ticket at his barred window, while the telegrapher, wearing a green eyeshade, jotted a note on a yellow desk pad. Several waiting passengers glanced up curiously as the Presidential party passed through and out the other door to the station platform.

Mulroy had a sudden urge to break this placid air by running inside and shouting that President Abraham Lincoln was about to be overpowered and kidnapped. Then he realized where he was. Most of these men would probably offer to help with the abduction. And, besides, there was the threat against Billy and Cal.

Shepherd glanced again at his watch, waited about two more minutes, then ambled inside the lighted room. He pretended to examine the chalkboard on the wall listing the arrival and departure times of the various trains. Then he hooked his thumbs in his vest pockets and sidled toward the door leading to the platform, keeping Meg and Mulroy in front of him. Outside, in the dim light, they saw the two red lanterns glowing on the last car of the four-car train that was parked evenly with the corner of the depot. The locomotive panted softly, steam up. The two civilians in dark suits who had accompanied the President stood on the rear platform of the car, their low voices indistinguishable.

Mulroy was both amazed and irritated. Why weren't they guarding Lincoln more carefully? Office seekers and petitioners of every sort thronged Lincoln's White House office daily. No attempt was ever made to shield the President from the public. Probably because this man was unpretentious and wanted no fuss made over his safety, even though someone had earlier taken a shot at him when he was riding to the old soldiers' home near Washington City. On that occasion he'd remarked that the hole in his stovepipe hat was only the result of some hunter's stray bullet.

Shepherd seemed in no hurry. He ambled away

from the Presidential train to the opposite end of the platform and gazed intently into the darkness of the rail yard. Was Aston watching, ready to light the fuse? Did Bowen have the derelicts mounted and poised to ride?

"Stay close, and keep your mouths shut," Shepherd whispered, and drew the .32 Moore from his belt and checked it, making sure the others observed his action. "Let's go," he said, and shoved the small pistol into his waistband, then hefted his small black bag and started toward the train with a purposeful stride.

"Gentlemen!" Shepherd addressed the two men on the rear platform. "Is this Mister Lincoln's train?"

"It is. What can I do for you?"

"I'm Doctor Shepherd, a physician assisting General Buell's staff. I was told one of your train crew is ill. I'm here to examine him."

The two civilian guards looked at one another. "Don't know anything about that, but we just arrived with Mister Lincoln's party. What's the man's name you're looking for?"

"I wasn't told. Perhaps a porter? Would you mind making inquiry for me?"

"You have some identification?"

Shepherd slipped the bogus letters from inside his coat pocket and handed them over.

The guard examined them briefly in the half light. "And who are these people?" He asked suspiciously, gesturing at Meg and Mulroy.

"She's my nurse and this gentleman is assisting me as part of his medical training," Shepherd responded somewhat impatiently. "Now, if you'll locate that sick member of the train crew. . . ."

The guard nodded, handing the papers back. "I'll go forward and check." He stepped off the platform and strode forward alongside the train.

Voices and clumping of hoof beats sounded behind them. Three soldiers of the dismissed honor guard were riding slowly across the tracks nearby. An iron shoe *clanged* against a rail.

"I've been a great admirer of Mister Lincoln for years," Shepherd continued. "If he hasn't already retired, would it be possible for me to obtain his autograph while I'm here?"

"I'm afraid not. He's had a tiring day," the remaining guard said.

"That's unfortunate." Appearing disappointed, Shepherd turned away, removing his gold-rimmed spectacles and slipping them into his vest pocket. At the same time he smoothly drew the .32 Moore from under his vest. Pressing the muzzle into Meg's back, he whispered something to her.

"I'd certainly love to meet the President," she said, coming forward and smiling up at the Pinkerton man.

"And who might you be, young lady?"

"I'm Miss Sartain, Doctor Shepherd's nurse."

"Oh, really?" The man put a foot on the lower rung of the iron railing and swept back his suit coat, hooking his thumbs in his galluses.

Mulroy saw the butt of a small pistol jutting from a shoulder holster.

"Maybe you could nurse *me*," he said, eyeing Meg up and down. "I been feelin' a mite poorly of late."

"I'll have to give you a thorough examination." She gave him a dazzling smile. "But I'd like to meet Mister Lincoln first. Anything you could do would really be appreciated. We'll only take a minute of his time."

The man hesitated, distracted by three cavalry-men riding slowly beside the tracks in the direction of the train.

Mulroy turned at the sound of footsteps scuffing along the platform. His stomach contracted at the sight of Cal and Billy.

Cal was clinging to Billy's arm, pleading in a stage whisper. "Billy! We can't go down here. Come on!" But the young man shoved the weakened boy aside like a pesky fly, and kept going.

Cal scampered after him. "Billy! Listen. This ain't the time."

"I won't let them hurt Meg!" he blurted.

"Shit!" Shepherd hissed under his breath, glanc-ing at the horsemen, then at the two young men approaching.

Billy jerked to a halt, staring toward the three cav-alrymen. His breath was coming in quick gasps.

Mulroy sensed something coming, and reached to calm the young man. But he was a second too late.

"*Aauughh!*" An anguished cry ripped from Billy's throat. He snatched the revolver from Shepherd's waistband. *Bam! Bam!* Flame jetted toward the sol-diers. "Yankees! Stop 'em!" Billy screamed, firing again.

Shepherd cursed and lunged for him, but Billy skipped nimbly out of the way.

As if everything slowed down, Mulroy saw the guard on the train reaching inside his coat, a screaming Meg trying to grab Billy's arm, the troop-ers drawing their Colts. Weapons blasted and bul-lets *thudded* into the depot wall.

Trying to avoid Shepherd, Billy fell backward off the platform and under the snorting, rearing horses. Yells drowned in booming gunfire. A cloud of white gunsmoke fogged the scene.

Mulroy blocked out everything but Shepherd. Crouching, he launched himself, his shoulder slamming into the doctor's side. The two went down, tumbling, rolling. Mulroy felt a fist slamming the back of his neck—saw a burst of stars. Locked together, they rolled over and over in the cinders, neither able to gain an advantage. Shepherd had the strength of desperation, and Mulroy felt his own weakened body being overpowered. If he could only hold on until help came. . . . With a sudden twist, Shepherd broke loose and grabbed his knife. Mulroy pushed back as the blade slashed upward, ripping his shirtfront and slicing across his belly. Before he could scramble away from a second thrust, he saw Shepherd clubbed by his own bag. He fell sideways, striking his head on an iron rail, and lay still. Cal dropped the bag, ripped the straps open, and drew Shepherd's Smith & Wesson.

BOOM!!

An explosion lit up the rail yard like bombarding artillery. The concussion knocked down the struggling figures. Stunned, Mulroy got to his hands and knees, partially deafened by the blast. He saw Shepherd inert between the rails, while Cal was spraddled on the platform, holding the doctor's gun. Billy lay flat on his back, with Meg crouched beside him, gripping the .32. The cavalrymen were afoot, trying to capture their panicked horses.

Chuff! Chuff!! Chuff!

Mulroy shook his reeling head. The train was

moving—pulling out of the depot. The guard slumped on the rear platform of the last car. The train began picking up speed, its two red lanterns receding into the murk.

Mulroy rose shakily. "Meg! You hurt?"

She sat beside Billy between the tracks. "I'm all right. Billy got kicked by a horse."

"How bad?"

"Barely clipped him. Scalp wound's bleeding." Her voice sounded strange, as if she were in shock.

Mulroy staggered the last couple of feet and sat down next to Meg, putting his arm around her. She cradled Billy's head in her lap, his blood staining her silk dress.

Men were creeping cautiously out of the depot to see what had happened.

"If it hadn't been for Billy . . . ," Cal began, crawling to the edge of the platform.

"I know," Mulroy said. "And your quick thinking."

"Did Billy shoot any of those soldiers?" Meg asked, her voice trembling.

"No, he was just firing wild. Looked like the guard was wounded. Thank God, Lincoln is safe." He glanced in the direction of the departed train. Warm blood wet his shirtfront and he felt a stinging sensation where Shepherd's knife had raked his rib cage. But he knew it wasn't serious.

Running feet thundered on the depot platform. Official authority was arriving, and Mulroy braced himself for the long ordeal of questions.

"Oh, I want to go home," Meg whispered, leaning her head on his shoulder.

EPILOGUE

When the story of the thwarted abduction broke, Meg Sartain, John Mulroy, Billy Sartain, and Cal Blackwood were treated as heroes. Newspapers around the country reported every detail of the near kidnapping, and most of them got it wrong. Some witnesses swore Billy had been shooting at Shepherd and missed. Men in the depot who came on the scene after the shooting stopped gave their conflicting versions of what occurred, some stating that the cavalry was involved. But most accounts did agree on the fact that Dr. Amos Shepherd and two escaped accomplices had used hostages to attempt a kidnapping of Abraham Lincoln, and been foiled by these same hostages.

Shepherd recovered from a mild concussion and was later put on trial and convicted. He was sentenced to twenty years in prison. After nine years of good behavior, his sentence was commuted to time served. Willis Aston and Charlie Bowen were never apprehended. They didn't attempt to retrieve their saddlebags at the livery, nor did they return to Canfield, Alabama. They simply vanished. Rail yard switchman Howard Kenny fled Nashville that night and remained a fugitive, sending money to his family by an intermediary. Eight months after the war and the death of Lincoln, charges against Kenny were dropped.

After several weeks of recuperation, Sergeant John Mulroy rejoined his unit and was promoted to lieutenant for his part in saving the President. He served out the rest of the war away from the battlefield and was honorably discharged in May, 1865. A much changed man, he returned to Iowa, where he helped his brother operate their family farm.

Because of press coverage, Zack Palmer managed to locate John Mulroy and he related the fate of their Andersonville messmates. On August 13th, following several days of hard rain, a spring burst forth from the hill inside the stockade. The gushing spring flowed at the rate of eight to ten gallons per minute, providing plentiful clean water for all the prisoners. To the desperate prisoners, the appearance of this life-giving spring was no less than an act of Divine Providence. Thus it was named Providence Spring. In later years a shelter was built over the spring and it still flows to this day. However, the spring appeared too late for Luther Salsbury who died in early August. As Sherman's Army drove South, the Confederate jailers transferred several thousand prisoners, including Rob Miller and Palmer, to another stockade near Savannah, Georgia. There, Miller succumbed to disease and despair, but Palmer managed to escape and make his way back to Union lines just before the war ended.

Although President Abraham Lincoln was saved from abduction on several occasions and lived to see the end of the war, he was assassinated on Good Friday in April, 1865, by a rabid Southerner who thought he was visiting retribution on an evil man.

Henri Wirz, commandant at Andersonville, was put on trial by the Federal government, charged with the inhumane treatment of prisoners and murder. Convicted, he was executed by hanging on November 10, 1865.

In a flush of gratitude, Congress appropriated a sum of money to pay off Meg Sartain's mortgage. She returned to her Alabama farm where she became Cal Blackwood's legal guardian. He recovered from his hepatitis, while the malaria went into remission. Later, as a grown man, he chose the career of railroad conductor. Throughout the injustices of Reconstruction, Meg continued to live quietly with Cal and her brother Billy. She and John Mulroy corresponded often by letter, and he visited every few months. Seven years later, in March, 1871, she petitioned the court to declare her absent husband Sam legally dead. The petition was granted. She and Mulroy were married a month later in a Canfield church. The couple had no children, but cared for Billy the rest of their lives. In the late 1870s they collaborated on a story of their adventures, which was serialized in the *Canfield Clarion*. The articles were later collected into a book that remained in print for forty years.

ABOUT THE AUTHOR

Tim Champlin, born John Michael Champlin in Fargo, North Dakota, graduated from Middle Tennessee State University and earned a Master's degree from Peabody College in Nashville, Tennessee. Beginning his career as an author of the Western story with *Summer of the Sioux* in 1982, the American West represents for him "a huge, ever-changing block of space and time in which an individual had more freedom than the average person has today. For those brave, and sometimes desperate souls who ventured West looking for a better life, it must have been an exciting time to be alive." Champlin has achieved a notable stature in being able to capture that time in complex, often exciting, and historically accurate fictional narratives. He is the author of two series of Westerns novels, one concerned with Matt Tierney who comes of age in *Summer of the Sioux* and who begins his professional career as a reporter for the Chicago *Times-Herald* covering an expeditionary force venturing into the Big Horn

country and the Yellowstone, and one with Jay Mc-
Graw, a callow youth who is plunged into outlawry
at the beginning of *Colt Lightning*. There are six
books in the Matt Tierney series and with *Deadly
Season* a fifth featuring Jay McGraw. In *The Last Campaign*, Champlin provides a compelling narrative of
Geronimo's last days as a renegade leader. *Swift
Thunder* is an exciting and compelling story of the
Pony Express. *Wayfaring Strangers* is an extraordi-
nary story of the California Gold Rush. In all of
Champlin's stories there are always unconventional
plot ingredients, striking historical details, vivid
characterizations of the multitude of ethnic and cul-
tural diversity found on the frontier, and narratives
rich and original and surprising. His exuberant tap-
estries include lumber schooners sailing the West
Coast, early-day wet-plate photography, daredevils
who thrill crowds with gas balloons and the first
parachutes, tong wars in San Francisco's China-
town, Basque sheepherders, and the *Penitentes* of the
Southwest, and are always highly entertaining.

TWISTED BARS

He was known as The Duster. Five times he'd been tried for robbery and murder, and five times acquitted. He'd met the most famous of gunmen and beaten them all. Before he gives it all up, he's got one battle left to fight. The Duster needs a proper burial for his dead partner, but the blustery Rev. Kenneth Lamont refuses to let a criminal rest in his cemetery. The Duster knows if he can't get what he wants one way, there's always another. And this is a plan the reverend won't like. Not one bit...

ISBN 10: 0-8439-5871-5
ISBN 13: 978-0-8439-5871-3

To order a book or to request a catalog call:
1-800-481-9191
This book is also available at your local bookstore, or you can check out our Web site **www.dorchesterpub.com** where you can look up your favorite authors, read excerpts, or glance at our discussion forum to see what people have to say about your favorite books.

NIGHT HAWK

STEPHEN OVERHOLSER

He came to the ranch with a mile-wide chip on his shoulder and no experience whatsoever. But it was either work on the Circle L or rot in jail, and he figured even the toughest labor was better than a life behind bars. He's got a lot to learn though, and he'd better learn it fast because he's about to face one of the toughest cattle drives in the country. They've got an ornery herd, not much water and danger everywhere they look. The greenhorn the cowboys call Night Hawk may not know much, but he does know this: The smallest mistake could cost him his life.

ISBN 10: 0-8439-5840-5
ISBN 13: 978-0-8439-5840-9

MEDICINE ROAD

WILL HENRY

Mountain man Jim Bridger is counting on Jesse Callahan. He knows that Callahan is the best man to lead the wagon train that's delivering guns and ammunition to Bridger's trading post at Green River. But Brigham Young has sworn to wipe out Bridger's posts, and he's hired Arapahoe warrior Watonga to capture those weapons at any cost. Bridger, Young and Watonga all have big plans for those guns, but it's all going to come down to just how tough Callahan can be. He's going to have to be tougher than leather if he hopes to make it to the post…alive.

ISBN 10: 0-8439-5814-6
ISBN 13: 978-0-8439-5814-0